THE MAN WHO LOVED HIS WIFE

THE MAN WHO LOVED HIS WIFE

JENNIFER ANNE MOSES

MAYAPPLE PRESS 2021

Published by   Mayapple Press
                362 Chestnut Hill Road
                Woodstock, NY 12498
                mayapplepress.com

ISBN 978-1-936419-96-8
Library of Congress Control Number 2020948523

ACKNOWLEDGEMENTS

Twelve of these stories were published in slightly different form in the following: "The Uncircumcised" in *The Sun*; "The Holy Messiah" in *ACM*; "Next of Kin" and "I'm Getting Married Tomorrow" in *Commentary*; "Skipped" in *The Southern Review*; "The Niece" in *Fiction*; "The Man Who Loved His Wife" in *St. Katherine's Review*; "The Teacher" in *Feminist Studies*; "Do This Together" in *New Letters*; "My Cousin's Heart" in *The Gettysburg Review*; "The Story of My Socks" and "Sol's Visit" in *Tikkun*.

Cover art by Jennifer Anne Moses. Photo of author by Nick Levitin. Book designed and typeset by Judith Kerman with titles in Hypatia Sans Pro and text in Adobe Caslon Pro.

CONTENTS

In loving memory of Lisi Oliver, and for Kris Fischer

THE UNCIRCUMCISED

Three months after his aging daughter Rhonda gave him a one-year-old poodle-Lab-golden-retriever mix to keep as a pet, Felder came to believe that the dog—who looked at him mournfully whenever he went to the bathroom and waited for him by the door, as still as a statue, until he came out—was in fact none other than the reincarnation of his sister, Esther, may her name be a blessing. Esther, who was seven years his elder and his de facto mother, had been taken to Bergen-=Belsen during the war and had never been heard from since. Even those survivors who had been at the camp at the same time as Esther had no recollection of her: not even her name rang a bell. Esther—there were lots of Esthers. Lots of Esthers. Lots of Ettas. Lots of Emmas and Ellens and Yettas and Evas, and most of them didn't come out, may their souls rest in Paradise. And now the survivors were dead, too—most of them, anyway. Felder himself had avoided the camps by dint of sheer, stupid luck, having hidden in the linen closet with their maid, Minnie, until the SS had finished rounding up the rest of his family and herding them and others like them into the central square. Minnie, who'd once been his nursemaid, had felt delicious to twelve-year-old Felder in the confines of the warm, fragrant closet, her breasts against his chest, her breath in his face. As darkness fell she'd led him to the edge of town, where she lived in a small, decrepit, sour-smelling flat with her parents, two brothers, three sisters, and maternal grandmother. An argument had broken out in a jumble of Polish and German, the gist of which was that they couldn't keep him: they'd all be killed. Then Minnie had whispered to her mother that Felder could pass for Christian and something else he couldn't hear, and that night he was allowed to sleep in the corner next to the stove and told to pretend he was deaf. They'd think of a cover story for him: he was a cousin, a second cousin even, an orphan of the war.

There was no plumbing in the flat. To get water you had to go to the courtyard of the building and pump it. The neighbors emptied their slop buckets out the window sometimes, especially at night, into the courtyard, where the Christian children ran like wild beasts, braying and hooting into the wind, their pink-white faces going almost blue as the fall changed to winter, until they looked like potato water.

"Black Donkey! Black Donkey!" they cried, pointing at Felder's thick black hair and chasing him around the courtyard, the bigger boys pulling his trousers down so that the pale blond girls with their pale blue eyes could look at his thing and laugh. "His pecker sure isn't as big as his nose!" they cried, shrieking insults from house to house until the entire courtyard resounded with them.

Because Felder's parents were—had been—radicals, he had a foreskin, as wrinkled and sour smelling as any German peasant's. Socialists who believed that the old religions were dead and that the way forward was through technology and education and a radical redistribution of wealth, his parents had not only insisted on having a civil wedding at city hall, but when their first and only son had finally come along—years after they'd given up hope of ever having a second child—they'd adamantly refused to circumcise him, calling the procedure "barbaric" and "atavistic," a symbol of all that had held the Jews back, of all that was wrong with Jews and Judaism as a whole. They'd met as students at the university in Mainz, where she'd majored in literature and he in biology. After they were married, they'd taken teaching positions at a provincial secondary school renowned for its progressive policy of educating both sexes under one roof. And there they'd held on to their beliefs in the progress of mankind—until they'd been dragged from their dinner on the Christian Sabbath.

In Minnie's flat, Felder, now renamed Tim, was moved from the spot beside the stove to a corner next to the washing. The family ate cabbage when they had it, potatoes when they didn't and then, as the war ground on and even big towns like theirs fell into desperation, not much of anything at all. Bugs. Roots. Frogs. River plants, which Felder pulled up from the banks, careful not to go in too deep, where he might be swallowed up and drowned, the waters closing over his head.

"Where did you come from, Black Donkey?" the other children yelled, sticking out their tongues and laughing until one of the mothers came down to do her washing at the pump and, curses flying, scattered the children like so much chicken feed. "Brats! Idiots! I'll flay every last one of you alive!"

One of the mothers in particular was fierce, with a huge bosom, red hair, arms like two ham hocks, buttocks that strained against her dresses, and a tattered sweater—always the same one, black with black buttons—barely covering her chest. Whenever she appeared, the children froze as if in a stuck movie reel and then ran off. Only Felder would remain, too terrified even to run, too terrified to do much of anything other than look at his feet and hope the woman wouldn't notice him.

"What are you looking at?" she'd snarl.

"Uh-yuh," he'd stammer, pretending to be deaf, as he'd been told.

She'd return to her work, and he'd slink away only to dream of her over and over as he slept in a sweat of longing in his corner by the wet washing and his penis rose and stiffened and finally burst.

Then the bombs began to fall, and Felder found himself up to his neck in the river and then in over his head and then above the water and then below it again as the reeds took him and the bombs burst until he was scrambling up the bank to the woods on the other side. He was all but dead of starvation, covered with suppurating sores and insect bites, when he stumbled upon the Americans. Then the displaced-persons camps: their jaunty flags and Yankee

Doodle dandy. Three years later he was in New Orleans, Louisiana, working on a loading dock. A rich Jew by the name of Bernstein, a cousin of a cousin, had given him a job. Felder wasn't particularly grateful. He wasn't particularly angry either. Bernstein kept telling him how lucky he was to have survived.

The dog had come with a name: Goldie. Of course her name was Goldie. She was part golden retriever, so what else would she be called? But from the moment she'd looked at him with her large and luminous black eyes, Felder had known the name was a lie, a stupid and obvious concoction his daughter had given her, thinking it would sound Jewish. No sooner had Goldie come up to Felder and sniffed his feet and legs and crotch and finally his hands than he'd changed her name to Esther. He didn't need to explain it to anyone, not even to the rabbi: he knew what he knew. And what he knew was that, somehow, *baruch Hashem*, the dog was a vessel of his sister's soul.

"Who names their dog after their dead sister?" Rhonda wanted to know. She was a large woman, his daughter, and now that she was on the far end of middle age, no longer particularly lovable, even to him. She looked like her mother, Sarah, only without her mother's grace, dignity, and determination. Felder and his wife had fought bitterly for the fifty-nine years that their marriage had lasted, until one day she'd come home from synagogue with a bad headache and died a few hours later. At first Felder hadn't known if he was too numb with grief to properly mourn, but as time went on, he'd come to understand that mainly he was relieved. A survivor, Sarah had wakened every night screaming about the bayonets and had been, at best, an indifferent mother. Worse, she'd bitterly resented living in Baton Rouge and not New Orleans, where they had met and married, even though it, too, hadn't been to her liking—too hot, too American, too Catholic, too many drunks, too many *shvartzes*. And she'd persistently reminded Felder that back in Vienna she'd not only been a typist at *Wiener Zeitung* but also had been admired by both the paper's chief opera critic and the wealthy heir of the city's leading Jewish banking family. Such a beauty she'd been, so feisty, so ferocious, she could have had anyone, but instead here she was, stuck in a small, lousy house in a small, lousy town, and who had she married? An intellectual? An artist? A professional of any sort? No, she'd married Felder, eight years her junior, the uneducated, uncircumcised manager of a shrimp-processing factory. "Thank God my father isn't around to see what's become of me," she'd mutter as she padded around their cramped kitchen, wiping the sweat from her broad forehead and eyes.

But she'd had something, some kind of grit, some kind of class that Rhonda lacked. Sarah could give as good as she got, and when she was drunk, she would get misty-eyed and sing in German the songs of her childhood. She was very religious: very *frum*. She lit candles, sang the Shabbos songs. She was a good-looking woman, too—much better-looking than Felder, who had a long, thin face dominated by an oversized nose, eyes that were set a bit too close together, and hair so thick he couldn't get a comb through it. Sarah had a perfect oval of a mouth and was padded in all the right places, with a bottom so round and pink it had a life of its own. Now he was nearly bald and so thin that his clothes flapped on him, and she was in the ground. A year after she'd died, he'd sold the house and moved into a one-bedroom apartment on Perkins Road.

Years ago he'd read a story, or maybe someone had told him a story, about a man whose wife is dying slowly of cancer. Every day the wife gets a little sicker. For years the man told everyone who would listen that, once his wife died, he would have nothing to live for. And, lo and behold, one day the wife doesn't wake up, and the husband takes a gun from the kitchen, loads it with a single bullet, goes out into the backyard, and shoots himself in the mouth. That was quite a story. But Felder didn't believe it.

"Daddy?" Rhonda said when he didn't answer. "Have you thought about getting a hearing aid?"

"Why should I get a hearing aid?"

"It's just that with you living here all alone . . ." She spread her arms wide to indicate his lemon-colored living room, or at least that's what she called it: "lemon-colored." It was really more beige: beige wall-to-wall carpet, a beige-brown sofa, and two vaguely beige-orange chairs, stained with age. She wanted him to move into an assisted-living facility on Florida Boulevard and couldn't understand why he hadn't done it yet.

"What if someone tried to break in on you?"

"So let them," he said.

"This is serious, Daddy! What if someone breaks in here one night, and you're asleep? God knows what could happen. It's happened before, you know. Right here in this very building. Do you have any idea how *old* you are?"

"Old enough, that's what," he said. "And anyway, I have Esther here. You think she doesn't know how to bark?"

"I wish you wouldn't call her Esther," Rhonda said. "Do you have any idea how sick that is?"

"I don't think she minds," Felder said, scratching Esther between her ears. "Do you, girl?"

Esther wagged her tail.

The truth was he didn't remember all that much about his sister. Mainly he remembered the way she'd smelled: like baking potatoes mixed with some elixir that he'd always thought of as a byproduct of her life in the city. When she was seventeen, she'd gone to Berlin to study in the university there, and whenever she came home to visit, she brought with her not only books and friends and excited talk about Schopenhauer and Schelling, but that strange, alluring scent. She was beautiful—that, too, he remembered—with long, thick black hair that she pulled back into a bun and very white hands. She fought with their mother about some boy she was seeing in Berlin, a boy who wasn't Jewish. Emil, that was his name. "Why do they care who I see?" she haughtily declared to Felder, tossing her black hair, brushed and loose for bed. "Hypocrites, the both of them!"

Why did Felder remember that moment and not the countless other minutes, hours, days that he'd spent with her: at breakfast or dinner, or walking to school, or watching her choose her clothes for the day ahead, laying them out on the desk chair in her bedroom? He just did, that's why. That's all he had of her, too, because once she'd been taken to Bergen-Belsen, that was it: he'd never been able to trace her further, to find out whether she'd been gassed or had merely died, as so many had, of starvation, or disease, or bullet wound, or execution of another kind, in a pit or in a forest. Or had she been raped? Raped and then murdered? She'd been a pretty girl, his sister—a beautiful girl. Had some Nazi forced himself on her and then pushed her into the gas chamber?

He didn't like to think such thoughts and tried his best not to. Even so, they came to him uninvited at all hours of the day and night. Sarah had been plagued with such nightmarish thoughts as well. He could always tell when she'd had a particularly tortured day, because there would either be no dinner on the table or so much food they'd be eating leftovers for weeks.

It was a miracle they'd managed to have children at all—first Rhonda and then, a year later, Kate. Sarah thought the name Kate sounded more American than Rhonda, which had been Felder's idea. Kate lived in Atlanta now, and only came to see her father when she had to; they'd never really gotten along. But her birth had been a miracle—both girls' were. To make love, to have someone to hold and be intimate with, to kiss and grunt and moan and then, after all they'd been through, after all that their bodies and souls had been deprived of—food and water and warmth—after they'd been battered and exposed to humiliation and deprivation, to watch Sarah's belly swell up just like any other woman's: such was the way of the world. He couldn't have cared less about the sex of the babies. He'd merely marveled that they were there, in his house in Louisiana—four thousand miles and a million years away from the ruination of wartime Europe.

Two months after her arrival, Esther began to speak to him in Yiddish. At first Felder assumed he was dreaming—either that or he'd suffered some kind of stroke, or he wasn't in his right mind, or his neurons were misfiring and his synapses collapsing. Or perhaps he was merely willfully hearing what wasn't there: her *rrurffs* and *arrrs* sounding, to his delusional ears, like *Di Rusishe ongeyn*—the Russians are coming!—as if his parents' dreams of a socialist paradise might sweep the Nazi contagion away.

He patted Esther's head. "We're in America now. It's OK. Go back to sleep."

Tsu vartn!

"What did you say?"

Schlump! Shmegegge! Shmendrik!

It was odd that she insulted him in Yiddish, because at home they'd mainly spoken German, the language not only of literature and the Enlightenment but also, of course, of university-level studies. Both parents also spoke some Polish and some Ukrainian, but not enough, they said, to really carry on a conversation—or, at least, not at an elevated level. Felder's grandfather, a grain merchant, had wanted Felder's father to be a lawyer. The older man had all but cut his son off when he'd gone into teaching. And then, when Felder's father began handing out leaflets and attending rallies for the Socialist Workers' Party, Felder's grandfather had suffered a heart attack and died.

Usually Esther slept on her doggy pillow in a corner of Felder's bedroom, but after she started barking in Yiddish, he invited her to join him in the bed. After all, there was plenty of room—all of Sarah's side, plus spare room on his own; even after decades of living in America, he couldn't stop sleeping as if he were curled up in the corner next to the dripping wet laundry.

Bounding up, Esther licked his face, and then she fell asleep and ran in her dreams, her dainty paws padding against the blanket.

It was nice having someone to talk to again, someone who understood, who'd been there, who had, in point of fact, known him since birth. It was also awkward at first. After more than sixty years of separation, where did you start? Small talk seemed idiotic, but going right to the big questions, the big unknowns, the terror of the war years, seemed downright rude. So they struck an unspoken bargain to start with the present, with his two daughters: Rhonda in her giant house in Bocage, with a kitchen that was bigger than his whole apartment and a swimming pool that she didn't swim in; and Kate in Atlanta, working with mentally disabled children, teaching them how to paint. Both daughters had grown children of their own and lazy American husbands. As for Sarah—well, what could he say? They'd met at a time when neither of them could quite believe that they were still alive, and within days they had agreed to marry. Neither had any living relatives (none that they knew of, anyway), and on their wedding night, rather than fall into the delights of bride and groom, they'd clung to each other, fearful and crying, like small children during a thunderstorm. Only later, once they'd gotten used to each other's ways, once they'd each learned to trust that the solid, foul-mouthed Americans they met at the grocery store meant no harm, that their smiles didn't hide menace, that their accents betrayed only where they'd been raised, did Sarah and Felder become entwined in each other's bodies. They were all over each other like starving beasts in winter. As he kissed her mouth and lunged for her breasts, Sarah would babble in a mixture of German and Yiddish and Russian and Polish, saying unspeakable things, wretched things, perverse things, things no whore could conceive of. And he, engorged and excited, rose up like the beast that he, too, had become, with strong shoulders and skin made dark by working on the docks. Then, in the morning, they'd rise and dress without talking or even looking at each other. At night, before falling into bed, they fought.

"And that's how we got the girls," he explained.

Ye, gut.

"And when she died . . ." He shrugged, palms turned upward, allowing the heavens to complete his sentence.

By this point Esther didn't need a leash. He could trust her to walk by his side, neither in front nor in back of him, and he had to be on the alert only in case a bicyclist came up too fast from behind them, which could scare her and make her dart between his legs. It was hard for Esther to get used to the traffic and the noises in Baton Rouge. Who could blame her? What kind of person, raised in a provincial town in Germany and then killed by the Nazis, could so much as fathom the tangle of roads with their roaring, beeping, honking, exhaust-spewing vehicles, the rap music and country rock and Christian contemporary blaring out of every other car and truck? Even in City Park, which was his favorite place to walk her, there were teenagers on rollerblades and students on bikes. And the pickup trucks—you'd think after almost a lifetime of living in Louisiana, Felder would have gotten used to the trucks outfitted with giant wheels or gun racks speeding down the highway, but he never did. To him they felt threatening.

"What about you?" he asked, as Esther sniffed around one of the public trash cans that lined the walking path in City Park.

"Trust me, you don't want to know," she answered, this time in proper Berliner German.

"But I do want to know about you. I've never stopped wanting to know about you."

"Well, for one thing, I've been dead awhile now."

"This is news?"

"Wise guy. You think I traveled through time and space and consciousness itself for your smart mouth?"

The phone rang. It was Kate, the younger of his daughters. She was worried that he wasn't taking proper care of himself.

"I'm fine," he said.

"That's not what Rhonda says."

"What does Rhonda say?"

"Rhonda says that, for starters, you need to get your hearing checked."

"My hearing's fine. I can hear you, can't I?"

"Daddy, I'm shouting into the phone."

"Well, I can hear you."

"And what about the dog?"

"She's a good girl, Esther is." Hearing her name, Esther got up from her place by his feet and lowered her head onto his lap.

"Rhonda says that you talk to her."

"So what?"

"Rhonda says that you have long conversations with her."

"I'm old. I'm allowed to be eccentric."

"That's exactly the point, Daddy. You *are* old. And you're lonely. Why are you living in that cramped apartment when you could have a better apartment in assisted living, where you wouldn't have to cook for yourself and where you'd have some company? I just don't understand."

"I have company."

"Who?"

"The rabbi," he said. "The new one. Kaplan. That's who. All the time, he visits."

"Kaplan was the rabbi when I was growing up."

"This one is Kaplan, too."

"For your information, his name is Kaminsky. Rhonda talked to him yesterday, and he told her that you refuse to see him."

"Kaminsky, Kaplan. At my age I confuse names."

"Rhonda says that's not all you confuse."

"You girls have been talking about me."

"We're your daughters, Daddy, and we love you. Of course we've been talking about you. Ever since Mom died—"

"This has nothing to do with your mother."

"You may not think so, but since her death you've been acting stranger and stranger. You never even go to synagogue to say kaddish for her, which, may I remind you, is what we do to honor our loved ones who have passed."

"She died, is what she did. 'Passed' is what you do with a kidney stone."

"The point is, you've isolated yourself from the community."

"What community? All my friends are dead."

"That's what I mean. It isn't good for you to live alone. And, frankly, it isn't safe."

"It's perfectly safe."

"Rhonda said there was a break-in at your complex a month ago, and three last year alone."

"So what? They want my TV? They can have it."

"At least get a burglar alarm, OK?"

"You worry too much," he said.

Eventually Esther filled him in on the last few months of her life: She'd moved into her boyfriend Emil's flat in Berlin and pretended to be his sister until they were both taken away—him to the police station, her directly to the depot. By then she'd missed two periods in a row and knew she was pregnant, though she wasn't showing yet. At the time she was gassed, her belly was just beginning to round outward, and she'd held it, weeping, until she was no more. "I was going to name it Ruth if it was a girl," she said. "And Joseph if it was a boy."

"For me?"

"Of course for you. Who else? I figured you were dead, too."

Not that she'd really thought she would be able to carry a child and then give birth to it in a concentration camp, not with the starvation, the filth, the daily rounds of death. Sometimes she'd prayed to miscarry. At night, just before she fell asleep, she'd beat her belly, thinking that if it could come out— if it might slip out between her legs in a knotty gush of blood—she herself might escape notice, might even be strong enough to endure. Other times she prayed only that her death might come soon. In the end both she and her baby had died, and her baby's soul was still waiting for another chance to be born.

"So reincarnation is real, then?" Felder said.

"It's not that straightforward," she explained. "It's more like—the human idea that people vanish isn't accurate."

"Oh," he said, but mainly because he didn't want to leave an awkward pause hanging in the air between them.

As their conversations got longer, so did their walks. At first Felder had confined himself to City Park, but now he and Esther did at least one trip around the golf course, and sometimes they even went as far as the I-10 underpass. Although Felder explained that the roaring traffic overhead couldn't possibly hurt them, Esther would sit on her haunches, trembling, and downright refuse to cross under the highway with him. Nor did it matter to her that on the other side were yet more vistas: of the university campus on the far shore, and egrets and pelicans and ducks. "You'd like it," he'd say. "And you don't even have to walk on your own four paws. I'll carry you."

"Thanks, but no thanks."

So adamantly did she refuse that, the one time he tried to scoop her up against her will, she bit his wrist and ran in the opposite direction. Of course, she stopped at the bend to wait for him.

"You don't trust me," he said, angry.

"Trust has nothing to do with it."

"Even so, I'm alive, and I live here, and highways and cars are something I know about. And still you don't trust me."

"I don't trust anything or anyone," she said.

"Why did you even bother coming here, then?"

"To tell you the truth," she said, "it was God's idea, not mine."

That gave him something to think about, because even with his miraculous escape and his having had work and a wife and a family and a house and a community in Louisiana; even with the knowledge that his five grandchildren had been raised as Jews and would, most likely, have Jewish children of their own; even after Esther herself had come to him and filled him in on everything that had happened; even after all that, he hadn't believed, let alone trusted, in God. But then something began to change in him. He thought maybe there *is* a God after all, a God who somehow pervaded the universe in a way beyond anything Felder could so much as intuit; a God who was in his cells and in his pores and in his sweat and in his shit; a God who had come spurting out of his uncircumcised member when he'd climbed on top of or lain under Sarah and thrust life into her womb.

It was with this thought on his mind that he woke one night to Esther's frantic barking. "What is it?" he mumbled in Yiddish, to which she replied, also in Yiddish, "A thief!"

She darted into the beige living room, barking, with Felder following after, tripping slightly in his too-big pajama pants, banging the little toe of his right foot against something—a table leg?—as he tried to keep up with her. He cursed; she howled. Everything was dark. Then he heard something fall over, followed by the sound of throaty breathing.

"Motherfuck!"

16

A moment later whoever it was was gone, and Esther was on Felder's lap, the two of them together on the sofa.

The next day he had to call the building manager to get his door fixed—the lock was broken; the chain, too—and the day after that, both Kate and Rhonda appeared at his door, saying that they would no longer allow him to live where he was, that he was in danger there, but he was also in luck, because the assisted-living facility on Florida Boulevard that had been Rhonda's first choice for him, and that was almost impossible to get into, had an opening. One of the residents was moving to South Carolina to be closer to his son, and Rhonda had already put down three months' rent on the vacant apartment. It was Felder's as soon as he was ready to move.

"You did what?" he said.

She explained again.

"I'm sorry," he said, "but I'm not moving. I like it here."

"Essex Homes is the best in the business," Kate said. "Do you have any clue what kind of strings we've had to pull, how many hours on the phone we've put in to clinch this apartment for you?"

"So who asked you to?"

"Actually," Kate said, "you did."

"Ha!"

"Show him," she said.

At which point Rhonda reached into her oversized purse, brought out an oversized envelope, and showed him a copy of some legal document that he had signed. It was, she explained, a power of attorney, granting her control over any legal or financial decisions made in regard to his welfare.

"You really don't have a choice," she said.

And now he remembered how, in the confusion over selling the old house, he'd allowed his daughter to take over not only with the realtor, a dyed-blonde named Judy or Jody or Jennie—one of those *J* names—but also with the bank and the closing lawyer and others. He remembered how she'd sat him down one day and explained to him that, when he signed the paper, he would in effect be handing over the right to make important decisions to her. And what had he done? He'd nodded and said, "Yes, yes. I understand. I'm not senile, you know. Not yet, anyway."

He didn't even really care about staying in the one-bedroom apartment. It was just that he didn't particularly like old people, never had. It was bad enough that Sarah had grown old; worse still that he had. Old people tended to be ugly and to have bad breath, and to enjoy prattling on about the past and showing you pictures you didn't really want to see of their grandchildren and great-grandchildren. Who needed them? Certainly not him. Plus he hated being bossed around, particularly by his own daughters.

"No," he said.

The girls looked at each other in a way that reminded him of their mother when she was about to start shouting.

"Really, Daddy," the younger of the two—the one who had never even pretended to understand or respect him—said. "You don't have a choice. It's all arranged."

That's when he knew they'd beaten him. He hung his head. He squeezed his eyes shut. He opened them again and, as Esther rubbed against him, said, "Looks like we're moving, Esther."

"Except, Daddy?" Kate said. "That's not going to work."

"What?"

"Essex Homes doesn't allow pets."

"But don't worry," Rhonda said. "Esther is coming home with me, and you can see her as often as you like."

An hour later, as Felder and Esther walked toward City Park, he said, "Don't worry. I wouldn't let you go to live with Rhonda in a million years, no matter how big that palace of hers is, no matter that she has a television set bigger than the dining-room table at home. You remember that dining-room table, how Mama and Papa used to argue about politics there? Even if she takes you to the doggy beauty parlor every week to get your fur shampooed, I won't let her take you away. No! Over my dead body. They think they can just do this to us, but they can't. Who do they think they are? God in heaven, what am I going to do? Oh, Esther, Esther! What are we going to do, Esther?"

"Arf," she said.

"What?"

"Arf," she said again.

Then he heard the sound of a cyclist coming up from behind them on the bike path, and then the bike was swerving around them on their right while, on their left, a car came speeding up the hill, music blaring from its open windows, making the air shake and causing Felder to feel a sudden unpleasant sensation in the hollows of his bones. The next thing he knew, Esther, scared and skittish, darted into the road, where, before his eyes, a second car coming from the opposite direction squealed and skidded but hit her just the same.

"Esther!"

Felder ran into the street and, bending over, saw that she was badly hurt, that she was bleeding from her eyes and ears, that her breaths were agony, that she was dying. Behind him he heard someone say, "Oh, no. I'm so sorry, man. I braked as hard as I could," and someone else say, "Yo, someone help the old dude. It looks like he's going to faint," and a third person say, "Does anyone have any water?" But they were as nothing to him, and he refused their offers of help. He sat down in the road and pulled Esther's body onto his lap, stroking her face as his tears fell on her muzzle and into her terrified eyes. And even after she'd stopped breathing, he held her limp body and wailed over her as, one by one, more people came to help and the crowd surged around him, and he stood over Esther's body to say kaddish while the other mourners rocked back and forth endlessly.

THE HOLY MESSIAH

Can you believe it, there are Jews here living among us on this sliver of desert hugged on the one side by the Mediterranean and on the other by enemies too numerous to count, who do not recognize the State of Israel, or plain old "Israel," or even "*ha-aretz*," like the name of the newspaper, which also means "the land," as in "the land which I will show you," the "I" in this case being the Almighty Himself—referring to the place that would take them in after the scourge of Europe and the millions reduced to ashes as "the Land of Israel," as if our liberation, our great moment of self-definition, our casting-off of the shackles of second-class citizenship had never come? And this because they are religious fanatics who don't believe in the legitimacy of the secular, democratic(ish), freely(ish) elected state, because they are still waiting for the Messiah to come and wave his Magic Wand and establish the dominion of His people, as stipulated in the Book of I think it's Isaiah, and encompassing that vast stretch of dry yellow wasteland now claimed by the Palestinians, who, having no better place to go to and rejected by their Muslim so-called brothers across the Jordan so-called River and, for that matter, every other Arab country too, moan and howl over their rights to it as if it were Gan Eden. Let them have it, I say. Let them have the whole over-baked, filthy, barren place—and good riddance and also, heaven forbid I should forget to say, live in peace. Make babies. Bake bread. Watch your favorite programs on TV. Just leave us alone already, and we'll leave you alone, and all will be well. In this fantasy land, that is. Because our fundamentalist Jews—those *shtreimel*-wearing long-beaded God fearing Talmud-drenched lunatics? Never will they let this happen. *Salaam salaam.*

And did you know furthermore that the rabbis taught that we were sent into exile and ruin not because the Roman legions with their weapons of mass destruction and crucifixion-compulsion burned our cities to the ground and slaughtered those who weren't already dead but because we ourselves—we Jews, who were then divided and sub-divided not into Reform, Orthodox, Conservative, etc. etc. but rather into Pharisees and Sadducees and Levites and zealots and so forth—turned on ourselves. "Jew-on-Jew hatred is what caused the great calamity" is more or less what the later rabbis, who of course weren't there but rather nestled in their cozy nests in places like Pinsk and Minsk and Sura, terrible places, places where they hated and slaughtered Jews, but go figure, they said that it was baseless hatred that brought catastrophe down on our heads, not the Roman Legion.

So, *nu*, hatred: we, by which I mean myself and my siblings and all the other kids on our kibbutz (Bet Zion) were taught to hate such people, by which I mean religious fanatics dressed in their weird and hot costumes, clothes so oppressive and out-of-time that you'd die of a heat stroke, wearing those long sleeves and long beards and long heavy black dresses in our Middle Eastern heat—or rather, not to hate the people, not the religious per se, but their ideas, those radical, fanatical, rigid and doctrinaire set of doctrines and strictures and rules that kept them—and by association, us—stuck in a netherworld of neither-nor. With their taking over great swaths of central Jerusalem and then spreading like a wave of black crows as far as Bnei Brak and Bet Shemesh and up and down and east and west (which, in Israel, is only a matter of fifty miles, Israel being more the size of a large ant hill than an actual country). Anyway: what could we do?

I was from a different class and time and place and history and philosophy and even skin tone entirely: meaning, if they were the descendants of crazed Eastern European *tzaddiks* and *hasids*, I and my siblings were the progeny of what in Israel passes as royalty, or, if not royalty, then the upper class: namely, the *Halutzim*—the pioneer generation, themselves the product of the Jewish Enlightenment who, educated in Freud, Einstein, Marx, Buber, Aristotle, Shakespeare, Bach, Goethe, Tolstoy, Dostoyevsky, Schiller, Mahler, Lincoln and Liszt, American movie stars and American jazz, all of them, and they came to this place—leaving their homes in Europe for the rigors of the desert and the company of impoverished Arabs—and built the first kibbutzim, drained the swamps, cleared the land, irrigated, dug, learned to shoot a gun, shot and got shot at.

I, Yoni Benavi, am of the third generation of the *Halutzim* class, and on our kibbutz, founded by my grandparents before Israel was even Israel, we hated every idea, every notion, every prayer, and every intention that originated among the fanatics, in all their varying costumes and degrees of fantasy and fanaticism of the 18th century Polish ghetto: i.e. our own religious Jews.

Religious, you say? What's religious? And when there are so many shades, so many tones and semi-tones of religious, who really qualifies as merely religious and who, as a nut job? Especially here in the Holy Land, God help us, where you could argue—and you'd be right!—that pretty much everyone is a nut job. But I digress. Or rather, I stray, I stray, when in fact I need to get down to brass tacks, which is to say the story itself, what you've come to these pages to read, the what-happened, the when, the why, the who. Speaking of the who—which is to say, our own homegrown nutcase Jews—most of them, they don't even speak Hebrew. Or rather, though they can speak it, they use Hebrew for the holy books only. For the everyday, for the here and now, they use Yiddish. They even write in Yiddish. You speak to them in Hebrew, most of them will reply: "I am sorry but I do not understand." Only they don't say "I'm sorry." Instead, they look at you like they're going to spit in your face. Most American tourists speak Hebrew more readily than they do, and trust me that isn't saying much. So why, given that I've lived in Israel with my co-religionists all my days, am I ranting? I'll tell you why. It's because of Itai. Who is Itai? I'll tell you. He is my son, my own and my wife Devorah's second child, the first wasn't a son, she was a daughter, a lovely girl, an accountant, she's engaged to be married to another accountant, they met in school. We live in Tel Aviv. Yes, I left the kibbutz. After I got my degree, I didn't go back. I studied biology at Hebrew University and continued with my advanced degree at Be'er Sheva, but Devorah, my wife, who also I met when we were both doing our first degree, me in biology and Devorah in psychology, she is from Tel Aviv and didn't want to live on a farm with the chickens and the citrus trees. We bought a two-bedroom apartment two miles from the sea, it's beautiful, the sea, not so far if you ride on a bike.

Itai loved the sea; he and his friends would spend whole days there. Even in the winter, off they'd go on their bicycles, to the beach, or to sit on a park bench eating peanuts, listening to the birds caw above them; talking; looking at girls. The usual things. There was nothing unusual about him; nothing that hinted that his soul was hindered, that things were amiss, that Devorah and I hadn't managed to provide for him some essential something that his inner self required. And what was essential something? Did we not coo over his cradle, change his diapers, attend his school performances and so on and so forth until the day he was drafted into the army like every other able-bodied Israeli boy and girl and, at the age of eighteen, put on his uniform, his boots, his gun, his cap, and did service? This is not in Israel such a hardship as it is in America; everyone does it; it's even a point of pride, something to look forward to, a necessary stop in one's development as a full-fledged citizen. Not that it's such a joy, either, let me tell you—not with your commanders screaming at you as you crawl on your belly through the desert at night with nothing but your wits to guide you, and that's only in training, but you get the idea; not with the terrible food, the endless tuna sandwiches, you eat so many tuna sandwiches the sight of it later in life makes you sick; not with a bullet aimed at your head if, God forbid, a war should come.

I myself was in Lebanon in '82, and let me tell you it wasn't nice. Even so, Itai: off to the IDF he went, he was a medic with the infantry, in Golani, a top brigade, the best he was in, we were so proud, and when his three years were up, he and his girlfriend went to Turkey, saw the Blue Mosque and the fairy chimneys and sand towers of Cappadocia—our Israeli youth, how they love to travel—I myself went to India, for ten months I was there, in India, what a place I could barely tear myself away but I had to, I had a place waiting for me at the Hebrew University, and God forbid I didn't take it, then what would my future look like? (Because even on the kibbutz—or perhaps I should say especially on the kibbutz—we prize education. Thus we have our poets on the kibbutz, our physicists and mathematicians and cellists as well as our agronomists and fruit-pickers and dairymen.) His own three years weren't the worst three years Israel has ever seen but not the best either, trouble in the territories but no outright war, a couple of busses blown up, a handful of Jews stabbed, but, nu, what else is new? He came out of it without a scratch, and also, in those three years he grew; he grew from a scrawny lad of no more than one hundred and sixty centimeters to nearly two meters tall, and broad and strong, with a thick tangled black mop on top of his face like some exotic obsidian animal had taken up residence there—and true, he's not so much to look at, or rather, his looks don't make him any kind of movie star, but he's solid, a solid, healthy, strapping Israeli type, he could almost be Italian, an Italian Mafiosi in New Jersey or Staten Island, America—but his girlfriend, they met on the base, what a beauty!

A rare find, this girl, this girlfriend of his, Tamar, a jewel, blonde no less, with long blond hair and her dirty feet in sandals, straight from the countryside this one, her family thinks ours is sophisticated and worldly, this is how simple was her upbringing in a small town in the north, just under the belly of Lebanon, where her family made olive oil and soap from their own olive grove for export. And she was crazy about him too; you could see it, the way she looked at him; and how agreeable she was, always saying yes, never no, never "I don't feel like it," never "I'm tired." Yes, of course, we gave them our blessing—or if not our blessing, not technically, our consent, our support, we are more secular, we don't go in for giving a blessing per se—when they went off together to explore the wonders of Turkey, and, later, when they were both in school, they decided to live together. Because this is Israel, and if you're not a religious fanatic, we are very accepting here, very relaxed about matters of sex and love, of boy-and-girl: we figure that if they're old enough to serve in the armed forces, they're old enough to navigate their own personal lives. This girl—I'm telling you, she's a gem, an angel from heaven, she helps Devorah in the kitchen, she and Ruti huddle together on the sofa, the two of them chatting like old friends and so lovely to look at, and what happens? It doesn't work out, is what happens.

The old story: she's living with him, they share their lives, she wants some kind of commitment, she isn't asking for a wedding ring or even a date or even a year, but just some sort of commitment, that he will be there, for her, by her side, in some kind of official capacity: she'll want children. Not now, but later. She'll want what most women want: her own home, her own little ones, laundry hanging out on the line. This is Israel: we are in and out of each other's homes constantly. No one has a lot of space, no three-and four-bedroom mansions or two-car garages or bright green back yards with a swing set and a swimming pool, and no matter what, you can never be far from home, even if you settle in the far south, on the border, you are only spitting distance, so what do we do? We pile into each other's houses, every day, every week we do this, and then we eat. Which is all to say that their romance wasn't conducted entirely behind closed doors, because in Israel, as I just said, closed doors aren't so easy to come by.

It got so bad that towards the end she even confided in my wife, in Devorah, that she loved him, she loved our son, she wanted a life with him—but Itai, he wouldn't say anything, he'd only shrug and say "maybe" or "we'll see," or "who knows?" So she moved out, and Itai left the university entirely and went to work on the kibbutz, which is to say my kibbutz, where I'd grown up. For a year, he picked lemons. Then he began to study Talmud, at first just once a week, at a nearby town where recently the *haredim*, religious wackos, had been coming to live, because of course they breed like rabbits, our religiously endowed, they're spilling out of their cramped neighborhoods in Jerusalem, out of their cramped apartments hovering above cramped alleyways stuffed to the brim with all matter of things that people throw out when they no longer have any use for them—barrels of rotting vegetables, tallow, chicken bones, candy wrappers, plastic bags, net bags, sneakers, aerosol bottles, and the ever-present baby buggy, the buggies and push-strollers parked end to end on every sidewalk and every doorway from Mea Shaarim to Ezrat Torah and in between in every direction: pregnant women pushing babies and more babies, so many babies you'd think they were farming them. The town, like so many towns of the same type, was new; it sprang up out of the desert like the gourd in the Book of Jonah. One day, no town; the next, a metastasis of concrete-block apartments, a blight on the landscape, a cold sore on the lips of a virgin.

This one they called Kiryat Yisroel, and like all such towns, it was filled with anger, self-righteousness, dirty diapers, squabbles, envy, venom, and not-enough: not enough money, not enough food, not enough space, not enough quiet, not enough peace. Prayers, yes; peace, not so much—because how do you attain peace when you and your wife who you married after meeting once, for a single hour, live in a two-bedroom flat with seven children and one-on-the-way? For this, my friend, you have to go to the study house; you have to study Talmud while your wife works at whatever work she can get in between birthing babies and washing their nappies. A disaster, is what it is. And, plus—and here I'm getting to the main point—they don't serve in the army. This is the law in Israel, that the Orthodox, busy serving the *Am* in their own way, i.e. studying Holy Writ, are exempt from the army. Why this is so is a whole long story, a historical fact dating from our earliest and first government, and the rest, as they say, is misery....

So yes, as I was saying, he'd go and study: first once a week, just dipping his toes in, he said, like many secular Israelis he'd never studied the ancient books, he was curious to know where he had come from, he said, where his people had come from. To which I said: your people? Your people come from insanely terrible little towns in what is now Ukraine and what is now Poland, where they were tanners, and starved to death, except when instead of starving to death, they froze to death, or were murdered by peasants.

No, he said, and you know what I mean, Abba: my people, our people, the Jews. Going all the way back: like, what's our story? And I'd repeat the story or rather cycle of stories I'd told him (and his sister, Ruti) since childhood: our story, our story—we came out of the desert, a little tribe infused or infected, whichever way you want to put it, by God, by some notion of God, by some notion of right-and-wrong and of being apart and selected and elected by None Other than God Himself. What followed was—who knows for sure, because the Bible isn't exactly an accurate historic record, though archeology is?—but what followed was we landed in Jerusalem, had a bunch of kings and endless inter-tribal warfare and skirmishes, and a bunch more of this faction saying that this is the way to worship God while that faction said, no, you're wrong, it's this way, and all this was punctuated by various empires rising up in the east or the north and deciding that little old Israel (which wasn't called Israel then, it was called other things, but wasn't even a country, because countries as we know them today hadn't yet been invented) was in the way, or rather, that they didn't like its inhabitants—those Hebrews with their own God and their own language and own tongue and, depending on the century, their own Temple—and either killed us or enslaved us or exiled us or burnt us to death but in the meantime people kept talking and arguing and writing, and then the Romans came, and we spread to Europe in the north and the desert to the south and east and eventually came to live either under the Muslims or the Christians, and for a long time, things were okay, living in Muslim lands, but not so good in Christian lands, and finally after another dozen disasters involving the wholesale slaughter of Jews, culminating, naturally enough, with the Shoah—with the murder of the six million by that butcher—we came here.

Your great-grandparents, I'd say, they came from Poland and from Lithuania, young and on fire, they came to a backwater, a desert, an impoverished nothing of a place nominally governed by the Ottoman empire, and they built a kibbutz.

But no, that's not what Itai meant. He meant: why and how did we Jews come to *be?* What is the essence of the Jew? Why is there consciousness? What is consciousness? Is there any way to address the cosmos from within our puny framework?

Thus his weekly and then twice-weekly and finally nightly retreat to a *chevra*, a holy circle, to study the holy books, and all this under the auspices of someone whom my son called Rav Eli, who later became his father-in-law, but I'm getting ahead of myself.

In America, when this happens—when an otherwise reasonably well-rounded and well-grounded young person goes religious—they call them *baal teshuva*, "master of return," or "master of repentance." Here we just say he or she is lost—lost!   So too with our son, with our strapping, black-eyed and black-haired Itai. He becomes strange to us; he grows a beard; he covers his head; he wears a black coat and then a black suit and then a black gabardine and then a black hat. He will not eat in our house; we aren't sufficiently kosher (though, unlike most secular Jews, we do keep kosher—a remnant of my wife's upbringing, and trust me, it's not so easy to keep kosher in Tel Aviv.) He won't shake the hand of my wife's friend Elena even though he's known her since he was in diapers. He won't even kiss his own mother, not without his rebbe's permission. By now of course he's moved off the kibbutz and into a kind of men's dormitory attached to the rinky-dink ramshackle yeshiva that Rav Eli runs out of a former petrol station, or maybe it was a warehouse, something left over from when Kiyrat Yisroel was no more than an intersection on the road from Gedera to Tel Aviv, a truck stop, a place where you could get the bus. In any event, nu, you get the picture. Our son had become one of them: infused with blinding certainty, committed to Talmud, convinced that the only way to be a Jew and to do a Jew's work in the world was by studying the Holy Books, six, seven, eight, nine hours a day, except on the Shabbat, a day given over to prayer and rest. And what is the work of a Jew? The real work that the Jew was put on earth to do? Only to invite the Messiah to come visit already, we've been so patient—to perfect the world as much as he can, which isn't saying much, but a little is better than nothing at all, and thus to bring unending peace, the world-to-come on earth. We await the Messiah, may he come soon and in our day, etc.

Of course all of this caused endless amounts of angst and hand-wringing in our own home, amongst us, the *us* now including Ruti's fiancé, a fine young man, Ori, he's an accountant, I've already mentioned this, but forgive me, I mention it again: because accountancy, unlike lunacy, is a sure, certain, calm and practical occupation. People need accountants; businesses couldn't run without them. The very government couldn't! Numbers are certain, they are facts unto themselves. And the job goes with a decent salary, too, more than decent if you have your own firm or the right connections or both. So yes, I am pleased that Ruti will always be able to work at something solid, which she's good at and which gives her satisfaction, and that her future husband also has this profession. Versus needless to say the God business, which even during the best of times is iffy.

Long story short: we lost him. We lost him to that tribe of pale, impoverished, underfed, poorly-dressed, God-maniacs. He cut off all ties to his former friends at the kibbutz. He cut off all ties to his former mates—his brothers-in-arms—from the IDF. And if we hadn't agreed to come to him, on his terms, he would have cut off all ties to us, his family, as well, only where in the holy books it says it's kosher to turn your back on your mother and father, your sister and brother-in-law, your aunts and uncles and cousins, I don't know. And what were those terms? Endless, is what they were, starting with dress code: my wife, his mother, had to cover her hair, and not with a simple head scarf: no, not a wisp of hair could escape. She had to wear long sleeves, a long skirt, and nothing that would show that she is a woman and not a man. Ditto for his sister. For me, it wasn't so onerous. I merely had to wear long sleeves and long trousers, didn't matter what time of year it was, no short sleeves, no sandals.....nothing that would make sense in a desert country under a broiling sun such as ours is. If we came to visit on the Holy Shabbat, God forbid we should drive, use electricity, cook, check the mobile device, until Shabbat was over, meaning by the official God-calendar, meaning not until three stars appeared in the night sky. It's a plague, this kind of thinking, this way of life. Life? What kind of life, may I ask you, when not only your every minute but your very imagination, your very intelligence, is forced into strictures too numerous to count?

And yet, he swore by it, saying he was more at peace, happier, more content than he'd ever been. And we, his family, could see that it was so: his voice had taken on a calm, resonant tone; his eyes, which once flashed fire, now flashed sunlight; even his bearing changed. Whereas once he'd walked with a ferocious step, his arms swinging athletically by his side, his strides hurried, now he slowed, took in the scenery (not that there was much to see in that drab little town), breathed as if the air felt good in his lungs.

Then he announced his marriage, to, as you already know, his rebbe's daughter; actually, there were four daughters. He married the second. She was eighteen, he was twenty-eight. How it was arranged I don't know, though we could only assume it was via the usual channels of matchmaking and negotiation, but it was clear that though Itai didn't love his wife, or at least not at first, he was pleased by the arrangement. What can I tell you about Hannah that you don't already know? That she was young; that she lacked education; that she'd never read a novel or even a real newspaper; that she could cook and sew; that she wore a full veil and a white satin long-sleeved wedding gown; that on this same occasion she didn't dance with Itai at all, but only with the other women; that she was pregnant within a few months of their marriage; that she was pale and delicate, with huge terrified dark eyes; that she awoke on the first day of her life as a married woman to don a wig.

The baby—our first grandchild—would be named Dafna. Both mother and father were slightly disappointed that Dafna was a girl and not a boy, but what can I say? Another would come along soon enough, and this one, this Dafna, they loved her. Of course they did. And meantime, he immersed himself in the Talmud, and she nursed the baby, took her on walks, baked challah, did the laundry, and worked along with her mother and sisters in the family business, which in this case was internet retail. I've failed to mention it, but the women of the family were nothing if not entrepreneurial. They saw a hole in the fashion market and filled it, contracting with makers of Orthodox women's apparel to sell outfits online, and a nice little business they had going, too, especially when you consider that the women of the family not only brought home the bacon, as it were, but also managed all the domestic

28

details. Anyway, it was enough to keep the little family of three (plus the many others who were sure to come) in circumstances above the usual poverty and misery and crowdedness. In short, they had a two-bedroom flat, with a modern kitchen and a washing machine in a nook by the bathroom.

We adjusted. What else could we do? Itai was—well, there was no going back was there? Not with a wife and a baby and whatever future babies there would be, which was as sure as sunrise itself. And then the next war happened. Which war, you ask? It was 2014. Rockets were being fired from Gaza into Israel. Some came as far as Tel Aviv. There were words, then escalation, and then our prime minister, excuse me but I cannot say his name without spitting, he ordered troops to the border and then ordered them to go in. And then our Itai, he was in the reserves, of course he was, everyone is. For decades—until you're forty if you're a man. There are exceptions, of course. For example, for the *Haredim*, who are so busy with their holy books, etc., that they can't be bothered. This didn't apply to Itai, though: he'd become a religious fanatic too late. His service had been with Golani brigade. Golani was sent into Gaza first, and then the losses began: the explosions in the tunnels, the blood. They lost them. They couldn't keep up with the blood. That's when Itai was called up. He was a medic. They needed him.

Two days later, Itai was dead. Dead in a tunnel where he'd rushed in, after an explosion, a big boom explosion, and the sound of gunfire, and he knew they were in there—the soldiers, that is, the eighteen-and-nineteen-and-twenty-year-old soldiers, and he ran in after them to help, but there was a second explosion. And that was that. He was given a hero's burial, at Mount Herzl. It's beautiful there. The smell of pines.

So now, yes, we too, we mourn. We mourn and wait for the coming of the Messiah, soon and in our day.

And I'm very sorry to have to tell you such a sad story, a sad story with an even sadder ending, but this is how it is for us Jews, here in the Holy Land, the Land which God promised to Abraham and his descendants, promising that one day, "I will make you a great nation; I will bless you and make your name great; and you shall be a blessing. I will bless those who bless you, and I will curse him who curses you; and in you all the families of the earth shall be blessed." I am of course quoting from the verses in Genesis, or as we call that book, *Bereshit:* "In the beginning." And what I'm thinking is: what if none of these stories had been written down? What if there was no Bible? What if there had been no Temple? No Second Temple? No Mishna, no Gemara. Where would I be living? Would I even be a Jew? Would Hitler have risen among us? Would there be a city where Tel Aviv now stands? Would my son still be living or would I and my son and all the rest of us be merely an idea, never to have been realized, in the Mind of God?

THE FIRE

Shortly after Christmas, my father lit the living room on fire. This is how it happened. It was snowing, the first heavy snowfall of the year. Dad said that now would be a good time to test out the fireplace in our new house, in Beth Page, which for those of you who don't know is on Long Island, about a forty-minute drive from Manhattan depending on traffic. Before that we'd lived in a much smaller house in Rego Park, surrounded by relatives. So there we were, our first winter in our new suburban house with its sunken living room and built-in shelving and paneled rec-room on the lowest-level, which wasn't even a basement. It was a five-level split level so even the lowest level was more above-ground than below. We didn't celebrate Christmas—we were Jewish and celebrated Hanukkah, albeit in a desultory fashion—but both my parents were drawn to what my mother would call "the holiday season" and my father called "winter wonderland." Thus the fire, where we'd sit roasting marshmallows, to remind us that we weren't merely a family, but a family whose father, though he'd had to scrape to put himself through college while he was working as a truck driver for his family's home-heating-and-cooling business, had now accumulated enough capital and success to own his own, comfortable, suburban house in a part of Long Island with very low crime and good public schools.

About a minute after Dad lit the fire, my older sister—already in junior high and our undisputed leader—said: "Dad, the flue is closed." But Dad ignored her. "Dad," she said again, "the flue is closed." This time Dad didn't like it and, waving her away as if she were an insect, said: "Hush, Dora." This made Dora turn bright red in the face. She persisted anyway. "I'm telling you, Dad, the flue is closed."

"And I'm telling you it isn't. Just give it another minute."

"In another minute, we'll all be asphyxiated," Dora said, using a word I happened to know she had just only recently picked up from reading H.G. Wells, whom she read compulsively and talked about at the dinner table, as if he were someone she personally knew.

"We'll die," she said.

She had a point. The room was filling with thick gray smoke, piles of smoke, smoking rising to the ceiling like billowing curtains, like waltzing clouds, combining and recombining in an endless variation of velvet gray. We children watched, entranced and horrified in equal measure, rooted to the spot and utterly transfixed until my baby sister began to cough, spurt, and scream, which made the dog howl, which alarmed our mother.

"Good God!" she said, coming down the stairs to see what all the fuss was about. "Open the windows! The flue is closed."

"It's not closed."

"One way or another, you need to put the goddam fire out, Harry!"

My father opened the sliding glass doors that led to the patio where earlier he'd cleared a path through the snow and grabbed a shovel. Shovel in hand, he walked inside to the fireplace, used it to pick up the burling log, and with the log still spitting flame, carried it on the shovel across the living room, where sparks ignited the rug, two chairs, and my mother's half-finished needlepoint project, a design of flowers and butterflies that she intended to use as a cover for the piano bench.

"Outside, everyone!" my mother shrieked as she grabbed my baby sister and quick-marched us to the patio, where we watched as the flames spread and our father, bewildered, blinked in all directions, as if blinking might put the fires out, as if blinking might prove some point that only he knew needed proving.

"Get snow!" my sister yelled.

By the time we'd hauled enough snow inside to put the fire out, all that was left was the soggy blue wall-to-wall carpet, now covered with ash and slashed with burn marks, and the remains of my mother's new living room set.

Even without the fire, the move had been difficult. For one thing, Dora had been adamant about not wanting to switch schools, arguing that at least she should be allowed to finish Junior High at home in Rego Park with her friends. She pitched several fits about it, her hands balling up, her face turning red, shrieks of misery filling the house. It was an awful and wonderfully mysterious sight to behold, when Dora did that, when she went up against our father that way. She'd let out a series of increasingly loud accusations punctuated by shakes of her head and what I later recognized as something akin to the Nazi salute, followed by endless arguments expressing all the reasons why she was right and should be listened to until finally banging on the door and throwing things, and all the while our father, who normally broached no nonsense and was known as someone who wasn't shy about handing out swift and brutal punishment, simply listened, shaking his head, before saying something like: "I understand that you don't like our decision, but it's our decision, and that's final." Not that she'd be placated by our father's attempts at buttressing her sense of having been accounted for, of *counting*, but eventually, she'd go stomping off to her room, taking her fury with her. In the end, of course, neither one of our parents was about to delay the move in order to made Dora's transition to a new school system easier. Instead Mom decided to placate Dora by giving her something she'd been begging for, in this case, a guinea pig, which she'd been asking Mom and Dad for ever since her friend Miriam Ginzberg got one for Hanukkah in the fifth grade. The guinea pig was purchased, installed in a cage in the rec-room, and named Ringo. My sister was given a long lecture on how owning a pet was a responsibility not to be taken lightly, that Ringo was a living creature who needed to have his cage cleaned once a day, his water changed, and so forth.

This lasted until Dora decided that since the rest of us played with Ringo too, she shouldn't be stuck with the daily cleanup and feeding, and insisted that we take turns, rotating from day to day the way we did with other chores—setting and/or clearing the table, washing up, drying—except that we never really shared chores and never had. Mom did most of everything, leaving us kids to laze around. The exception to this rule was weekends, when Dad would insist that I accompany him as he hammered and sawed or mowed or shoveled in the way of fathers with sons, except in my case doing chores with my father was terrifying. We'd be up on the roof, mucking out the drains as I'd imagine landing on the sidewalk beneath us, my brains splattered in the snow. Or fixing, which meant not-fixing, a broken light as it spat electricity which sizzled in my hand as my father insisted that I stop whining and be a man. So the prospect of yet more chores in accordance with the size of the new house with its surrounding front-and-back yards and my father's visions for it sent me into tizzies of anxiety. And those visions proved to be nearly endless as, over the years, he'd labor endlessly, laying bricks to expand the patio or hammering nails to build a fence or taking a weed-whacker to the bushes, which all might have been fine except that our father was also preternaturally clumsy, with a poor sense of space and zero hand-eye-coordination. More often than not, he either broke what he was trying to fix (the lawnmower, the toilet, the door handle) or left the thing unfinished.

I was his only son and not at all what he'd expected when he remembered his own boyhood and how he'd been a boy among boys more or less like him, which is to say: interested in sports, passionate about the Mets, and preferring the company of other boys and, eventually, men. But I only had sisters, and what's more, though in Rego Park we were surrounded by family, most of my cousins were girls as well. So it didn't come naturally to me, the swagger and sports-obsession and derring-do of boyhood. And our father's version of his own boyhood—recounted in endless stories about what he called "the old neighborhood," even though it was just a few blocks over, on the other side of Queens Boulevard—seemed like they were plucked from another time and place entirely, as far from my own life and as foreign to my own sensibilities as Calcutta under the Mughals or New York before the Europeans arrived, when it was still all streams and forests and happy innocent Indians living in peace with one another and trading moccasins for beads made out of conch shells.

And all this—my being the only boy and therefore subjected to our father's endless tinkering and fixing/breaking, combined with what was obviously, and from the very start, his utter incomprehension of me and dismay at my lack of sufficient boyishness; suffice to say that I dreaded those times alone with my father, when it was just the two of us doing manly things together.

What I did like were girls—all kinds, as long as they were pretty and were nice to me. I had a vivid imagination, so by the time I was in the fourth grade, which was the same year we moved, I was already imagining my future life in some flower-covered cottage with my classmate Amy or Susan or Rebecca or June. And in this cottage of ours (and I could see it, right down to the color of the flowers and the books on the walls,) not only would we be able to watch as much TV as we wanted to, but also, we'd have steak for dinner every night followed by tons and tons of sex. Sex every which way: from behind, doggystyle; or old-fashioned; she could even ride me from above, because that's what kind of guy I was, what kind of husband I'd be: women's liberation. I was all for it. It's all my mother and her friends talked about. Well, not all. They also talked about the usual things that women of a certain age and class and status talk about—their kids, their husbands, clothes, politics, movies, recipes, magazines, books. But they also talked about women's liberation, which had come, my mother lamented, too late for her.

Of course, when I thought about my own future sex life with my own liberated future wife I didn't think about real women like my mother and aunts and neighbors. I thought on the one hand about girls my own age, all those Amys and Susans, and on the other about the girls I saw in my father's stack of *Playboy* magazines, which I unearthed one day while going through his things, which I was doing because on a dare I'd made a bet regarding whether I or this kid down the block whom I hated named Bill Marcado could run to the corner and back faster, and even though I knew he'd beat me—he was bigger than me by several inches in both directions—I couldn't back down from the bet, even though the loser (me) would have to buy the winner (Bill Marcado) a pizza. Not a slice. A full, large-sized pizza. Hence I was going through my father's things, looking for what he referred to as his "secret stash of cash," when I came upon the dirty magazines hidden at the bottom of the nylon sack he used to take his dirty dress-shirts to the cleaner's. In the end Bill Marcado settled for three *Playboy* Magazines in lieu of pizza, and I became hooked on porn. And girls. Despite my father's misgivings regarding my lack of male fortitude, I was girl crazy.

So there we were, in our house in Beth Page with its burned-up living room, where everything and everyone was smoldering: the furniture, the rug, my father, Dora, my mother. I too was smoldering, but mainly for school to resume so I could win the heart of yet another new and wonderful girl, Gina Pearlstein, who in fact had just joined our class (Mrs. Tyler's) from the one down the hall (Mrs. Powtaki's) for reasons to do with—actually, I don't know. They didn't tell us, and cute, freckled, black-eyed and black-haired Gina

Pearlstein didn't seem to know either. She only knew that it had something to do with class size. Not that any of it mattered, because all that mattered was that I somehow find a way to make Gina Pearlstein love me.

Like many nine-year-old boys, I was hardly prepossessing, not with my fear of heights and dislike of sports and disinclination to get wet or cold or dirty. The best I can say for myself was that I wasn't threatening, not even in a way that a nine-year-old could be, which is to say too insistent, or knowingly cocky, or already certain of his own attractions. You could say that I was more like a girlfriend than a potential boyfriend, but that wasn't the case either, because while I understood such female realms as baking cookies, painting rocks, making jewelry with beads and string, and gymnastics, they didn't interest me either as things to do or as subjects of conversation. What I liked to do was tell stories. Sometimes I made them up entirely but more often than not the stories I told were reports of things that had actually happened but needed to be made interesting. I elaborated on them until even I was convinced that I'd made them up whole-hog, and I'd get so lost in these stories, so enraptured by their every twist and turn that there was no need to talk about anything else. Plus, it was the only way I knew to get girls to like me—to tell them things, even if they weren't true.

But Gina Pearlstein wasn't falling for it, not for any of my pratfalls or jokes or elaborate histories, not even when I finally got her to agree to sit by me at lunch and I told her the story about how my father had burned down the living room. Then I told her another true story, about the time my father hit me with a hammer. I was four or five at the time, I don't really remember, I just remember coming up from behind him when he was trying to fix something in our basement in Rego Park. Pound pound pound went his hammer as he cursed and sweated. I stood behind him, fascinated, as he crouched down on the floor, laboring. Then, boom! A blinding white pain. A screeching agony of heat as he swung his hammer behind his head, striking me. Then I was in my father's arms and he was carrying me up the stairs and someone's putting ice on my forehead and my father is explaining that he'd had no clue I was in the basement, let alone standing behind him. Then I'm in the emergency room, where the doctor is saying something like: "Okay, now, you got lucky, young man, you'll only have a small scar."

I told stories around stories, weaving biographical details with the fruits of my imagination. In the telling of my father hitting me with the hammer, he'd done it on purpose, in a rage—in a drunken rage!—continuing to threaten me with his weapon of choice whenever I didn't do what he told me to do. In the story of the living room fire, Dad had not just carried the spitting logs out across the wall-to-wall on a snow shovel, but had also dropped one of them on the sofa, which had instantly ignited, sending a volcano of sparks to the ceiling, such that all seven of us were trapped below it in an inferno, a hellish burning nightmare, and it was only a miracle that we all got out alive. Only it wasn't a miracle, not really: it was because I had had the instincts and the wherewithal to think fast. Yes, that was me: the boy with the heart of a lion, the heart of a warrior! Instantly, this boy—this veritable superhero hidden inside the scrawny body of a nine-year-old Jew—not only ushered his entire family to the safety of the backyard, but also, spotting an enormous icicle hanging from the eaves, broke it off to use as an icy sword to do battle with the flames until they died down in a tired hiss.

"I don't know," I said, shrugging with modesty. "Because it wasn't really like I was *thinking*. I just did it. Like breathing—you don't think about it."

Gina Pearlstein's eyes grew wider, her freckles more adorable, her chapped lips—lips the color of Band-Aids—glossier as she wet them with her adorable pink tongue.

"I carried the baby out," I added. "She's five, but she was too scared to remember how to walk!"

And with that, I finally—finally—got a smile out of Gina Pearlstein. "I wish I had a baby sister!" she informed me. "I would love a baby sister. But no. All I've got is one bratty younger brother."

I gave her my most adorable, most winning, most empathetic smile. "At least you don't have any older sisters," I said. "My older sister, let me tell you, she thinks she's Queen of the Universe. She's always bossing me around."

Gina made a what-can-you-do sound that sounded like "chhuu."

"I know, right?" I continued. "But the thing is, my sister, the older one?" And now my imagination really took flight such that even I didn't know who was doing the speaking, who was telling the story, the story-teller or the story itself, the words or the breath? It was as if I was touched by the angels, inspired by the same muses who'd inspired Shakespeare and before him the Prophets of Israel themselves when I said:

"My sister? Her name is Dora. Dora, as in 'adorable,' which is what my dad calls her, even though it's the opposite of what she is. It should be more like 'Door,' because she's as thick as a door, you know what I mean?" Gina didn't. Or at least she didn't indicate that she did, but rather stared straight ahead, and as I elaborated on Dora's door-ness, began to pick at her thumbnail. "Or maybe it's more like Bora, because she's such a bore." I thought that was a good one, but from Gina came only a side glance that indicated tedium, which indicated her desire to leave, which would mean that I'd probably never get another chance to be alone with her. My heart sank.

I needed to alight on a subject that would interest her, and I found it almost instantaneously, in Ringo. Not the real Ringo, who was left alone all day long in his newspaper-lined caged in the rec-room, pooping and twitching his cute little nose. But a more interesting Ringo, a Ringo who could . . . . I wasn't sure. I pressed on anyway.

"The thing is," I said as Gina continued to pick at her thumbnail and the clock on the wall showed that I only had two more minutes left until the end of lunch. "My sister wanted a dog, right? I mean, I wouldn't mind a dog, I'd love a dog, who doesn't want a dog?" Again, nothing. "But Mom was like: no dog. So she went out and got Dora a guinea pig, Ringo, and of course Dora was like: 'Ringo's mine! You can't play with him!' But then she totally stopped paying any attention to Ringo at all." Which was a lie, because while Mom had long since taken over the daily care and feeding, Dora continued to dote, if "dote" is the right word, on the furry little fellow, if he was a fellow, which was something else about Ringo we never knew: whether he was a he or a she. It was hard to tell. We'd turned him upside down many times in search of his elusive penis and/or vagina, but no dice, there wasn't enough there to tell. All we knew for sure about Ringo was that he was covered with light brown fur and had a sweet pink feet and a speckled belly.

Oh how I loved Ringo! Ringo, my heart! Poor dear Ringo, whose owner, so-called, didn't love him enough to clear out his cage or feed him slivers of carrots or pieces of shriveled lettuce, as I did, but who instead left him, for days on end…. "And," I said, "the thing about Ringo, only of course Dora doesn't know this, is that Ringo can—"

Gina looked at me blankly.

"Ringo can fly," I said.

"Ringo can fly," Gina said, repeating after me, only dully, with no intonation, not even a sarcastic questioning in her tone.

"I know," I said. "Hard to believe. Impossible, even, you might say, but it's true. He can fly. Only he won't do it for anyone but me."

She looked at me through the scrim of her lashes.

"*Chhu*," she said again.

"Fine then," I said. "I'll prove it."

"Sure you will."

"That's right."

"You're going to prove that your guinea pig can fly."

"Okay, listen," I said, hunkering down onto the slick flat of the lunch table like I was passing state secrets on. "Tell you what? I'll meet you—where? Anywhere—The Dunkin Donuts? Behind school? Or, I know, I've got it— I'll meet you at the playground, the one at Anders," I said, naming the park closest to my house that I thought was probably closest to hers, too, because even though I still didn't have the most excellent knowledge of Beth Page geography, I'd already done some background research on Gina, and I'd found out that Gina lived in a neighborhood of square wooden houses on the other side of the park from where my own house was.

"Okay, when?" Gina said.

I nodded slowly, thinking. "How about tomorrow? After school, say, at three-thirty??" We got out of school at two-thirty, which would give me a full hour to get back home, scarf a snack, sneak Ringo out of the house, meet Gina, and then get back in plenty of time for no one to notice Ringo's disappearance.

The plan, to the degree I had a plan, was to meet her at the playground according to schedule, climb to the top of the slide with Ringo on my lap, and, once there, convince the fair Gina to join me, so she could see Ringo fly with her own two eyes. And then, and this was the genius part of it, I'd confess all: how the whole story had merely been a lure, a trick to get her to come out and meet me, because—and here I'd be quiet and direct, dignified, but also somewhat sad—that's how much I loved her.

All of this, the whole plan, came to me in a flash, such that by the time Gina said, "Okay," my heart, which had been pounding with crazed anxiety, quieted down, suffusing my entire being with the certainty of the rightness of who I was and of where I was heading. One day, Gina and I would laugh about the guinea pig story after making hot crazy sex, while my thing stood straight up and spurted spurts of semen and she'd be like: oh, Josh, you make me so hot, do it to me again.

What happened, though, was that Gina went home and told her mother the story of how my father had hit me with the hammer, and her mother called the principal of the school. But I didn't find out about any of that until later, well after I'd snuck Ringo out of the house to meet Gina in the park. Just like I'd pictured it, she joined me at the top of the slide, so that the two of us (with Ringo on my lap) were snuggled close, side-by-side above the slushy snow. Gina didn't wait for me to tell her my true story of love and desperation, though, but instead took Ringo from my lap and tossed him out into the air, where he fell with a thud onto the blacktop below.

"I didn't think so," she said, a look of sheer disgust on her lovely face. "I mean," she continued. "What the hell?"

With those words, she became yet more alluring, making me love her anew, and in my desperate love I slid down the slide, scooped Ringo up into my arms, checked that he was still breathing, climbed back to the top of the slide, and said: "Sometimes it takes more than once for him to remember." Disdaining the laws of nature, I tossed him again into the icy air of midafternoon.

Where he again plopped onto the blacktop, whimpering in pain, while Gina, looking at me with an expression of disgust, headed back in the direction she'd come from. It was then that even I knew I was beat. Which didn't stop me from chasing after her—chasing after her with my bleating and bleeding guinea pig tucked into my jacket.

"Go home, loser," she said. "I know a loser when I see one, and if there was ever a loser, it's you."

That was cruel. It stung. It went right to my guts, which suddenly felt over-full and urgent. With Ringo snuggled up into the half-unzipped opening of my snow-jacket, I ran home, where I emptied my bowels, wiped Ringo down with a wet washcloth, and returned him to his cage. He was breathing. But by the time Dora got home from school, he definitely wasn't, which I knew when I heard her screeching up the stairs:

"Mom! Mom! Ringo's dead! He's bleeding and he's dead! SOMEONE MURDERED HIM!"

I felt awful. I felt worse than I'd ever felt in my life. But not so awful that I confessed to my crime, not even when Dora, her eyes puffy and her face streaked with tears, asked me point-blank if I had anything to do with Ringo's fate. With his sad little curled-up claws and non-twitching nose and trail of blood that extended all the way from his neck to the far corner of his cage.

"Me? No! How could I have anything to do with this?" I said.

"It's just that you play with him a lot," Dora said, the words barely getting out of her throat for all the mucus and misery there. "And you're a boy."

"So what?"

"And boys are mean."

"Not me."

But there must have been something about the way I said "not me" that clued her in, that gave her some hint of a feeling that maybe I had had something to do with Ringo, that at the very least I knew something I wasn't telling her.

"What did you do?" she said.

"Nothing."

"I'll tell Dad about your magazines."

"What?" I said, ignorant.

"How you and your sick little friends got your dirty little hands on some *Playboy* magazines, and how you hide them in your room and take them out and look at them."

I was gobsmacked. I didn't think she had it in her—blackmail that is. Actually, I didn't think she had it in her to know about my obsession with porn to begin with, because while Dora was bossy and theatrical and liked to get her own way, she wasn't sneaky. What she was was loud. Loud and insistent. Like a fire alarm.

"You can tell Dad anything you want," I fibbed. "Because you're making it up."

"Except guess what stupid? I'm not making it up. And I know where you hide them."

"Right."

"In the back of your bookcase behind your real books."

This seemed unlikely, completely unlikely, as Dora never set foot in my room (she said it smelled), and also, why would she be looking at my books, books which for the most part were too young for her and for the second part were mainly about knights, spies, true crime, and race car drivers. On the other hand, she'd named the exact spot where I did in fact hide my stolen *Playboy* magazines, which could only mean one thing: that she knew where they were.

"What do you want?" I said.

"The truth."

"The truth is that I'll tell on you, that I'll tell Mom and Dad that you've been going through my things and looking at *Playboy* yourself!"

We were at a standstill. And then we weren't. She pulled back and slugged me just under my eye, and I would have slugged her back, but she was a lot bigger than me. "I hate you," she said, walking out. "I hate you and always will."

And then it was over, except it wasn't over at all. First there was the ceremony of burying Ringo, putting his stiff little dead body in a shoe-box lined with tissue paper, then finding a soft-enough spot in the yard to dig a hole, then burying him there while Dora, crying, intoned predictions about how, one day, she'd find Ringo's murderer and force him (*him!*) to confess. And then of course I had to find a way to sneak my collection of stolen *Playboys* out of the house—a tricky business. And then of course there was the terrible business of facing Gina Pearlstein—Gina Pearlstein, who sat just two rows up from me, her sweet back bent earnestly over whatever piece of schoolwork our teacher had given us. She looked at me smirking. I looked at my shoes.

It wasn't until the next day, when the school principal came to get me, saying that he had a special visitor from the police department who wanted to talk to me, that I confessed it all: my crime against the truth, my crime against Ringo, my crime against Gina Pearlstein (if exaggerating can be a crime) and finally my crime regarding the stolen *Playboy* magazines. I was sure I'd be locked up.

"I'm sorry," I wailed. "Please don't put me in super-max."

"Super-max?" the man—he was young and had a beard—said. "What are you talking about?"

Had he not heard my confession? How I'd lured Gina Pearlstein to the playground at Anders Park to watch as I murdered Ringo, tossing him out into the air like a tennis ball? I burst into tears. When I was calm, the man said, "I'm here to ask you a couple of questions about your father."

"My father?"

"Your father—Harold, am I right?"

"Harry. People call him Harry. Except of course—well, I call him Dad."

The man waited a beat. "I understand that he likes to drink?"

"What?"

"Did he burn your house down?"

"What?"

"What's that, under your left eye?"

I hadn't noticed it before, but now that the man was pointing it out, I realized that there was a slight throbbing where, yesterday, Dora had slugged me.

"I guess I got hit?" I said.

After that, things moved pretty fast, so fast that I never could get the series of events straight, so fast that it seemed like a minute, but lasted for forever, until my father had been taken out of our house in handcuffs and my mother had hired a lawyer and had to get a babysitter several days in a row to watch us so she could go to wherever she had to go to straighten things out and then the days and weeks and months afterwards, with all the usual things, the expected things: the long walks I took with my father as he tried to explain, in his halting, uncomfortable way, how it was between men and women, and then more trips, this time with my mother, to see a child psychologist, followed by a couple of trips to the pediatrician, followed by my parents gathering us all together, regularly, to announce yet another new set of new rules, which were followed by more silences, and, finally, by all of us, even the baby, growing up and going off to college and learning to make mistakes of our very own devising. But even with all of that, with all the people my parents consulted on my behalf, all the resources they invested in me and in us, how was I to explain that I'd done it all for love?

NEXT OF KIN

Annie just wants her mother to die already. Is that so much to ask? The old woman no longer recognizes her, and anyway she hadn't been much of a bargain in the mother department even before she lost her short-term memory, her ability to control her bladder, and most of her jewelry. Why shouldn't she give up the ghost? Other people's mothers weren't so stubborn, so tenacious and difficult and selfish. Other people's mothers didn't insist on celebrating their ninetieth and then their ninety-first and ninety-second and ninety-fifth birthdays, even though they hadn't a clue what year they'd been born in or, for that matter, what were the names of their own children. Including Annie's, though Annie is the only one of Ruth's aging offspring who bothers to visit her, and even though she herself had been scheduled to die over three years ago. Which only goes to show you how much doctors know.

Well, it's a damn shame—a shame and a waste and a nuisance. Annie feels like a person trapped in a really bad late-night movie, or like one of those people who go about their business year in and year out only to snap one day and open fire with a machine gun in a crowded supermarket. She can picture it: herself pressing the trigger as middle-aged women in Ralph Lauren wraparound skirts and Gap capri pants drop like flies in front of the deli counter at the Safeway. And why, after all, does she—of all people—have to be the chosen one? Why not either of her distinctly cancer-free siblings, both of them on their third marriages, with grown children and grandchildren, not to mention hair?

Her brother, in particular, seems fully capable: an orthodontist who in middle age has re-embraced what he refers to as "the family faith and the faith of our fathers." Richard is solid, superficial, happy in his opinions, a contented mind in a robust body. Annie, by contrast, possesses neither health nor contentment, and her husband, though still her husband, has long since disappeared inside himself, where things are quiet and where he can think. He is a retired professor of public health, at Johns Hopkins, and mainly what he likes to do is read and take walks with Mutt, their very overweight black lab. When he gets back to the house, disposing of Mutt's business in the trashcan out back, he sits in his study reading, Mutt at his feet, or writing things on the computer. Annie doesn't know what he writes, or to whom.

"At least he didn't leave you," her sister Marion said some years back, after Annie had finished her third or fourth round of chemotherapy and Marion, in a rare display of maturity, had actually gotten on an airplane and flown to Baltimore to help.

"Why would he leave me?"

"Well," her sister continued, in the breathy, hurried way that she'd perfected as a child, and that, as far as Annie was concerned, had never ceased to sound affected and silly. "You know how men are. The second something goes wrong they trade you in for a jazzier model."

"Paul?" Annie said, thinking about her skinny, handsome, nervous, bookish husband, his inability to make small talk, his habit of picking his toes and sweeping the leavings onto the floor.

"Didn't you once tell me that every year there was some graduate student or another with a crush on him?"

"Paul is almost seventy."

"So?"

So? But that's just like her sister, always digging for dirt. Her sister had left her second and longest-term husband to marry her high-school sweetheart. The two of them now live in a new brick house in a suburb of Atlanta and take a lot of vacations. Marion looks the part, too: lots of jewelry, perfectly manicured nails, not enough lines in her sixty-eight-year-old face.

"Just be glad he's stayed put, is all I'm saying," Marion had finally said. As if the man would ever leave. As if the man could seduce anyone, let alone a bright young woman. He hasn't been interested in making love to Annie for years, long before her life became a series of trips to the oncologist. The truth is, the man is vaguely asexual, has been for some time. His balding head shines like an ornament; his eyes blink behind thick glasses; he wears soft old Dockers and button-down shirts. True, he and Annie still sleep in the same bed, but from habit and without connection. They don't even talk. A part of her wishes he would leave, let her get on with the business of being sick without his useless hovering: he hovers like a hovercraft, his face blank, his delicate hands (the hands of an intellectual, in a former life he would have been a rabbi) begging for something to do. He bothers her is what he does.

Or did; she's no longer so dismissive. These days she finds her husband's ineffectual worrying steadying, almost gratifying. She enjoys the idea of his making scrambled eggs and toast—the sum total of his culinary expertise— searching perhaps for his favorite blackberry preserves. She's come to rely on her sure knowledge that as silent as air, as amorphous as water, he is in his study, staring at the computer screen or lying on his beat-up sofa and—who knows?—perhaps dreaming, too. Dreaming of his glory days when his lecture rooms were packed, and every semester brought a new invitation to speak at a conference or contribute to some obscure journal. *Issues in Community Health. Public Health Law.* Dreaming of the early days of their marriage, when she was pretty—startlingly so, with straight thick black hair cut short like a boy's and a hard athletic body that rose to his touch—and he was promising. Oh, so promising. The wonder boy, the prodigy, the phenomenon, the genius. The two of them, together and apart, had possessed a kind of radiance.

Now Paul is retired, and she has an enormous scar from where the doctors removed her uterus and a large part of her bowel, a bathroom crammed with anti-nausea drugs, and a very expensive, not-very-realistic-looking wig that itches her but that she nevertheless wears whenever she visits her mother on the theory that, on top of everything else, she doesn't want the old woman to worry about her, even though she's well aware that Ruth no longer so much as recognizes her, let alone knows that she is once again in chemotherapy.

It has become her life, these drips administered via IV through the port the doctors have dug out of her chest just below her left collarbone, in that room filled with other women, some of them even worse off than she, all of them just sitting there and reading magazines as if they were in the beauty shop. Sometimes they talk. They talk and talk. They talk about husbands who still want to have sex even though their own insides are dry as dust. They talk about their children. They talk about their mounting bills. The religious ones talk about God. They talk about bowel movements: the distinct and newly unpleasant odor on the second day after Taxol, the slightly burned smell after being dosed with Carboplatinum. All those women, dying together.

But her mother knows about none of this. How can she? Her brains are all shriveled-up. She wears a diaper. She sits in a chair in the corner by the window in her room in the bonkers ward all day, reading the same page of the *New York Times* over and over again. Sometimes she looks up and says, "I'll take questions now." Sometimes, too, when Annie visits her, a look comes across her face that partially suggests, if not recognition, then at least familiarity. But then the look vanishes, and Ruth says: "Are you the nurse?"

It makes Annie want to scream—that blank, suspicious look that comes over her mother's features at the sight of her. It makes her want to pick up the paperweight on Ruth's useless and unused desk and bring it down right in the middle of the pale pink part in her hair. It wouldn't take much, and that would be it. Freedom. Peace. If that makes her a matricide, so be it. Anything would be better than this, this nothingness, this constant rerun of the present.

Which is why, when the chief administrator at the extremely expensive nursing home calls to say that Ruth has pneumonia and has been taken to the hospital, Annie feels a distinct rush of hope, like a girl who's been praying for months that a certain boy will notice her and call. Perhaps, Annie thinks, this time it's the real thing, and her mother will finally succumb. It is late November: a greasy, disappointing time of year.

"But I must tell you, Annie," the administrator continues, "that she's in a rather excitable state, confused, you know, poor thing. I worry, because of course with this infection she could throw herself into a fit, you know how she gets. I mean, even with the best medicine in the world, things can happen."

There is a pause, and then Annie, rescuing her, says, "Don't worry. My mother is never going to die."

Before she got sick, Annie was a guidance counselor. Unlike the days when her own children were in high school and what guidance counselors mainly did was help kids figure out what college to apply to, she had to get a master's degree in social work before she could so much as think about applying for a job in the public schools. But Paul had been disappointed. Why didn't she take that degree and work with the poor or help drug addicts, or grapple with the foster-care system? God knows, this was *Baltimore*: between the unemployment, the drugs, the teenage pregnancy, and the overall despair, there was enough work for an army of high-minded, college-educated women embarking on midlife careers. So why on earth did she want to work with a bunch of suburban kids from affluent homes?

In those days, Paul wore a beard and attended a lot of conferences in Arizona. Why, why, why? he'd say, pointing out all the opportunities that a woman of Annie's abilities, intelligence, and moral sensitivity might have, the difference she could make. Her mother, who was still in full command of her formidable persona, had sided with Paul, adding that Annie didn't have to settle for being what Ruth called a "schoolmarm." "Times have changed, daughter," she would say. "Why go backward?"

Because she wanted to, that's why. Because she liked kids, teenagers in particular; in fact she was fascinated by them, their wistfulness, their dreaminess, the way they reinvented themselves on a daily basis. Their moodiness appealed to her; she found their awkwardness endearing. She loved to watch them talk to each other, the girls unsure of what to do with their hips, the boys squaring their shoulders. They didn't make her feel young, but they did make her feel hopeful. Useful, too. The kids liked her—they *warmed* to her. She knew how to talk to them. She knew how to make them laugh.

Annie herself had been a carefree, happy girl, a girl to whom things—good grades, the right friends, admiration—came easily. She'd had, in her own youth, a wide-open heart, a beautiful mother, a father who loved her, and a lot of trophies, for basketball and softball and swimming, even diving, in which, during her last year of high school, she had been the district champ. Perhaps, she reasoned, if she could only get back in there, with the kids and all their hopeful anxiety, her former optimism—ah, but the world had once shined for her!—might return.

That was in the mid-80's, when the last of her daughters had finished college and Annie, like most of the women she knew in her generation, needed to find something to do. Several (Elsbeth Stuart, Hilary Levy) had started traveling around the world with their husbands: Japan, the Isle of Skye, Antarctica. They came back with beads, or small, smooth sculptures carved out of wood, or dense silk woven into extraordinary patterns. Annie felt a twinge of envy when they told her stories of their adventures but contented herself with the knowledge that she was doing something, if not sexy or glamorous, then at least commendable.

And it was a real job, too, with a regular salary and benefits, an office and coworkers, not merely a time-filler like the part-time positions in bookstores or on philanthropic boards that some of her women friends had. She wasn't the only woman in the world who preferred the routine and the concrete— her small, windowless, cinder-block office, the smell of chalk and nervousness and hormones, the principal's voice crackling over the school's P.A. system— to the promise of adventure or enlightenment or ease. She wasn't the only woman among her circle who had gone back to school so she could get an actual job—not that she had anything against women who dabbled or women who had married wealthy men who were able to pay for their wives' facelifts and put them up in four-star hotels in elegant European capitals. It was just that Annie hadn't married a wealthy man who could put her up in a four-star hotel in an elegant European capital. She had married Paul, and Paul was a professor of public health. Their vacations, when they took them, tended to be to laid-back, rustic places: a modest rental in North Carolina or Vermont, a cross-country trip to the Grand Canyon.

But handsome he had certainly been, her Paul: tall, thin, with an intellectual's beaky face and, in those days at least, a head of curly salt-and-pepper hair. He spoke softly but with authority. In the winter, he wore a woolen scarf. He was indeed the kind of man that graduate students had crushes on. Several young women—idealistic, bright, ambitious—had formed such attachments in the past. But it wasn't a graduate student he'd left her for. It was solitude.

As she rides the elevator to the fifth floor (geriatrics, pulmonary), Annie issues a fervent if somewhat hypocritical prayer: *Take her, please.* She doesn't much believe in God; nor does she believe in any kind of justice in the world. Just about the only thing she does believe in these days is her mother's amazing, persistent, obnoxious vigor.

The last time her mother suffered a medical crisis, Annie had been in New York, visiting her youngest daughter. She and Ellen had gone to Saks Fifth Avenue and then out for Chinese. When they got back from dinner, there was a message on the machine from Paul. Ruth had been taken to the hospital with a bad flu. "Looks like this might be it," he said. "You'd better give me a call." When Annie phoned, he said, "Don't you think you'd better come home?" She'd thought about it for a second, then said no. She didn't want to come home (how often was it that she was feeling well enough to go to New York?), and at any rate she didn't believe that her mother was on her way out. The hospital, however, failed to heed Annie's instructions that Ruth not be left alone, and the next day Paul called to report that she was missing. "Missing?" Annie said. An hour later, he called again to say that she'd been found in the maternity ward, where she was helping herself to somebody's leftover toast from a hospital trolley that had been parked near the stairwell.

Her mother is at the end of the hall in a small private room with a view of a rooftop covered with icy-looking dark puddles and a framed picture depicting European peasants working in a sun-washed field. Ruth is lying on her back with the covers pulled up neatly under her arms and an oxygen mask on her face. A nurse is standing over her, taking her pulse. The nurse is middle-aged, attractive, with a pretty, pampered mouth. All this Annie takes in with an apprehensive glance. The room is too hot. She takes off her coat.

"Knock knock," she says. "It's me, Mother. Your daughter. Annie."

Ruth's bright blue eyes slide toward her, then blink.

"How's she doing?" Annie asks the nurse.

"She's comfortable, I think, but awfully weak."

"Okay."

"But I think she's feeling a little better now, aren't you sweetie?" the nurse continues. "Your heart just goes out to the old ones."

Ruth's blinking again, a sign that she's either frustrated or excited, and a moment later she is struggling to rid herself of the mask. Before the nurse has a chance to turn around and readjust things or Annie has a chance to warn her, Ruth has it off her face. Annie hears hard rasping sounds as her mother struggles for air, sees her mother's mouth struggling to make shapes. A moment later, she succeeds. "You look like a witch," Ruth says.

"Well, I'm not a witch, Mother. I'm your daughter Annie."

The oxygen mask is back on now, the nurse patting things down, checking the tubing, making sure everything is as it should be. Through the clear plastic Annie can see her mother's mouth form the word, *Annie*, as if she were testing it out, tasting it on her tongue and deciding that after all it wasn't to her liking. Her feathery white hair splays out on the pillow. Her perfect oval nails are painted a pale, luminescent pink.

"She's a live one," the nurse says.

"That would be my mother."

"Try not to excite her, okay?"

Why did they always say that? Maybe it was just something they learned in nursing school or from watching hospital shows on TV. Why *not* excite her, Annie always wanted to ask. What's the worst thing that could happen? That she'd have an instant of clarity or, better, a fatal heart attack? This is such a tragedy?

"Don't worry," Annie says. "My mother will outlast all of us." The nurse, clearly unsure how to respond, puts a half-hearted smile on her face and exits the room.

"Well, Mother," Annie says. "I guess it's just me and you."

It was six years ago, at this same hospital, that Annie had awakened from surgery to discover that she was living in the land of the sick. She'd been taken back to her room with tubes down her throat. Her daughters had taped up crayon drawings made by their small children. "Get Well Soon Grandma." "I Love You." She shakes off the memory. It makes her too sad to think of herself then: still so hopeful, still so innocent.

At one point, early on, she'd believed that she would be one of the lucky ones, one of those miraculous cases that you sometimes read about who, against all odds, fight the good fight and come out on top. She'd actually told her daughters not to bother coming in for her first chemotherapy session. Though she wasn't looking forward to it, she claimed, she was eager to get going so she could put the whole thing behind her. She'd planned on returning to her job in a few days and then resuming full-time as soon as the treatment was over.

And then the chemo hit her, and she was bald and nauseated and shaking and sweaty and plagued by diarrhea and cramps and dry mouth and mouth sores and swollen feet like two wet loaves of bread. Her body shriveled up until she was smaller than she had been at the height of her high-school glory. And then her body bloated, becoming ungainly with fat and bulges, her muscles losing all tone, her skin becoming blotchy, until at last the brave black jokes she'd made at the beginning of her treatment seemed as absurd and awful as a laugh track.

It will be a long day, she thinks, made longer, no doubt, by quiet. Apart from Paul and her daughters (whom she trusts), no one knows that Ruth is in the hospital. She feels slightly guilty about this, but she just can't deal with either her sister's ongoing and unnecessary alarm or her brother's platitudes. She doesn't want to reassure either one of them. She's tired of being the good sport. And anyway she's fairly certain that Ruth is going to pull through. She knows her mother and senses, in her high color and the way her hands are curling on top of the clean white sheets, that the old woman has yet to give up her formidable will. She can tell by her defiance: *You look like a witch!* It's true though: she does look like a witch. Skin as white and dry as powder; eyes shrunken within folds of fat; a wig that could be part of a Halloween costume.

Ruth's eyes flutter open, then close again.

"Don't worry, Mom," Annie says. "I'm not going anywhere. At least not today." Ruth opens her eyes again, stares, then says: "Are you the nurse?"

"I'm your daughter, Annie."

A look of hurt bewilderment comes over Ruth's face.

"But you're a fighter," Ellen says on the phone from New York after Annie tells her that if she didn't have Ruth to look after, she doesn't think she'd bother to keep going.

"I'm not so sure about that."

There's a heavy silence. Ellen never did care for declarative sentences and hates being contradicted. Even as a young girl she preferred subterfuge, a certain amount of beating-around-the-bush, a certain avoidance, as if not saying bad or negative things flat-out would heighten the possibility of their not coming true.

"But, Mom," Ellen says. "Do you think Nana really might die? Do you think this is it?"

"I don't think so, but I'm praying it is."

"But, Mom, even if Nana goes, you're still young in spirit, and that's what counts." As if adding a second cliché to the first carried any kind of rhetorical weight. Ellen can't help it. Annie loves this third and youngest child of hers: loves her bouncy certainties, the ease with which she greets the world. But Ellen is an editor at a women's magazine, and her sense of language has been both flattened and distended from years of editing articles with titles like, "How Do You Know When It's the Real Thing?" and "Sex Kitten 101."

"Anyway, Mom," Ellen says, "they're coming out with new treatments all the time. You yourself said so."

Had she? Well, maybe she had, but then again, she's said a lot of things she never really meant. It's the curse of being a woman, she supposes. You just talk and talk and talk, sometimes for no other reason than to fill up the silence, and also because if you don't say something, everything might simply, mysteriously, fall apart.

At one point, Annie had loved her mother. Ruth hadn't been easy to love, either. Proud, haughty, domineering, she'd run her family as if always expecting photographers from *Life* magazine to burst through the door, eager to capture some quintessence of American-style domestic perfection: the three kids, the two dogs, the house swathed in chintz, the gardens blooming out back, the maid in the kitchen, the beautiful young mother in silk stockings and tailored two-piece suits.

Larchmont, New York: German Jews in love with high Wasp style is what they were. More English than the English. She was a piece of work, her mother: a woman who'd grown up as the daughter of Jewish immigrant shopkeepers in a small town in Kentucky and somewhere along the line had decided that she needed a grander space, some place that would do her justice.

As a young mother herself, Annie had dreaded her mother's visits, knowing she couldn't stand up to her sharp tongue or critical eye, the sheer force of her personality. Although she'd disappointed her mother by marrying Paul, a man from no background to speak of (his father owned a deli in Queens and used Yiddish) and no money either, she had managed to win Ruth's approval by pointing out that Paul was a true intellectual, a budding scholar, a *genius*, and that anyway neither she nor he wanted to live in grand style. And Hopkins? It wasn't Harvard, maybe, but it sure as hell wasn't Brooklyn College. Let Marion marry the hungry young lawyer (husband number one) and build an enormous modern house in White Plains. Let Richard cover his wife (wives) with jewelry. She, Annie, was happy with simpler things.

But when she came to visit, Ruth would invariably rearrange the furniture, fuss about the children's clothing and pass comments on the general untidiness of Annie's house and the parochial quality of Baltimore. All of which made Annie shrink into herself, see herself with her mother's eye: a daughter too stupid to recognize that there was a right way to do things, or perhaps simply without the charm, the grace, to get what she wanted. "You don't get bored here, daughter?" Ruth would ask. "No, I suppose you don't. You've always been resourceful that way."

But the truth was that Annie loved her mother, always had. She loved her with an instinctive, open-hearted, wet love, the love of a dog for its master or a child for its first teacher. She loved her just because.

"You sure she's gonna pull through?" It's her brother Richard on the phone, calling directly to Ruth's room. Paul, once again, directing traffic. "You sure you don't want me to come in, spot you some relief?"

"It's okay," Annie says. "She's looking pretty alert, for her. I think she'll probably go home soon."

"But if she doesn't, then what? How many days do you plan to baby-sit her? For Christ's sake, Annie-bananie, you have cancer. You need to take it easy."

"I know." Annie feels a distinct wave of annoyance creep up her spine. She's always hated Richard's childhood nickname for her, and it especially grates now, when, of the two of them, she is the one who is clearly more grown-up, wiser and more accepting of reality, while he is the one who is clearly full of shit. It's all an act, anyhow, all that I'll-be-there-for-you stuff. He wouldn't leave his comfortable North Shore house and his pretty third wife to sit by Ruth's hospital bed even if it meant points in heaven—or at his stuffy, downtown synagogue.

"Ugh," Ruth says from her hospital bed.

"You okay, Mother?"

"Who are you?" Ruth says.

On the other end of the line Richard is saying, "What is it? Is something going on there? Tell me," in a way that is so out of proportion to the reality of Ruth's brief burst of energy that Annie almost laughs. When in doubt, panic. Show that you care.

"Nothing, Richard," Annie at last answers. "Just Mother mumbling things. I told you that she's going to be okay. Or at least I think she is."

"She is amazing."

"That she is."

After their conversation, Annie resettles herself in the visitor's chair (covered, like most visitors' chairs in most hospitals, in a muddy pink) and takes out her needlepoint. She is making a pillow for her youngest granddaughter. When she's finished it will have a large white half-moon inside a starry sky and a legend that says, "Reach for the moon." But now all it has is a few rows of blue. Her hands don't work properly, is part of the problem. She works slowly, slowly, thinking of the look on the little girl's face. If her mother stays here much longer, perhaps she will make real headway. She'd like to finish it while she still can.

At eleven, a team of young doctors comes into the room. They bend over Ruth's body, look under her eyelids and down her throat, listen to her chest, bustle out again. At twelve, an orderly comes in with a full tray, then reads Ruth's chart and backs away. A little after that, Annie takes a walk down the corridor, then decides to do a complete lap. Perhaps when she returns to her chair she can start the novel that she's brought along.

"Really, Mother," she says as she settles back into the puke-pink chair. "You've got everyone all riled up." She does this sometimes—chats with the old lady, if only to brighten the air in the room and feel a little less alone. It reminds her of the one time she went to see a psychotherapist, back in the early 70's when she and Paul were having problems. On that occasion she learned two things about herself that she already knew. One, that her mother was very dominating and always had been; ergo, she, Annie, was accustomed to doing as she was told. And, two, that her husband had difficulty communicating anything more personal than the weather. After more than a year of listening to herself talk, she decided that her time would be better spent reading or playing tennis. She ended up taking piano lessons. (Another thing she can no longer do: play the piano.)

Taking up her needlepoint again, she resumes. "And for what? Because even if you're capable of fooling everyone else, you can't fool me. I know your tricks. I'm on to you, Mother." Her mother breathes, breathes, the oxygen turning her blood bright red, expanding the lining of her lungs, dancing through her veins. Amazing, how even now the old woman seems so sure of herself, so calm, so *grounded*. "I know how stubborn you are, how you always have to have your own way. But I'm losing patience, Mother. I'm just so tired. Look at me, if you don't believe me. Can you even recognize me? I barely recognize myself.

"At first it wasn't so bad. Not that I wasn't sick. My God, I was sick. But I was optimistic. I read all this stuff, you know, about the mind-body connection, how hope keeps you going, hope and something to live for, some goal or mission. It's a whole new industry, cancer. Not just the medical end of it, either. You should see the books on the subject. Eating right to beat cancer. Doing yoga to beat cancer. Meditating. Some women get into these all-women groups and do God knows what. Bray at the moon. Recite poetry. Journaling your way through chemo. Not that any of it works. But I read everything, and I was actually feeling upbeat. For a while I was even able to keep working. I marched off to school with my wig and my anti-nausea meds, and I drew my eyebrows on, and I was going to be one of those brave women who simply tough things out, beat the odds, surprise everyone. If I couldn't do it, I thought, who could? I was going to be the best cancer patient ever, you know, win a trophy for it or something. A blue ribbon. But most days I was too sick to do anything but lie on the sofa.

"And that was *then*, before all three girls were married or had families of their own. What's supposed to keep me going now? My marriage is boring, and that's the least of it. Not that you were right when you objected to Paul. You objected for all the wrong reasons. You actually thought the man wouldn't ever add up to anything, which, let me tell you, Mother, is so ludicrous that words fail to convey the total ludicrousness of your snobbery. The truth was the opposite. He was a big big star, you know. He just never added up to much of a husband. Not the world's worst, but not exactly the greatest. Steady, in his way. I'll give him that. But in bed? Forget it. He has more passion for Mutt than for me. Even when we were younger, there was a certain, shall we say *lassitude?*, about his love-making. Of course I didn't know any better. How could I? Like everyone else, I was a virgin. We both were. But you know, I always wanted a man who would sort of just take me—not violently, but with a certain firmness of purpose. Whereas Paul would just kind of lie there, his mind drifting off, and occasionally reach over or something, then drift back. Sometimes he'd just kind of stop in the middle and start talking about a problem he was having with his research, or some ethical dilemma having to do with how to allocate medical resources, or whether or not it's ethical to tie the tubes of retarded women, or I don't know. It's a miracle, really, that I had any children at all. And then of course, after Ellen came along—well, things just went splat. He just wasn't interested."

She stops, readjusts her needlepoint, and then glances up at her mother. Ruth's blue eyes are open and looking directly at her.

"Your father was a wonderful lover," she says.

"What did you say, Mother?"

"Is that you, Annie?"

"Yes."

"Well, I'll be damned."

"Mother?"

But Ruth has once again retreated into the innermost spaces of her reverie.

The phone call informing Annie that her mother has died comes in the middle of the night. "We're sorry to startle you like this," the doctor—who sounds young, and nervous—says.

"But as next of kin—" and she goes on from there, reciting all kinds of perfunctory things. She sounds tired, tired. Perhaps she's a resident, going on two hours' sleep. Perhaps she's just too tired to care. Or perhaps, more likely, she just can't get all worked up about the death of a woman on the verge of her ninety-sixth year.

Paul's side of the bed is empty, a sign that he couldn't sleep. Annie gets up, pulls a bathrobe around her, and pads down to his study, where she finds him dozing in his favorite chair, Mutt snoring at his feet. On the floor beside Mutt is one of their family photo albums.

"Didn't you hear the phone ring?" Annie says, waking Paul, who looks slightly guilty and slightly confused. Mutt remains asleep.

"Sorry. What? What time is it? Are you okay?"

"I'm fine," Annie says, seating herself gingerly on the edge of Paul's beat-up sofa. "But I just got a phone call from the hospital. Mother's gone."

A blank, wondering look—much like Mutt's, in fact—comes across her brilliant husband's sharp features.

"Dead," Annie says.

"Well, what do you know."

Annie lets the silence wrap around her, along with its implications. Funny, how she feels almost nothing at all, neither grief nor the vast openness of relief that she's so long anticipated. She supposes she should do something—make some phone calls, shed a tear—but nothing comes. She merely feels heavy.

She's about to get up and return to bed when Paul shifts forward in his seat, picks up the photo album from the floor, and says, "You know, I was just looking at this. Sometimes I do that, or rather, I used to. Just sit and look at these photos, from when the girls were small. For some reason I felt like doing that tonight. It's funny, though, how I can't really remember them, remember what they looked like, and more to the point, what they *were* like, how they smelled, how they sounded. I can't conjure them up in my mind except from the photographs. So now, when I think of the girls when they were little, what springs to mind is the images from the pictures. My own memory is just this wash. This watercolor. All impressions, no outlines."

"I know what you mean."

"Of course I know what they look like now," Paul continues. "And thank God I still have enough of my marbles to remember the grandchildren. But as for our own kids when they were little, it's all gone."

Annie doesn't know what to say. She is aware of how hard Paul is trying, how much he wants to comfort her. The truth is that she, too, can no longer remember the feel of a baby in her arms, or what it was like to nurse (alone among her friends and acquaintances, she had disdained formula) or to kiss a sleepy child goodnight. She can't remember what any of her daughters were like on their first day of kindergarten, or their frequent, unserious fights, or the smell of paste. She can't remember what they wore to their senior proms or the sound of their voices calling her from Paris or Los Angeles or Milan, telling her not to worry, everything was fine, I haven't run out of money, only gotta go, Mom, I don't want to miss the train. She can't remember whether or not they wore lace for their weddings. Perhaps tomorrow she too will go through the photo albums, trying to conjure up her children, and herself, before they disappear entirely.

"You're not going to give up on me, are you?" Paul says.

"I don't know."

"Please don't." The dog is wakeful now, alert, as if eager to hear the outcome of this conversation. His tail thumps back and forth. "It's just, dear, that life wouldn't be much fun without you."

"I know," Annie says.

She is very sad now, as sad as she's ever been. And how badly she longs for sleep, and what a big day she'll have tomorrow! Suddenly she is overcome with fatigue, fatigue like a drug, pulling at all her limbs, making her blood sluggish, her brain heavy. This is how she wants to die, she thinks: in this deep, slumberous peace, in this knowing that there is rest. She gets up to return to the bedroom, but Paul gets up too and pulls her back again, taking her by the hand and tugging her down to sit on the sofa beside him.

Skipped

When, at seven, I was skipped ahead from second to third grade, my older sister beat me with a belt. It was one of those plastic belts then in style among the well-to-do suburban set, bright pink with a hard and shiny silver buckle, a prized possession. Ava stood over me and hit me with it until I started shrieking and she got scared and stopped. No one other than the new maid was home, we could hear the roar of the vacuum cleaner coming from downstairs, and, as things turned out, the new maid was only to last a couple of months before our mother, who was picky, fired her. In any event, the beating hurt—I smarted for days, and it was weeks until the marks completely faded—and after it, nothing was the same.

Our parents were so incapable of raising children that I often think the three of us (I have a younger brother, too) would have been better served in foster care or even an old-fashioned orphanage, the kind I first read about in the fourth grade in a grisly story about Anne Sullivan, who was raised in a large and terrible orphanage where rats bit her while she was sleeping, before growing up to become Helen Keller's teacher. I loved that book with its grisly descriptions of the young Anne's deprivations, the beatings, the cold, and must have read it half a dozen times. In comparison, how lucky I myself was—how lucky we all were—because while our own father drank and stormed around the house, and, in an effort to keep the peace, our mother trained us to not to react, we not only lived in a large and well-run home, filled with art and books and music, but had a father who was a somebody, an author, a respected and well-known member of his field, psychiatry. Which of course made things all that much more confusing.

Mother would make us lie down on our backs so she could tickle us. If we laughed or giggled, she'd slap us, not hard, but hard enough that we'd stop. If we managed to lie perfectly still, betraying nothing on our faces, she'd let us have a treat: an extra half hour of television, perhaps, or an ice-cream cone. Eventually all three of us were able to pretend that nothing was amiss no matter what our father did, including when he threw things at us or smashed a lamp against the wall.

But for me, it wasn't any of these things—the strange ritual with the tickling; my father's alcohol-fueled rages; the sense that despite the regular violence that punctuated family events, we were distinctly superior to, better than, and special (nothing at all like the ordinary run of humanity with their petty ambitions and tacky taste in home decor)—that tripped me up. No, it was none of these things that flung me into something that, now, in my own late middle age, I recognize as a state of unmooring, of darkness so dark that I had nothing to compare it to, of utter collapse: a me that had unscrolled, unwound, collapsed in on itself, like an exploded crater. I was there one minute, and then I was gone.

"You show-off bitch! You show-off bitch! I'll show you who the show-off bitch is!" my sister said as she beat me with her pink plastic belt there in the light-flooded upper landing of our large, modern, airy house.

Until that moment, I'd been the smart one. I understand that in families such as mine, this appellation is typically reserved for the firstborn, and that any who follow tend to be saddled with labels both less intoxicatingly privileged and less binding. But in the case of my older sister, there were pronounced learning issues, an inability to focus, but these things weren't well understood then, so instead of getting her the help she might have been able to get had she been born at a later time, my parents resigned themselves to the disgrace of having a child who could not and would not succeed in the only place it counted, which was, it goes without saying, school. They were—both of them— the products of the Ivy League and its female equivalent, Harvard/Yale for him and Smith/Columbia for her (she had a master's degree in English). By the time I could read I also understood, as both my siblings did as well, that we were not only to acquire a higher education, but that to do so at an institution less prestigious than those that our parents attended would bring with it no uncertain shame. Such places—whether they be small Midwestern colleges or large state universities in sunny and lovely places—were for ordinary people, drab little people with drab little lives, so trapped in their own ordinariness that they didn't even know how second-rate they were.

We hated such people.

But I didn't know that yet, either. All I knew for sure was that being smart, or more to the point, being the smart one, caused all kinds of misery. It was my fault, then, the beating; and for that reason, before my sister had even finished beating me, I'd made a decision—as conscious as the decision I'm making now to write this story down—to never study or read or try again.

Long before I was in high school, I became the family fuckup, with a repertoire of behaviors suited to the role and an equally long history of increasingly severe threats and punishments. It goes without saying, of course, that punishment, in the form of punitive damages meted out by one or both of my parents, was entirely unnecessary; that I'd long since perfected the art of relentless self-punishment; that my every waking moment was a misery. On top of everything else, I was ugly, with a rash of purplish acne sprayed across my forehead and cheeks and enormous breasts that swung heavily, without the benefit of support of any kind, under the oversize men's shirts that I favored. (Here, too, my mother was oblivious; it wasn't until I was sixteen, and at my one friend's house, that her mother insisted on taking me bra shopping.) Though what I mainly did in high school was have a lot of mainly very bad sex, usually while stoned, I did manage to graduate, albeit at the very bottom of my class of one hundred.

Cliché that it is, the day after I finished high school I hitchhiked to Los Angeles, sometimes sleeping with my drivers, sometimes dozing or staring out the window. I figured that I'd find a commune to live in, only by the time I got to California most of the communes had long since closed, and anyway, I'd gone to the wrong part of the state. I had some vague ideas about writing poetry and ended up taking a room for thirty dollars a week at the back of a ratty house in the rattiest part of Hollywood. My landlady was an ancient black woman whom I only saw if I was late with my rent money. Mainly she watched TV. I'd see her in there, her chair moved up close to the screen, when I went back and forth through the alley that led from the sidewalk to my room. I myself was quite fond of TV, but not only couldn't afford one, I also would never have admitted to anyone, let alone my landlady, that I would have loved nothing more than to be invited in to watch *Three's Company* or *The Mary Tyler Moore Show*. Maybe she'd even give me some of the canned peaches that she seemed always to have on hand, in a pretty glass bowl from which she slowly scooped one slivered and glistening peach after another, eating each with a tenderness and delicacy that practically brought me to tears. I spent my days walking, a walker in a city of cars, walking to get to know the city—or at least that's what I told myself. In reality, I think I thought that if I stayed still for more than a few minutes at a time I'd simply vanish, cave in, collapse. That I'd suffer some unnamable catastrophe. Then my money, from my childhood bank account and sustained with cash presents from relatives, ran out.

The job I found was as babysitter to the six- and seven-year-old children of a man named Jacob. Jacob was a writer, raising the children on his own after his wife had left him. Actually, I never did find out if the children's mother was Jacob's wife or not: the subject didn't seem to merit even a moment of attention, in part, no doubt, because Jacob was not that kind of man, something he immediately made clear to me when he hired me despite my obvious lack of qualifications. He said: "It's just that I work at home. I need quiet, man, quiet and plenty of what I think of as meandering time. So you know: I'm here, but not here. It would be your job to get the kids from the school bus, give them dinner, get them ready for their baths. Because I need to work, and usually I don't really get into it, don't really feel it, until late in the day. And also?" he said, speaking directly to my bosom.

"What?"

"I can't pay a lot."

"How much can't you pay?" I said, biting my lower lip, tasting the bits of blood that were still there from when I'd played with my chapped lips, tearing them, the night before.

"Minimum wage."

"I can live with that."

We shook on it, and the next day, along with half the Mexicans and Chinese in Los Angeles, I took two buses, in my case along various parallel roads that led east toward downtown, stopping at the pale orange bungalow in Hancock Park that I'd later learn Jacob had been able to afford only because he had inherited it from his parents, who'd both died, one right after the other, sometime after his wife/not wife had left him.

It was his childhood house, in other words, which explained the decor: the light blue sprays of violets on the wallpaper in the master bedroom; the fussy, overly veneered dining room table and chairs; the faded curtains of a once-expensive lineage. Even the dishes were fancy, with gilt edgings and various curlicues. Whereas Jacob himself made a point of speaking without flourish or even much in the way of subtlety or intonation, and dressing as if to insist that he never was, nor would he ever be, bourgeois like the people from whom he sprang: a lawyer and a schoolteacher, Midwesterners who'd done well and wanted a large family but had to settle for their one son.

It was the late 1970s, the tail end of hippiedom, and people were still talking like that, spitting out words like *bourgeois* and *business* and *conventional* and *materialistic* as if the very words, held too long in the mind, might poison them. I, too, talked like that, greedily joining in any conversation whose point was to trash anyone who wasn't us, and when I say "us," I'm referring to me and Jacob, and then, me and Jacob and Jacob's friends, and then, me and Jacob and Jacob's friends' girlfriends or wives—and others. In the Southern California sun my acne cleared up. I cleaned up my act, too—I had to. In truth, I enjoyed my new role as the responsible one, the one who took care of the children, making sure they'd brushed their teeth and done their homework and the thousand other details that taking care of children brings in its wake. It's something of a miracle that I was able to do any of these things with any kind of clarity or proficiency, too, as my own upbringing had been so hurly-burly, so rumble-tumble, so fraught with violence, with suppressed and nonsuppressed rage. Still, I enjoyed and even came to feel deep affection for the children, a boy and a girl who were tender and bright and who called me by my name, treating me not with the reverence of a mother or the admiration of an older cousin, but as the oddball, hybrid nonmom nonwife nonsibling that I was. In time I began to act more normally, too, hiding out less and less in the fog that I'd become accustomed to and spending more and more of my day doing normal things, chatting with the neighbors—the weather, the cost of electricity, the drought—and getting to know the postman. I even considered adopting a dog, something I thought might complete the picture of our own weird and elusive family harmony, because while there was nothing like real family harmony, the picture—the picture itself—glowed. And I loved it, being a part of something so much prettier than the picture, however glamorous, that I'd left behind. Because while I'd been raised to believe in my family's strange superiority—how brilliant we were, and how magical; with our beautiful modern house filled with Early American antiques and our handsome, semifamous father with his accolades and awards and books; with our degrees (excepting mine, of course) from famous universities and our vacations to lovely spots on islands and in mountains—I was too conversant with its underbelly to want to return to it. Versus the fake family I now had, where there was nothing but sunshine, weed, and white wine, plus the gazpachos and grilled salmons and slivered cucumber salads that I learned to prepare.

We didn't discuss marriage. But then again, marriage—with its promise of stability, permanence, respectability, all the markers of having arrived at adulthood—didn't interest me. And Jacob? He seemed to appreciate my willingness to do things with him in bed that, eventually, he told me that his ex, that bitch, that frigid, selfish whore, refused to do. I took such acknowledgements as compliments.

I lived with him for ten years, pretty much raising the children for him, and then one day I got a phone call from Ava. Since the day that she had beat me with her pink plastic belt, Ava had gone to college and then got her master's degree in social work, and she was now busily counseling the confused children of the exact kind of upscale, bourgeois people that Jacob and I and, in fact, my sister herself had always loathed. She lived, with her husband whom I'd never met, in Long Island. I'd never met him because I hadn't been invited to the wedding, but even if I had been, it's doubtful that I would have gone. I hadn't been in touch with any of my relatives, including the one grandmother—my mother's mother, Nanny Judy—with whom I'd always felt a real kinship. I used to want to go and live with her, escaping my own family and our large modern house for her smaller but equally well-appointed apartment in New York City. She'd died not long after I'd moved in with Jacob, but I hadn't found out about her death until some years later, when my brother, the one member of my family who didn't seem to warrant a story line of his own, tracked me down to tell me that after I'd run away (his term, not mine), our mother's brown hair had gone white, and that now she had cancer.

"So you're saying that her cancer is my fault?" I had said.

"That's not what I said. I just thought you should know."

"And now I'm supposed to call that frigging bitch and apologize for all the pain I put her through, is that it?"

"She could die in a year. Or two. I don't know. I just thought you should know."

"Fine. You've done your job. Feel better?"

"Not fair."

"And?"

"Who's that guy who answered the phone?"

"Who, Jacob? He's Jacob."

"Is he your—"

"He's Jacob, is who he is."

A long pause. Then, from my brother: "It's just that actions have consequences, you know."

Then, as I was thinking about whether to hang up on him, actually thinking it through, the pros and cons, he said: "By the way, Nanny Judy died."

"What?"

"Three, four years ago. They found her dead on her kitchen floor. Heart attack, or wait. Maybe it was a stroke. She'd been dead like that, for a few days, when they came in."

But this time, it was Ava calling, and I knew her voice immediately—the same breathless, slightly Britishly infused intonations, the same implied insistence that there was a war between us, the same elongated pauses, invitations for me to rush in, to say something stupid that would heighten her sense of having won. It was, of course, an ancient, ancient battle between us, which of us was to distinguish ourselves to such a degree that the other one would be obliterated while we ourselves (whichever of us was the winner) would soar to such heights that the old traumas and ugliness would slough off of us like a lizard's skin. Strange how the battle had continued despite all the years since I'd taken off, all the years since she'd literally beaten me and I'd ceded the territory to her: because in fact, and despite whatever neurological or wiring difficulties she had—today no doubt she would have been diagnosed with attention deficit disorder and medicated—she'd managed, in high school, to be the straight-A student that I was supposed to have been. It had been something of a miracle, too, to see her go from the middling elementary and middle school student she'd been to becoming one of the bright and shining stars of our small private school with its rostrum of distinguished graduates. Her stellar SAT scores. Her meticulously written and rewritten papers. Her status, eventually, as one of a handful of top students in her own class of one hundred. And then, of course, her ascent to the big leagues, in her case, first to the small liberal arts college in Western Massachusetts that our father proudly called "the best of the little Ivies," and then to NYU for graduate school and so on and so forth—though until that day, and despite the phone call from my brother some years earlier, I hadn't known anything of her postcollege life.

"Dad wants to see you," she said.

"Is that so?"

"He's coming to Los Angeles, which is where you live, right? And he really really really wants to see you."

"Then why are you calling? Why isn't he calling?"

"He's going to be on television. For his latest book. It's gone big. Huge. Surely you know about this?"

I didn't. I hardly even glanced at the newspaper, let alone read any book reviews, although by then I had started reading in a way that I hadn't since my earliest childhood, picking up one and then another of Jacob's books, discarding the ones that didn't interest me but devouring the ones I did.

"It's a huge, big deal," my sister said. "He really wants to see you." Then she caught me up on all the family news: her own newborn twins, our brother's coming out as gay, our mother's frail dental health—she'd had to have bone grafting, periodontal surgery—and other bits of news, all punctuated with references to her children, career, town, husband, and house.

"So I guess Mom didn't die."

"From dental issues?"

"From cancer."

"You knew about that?"

"Obviously."

"She beat it back. Caught it early, you know. Thank God." There was a long pause. Who would rush in first? She did. "But there's a lot of other stuff you might want to know about."

"I doubt it," I said.

When I told him about the conversation, Jacob insisted that I find out what show my father was going to be on, so that we could watch it and he could "see the stud who sired me," as he put it. But I didn't know how to find out without calling my sister or one of my other relatives, and the *TV Guide* was useless, listing only the names of the programs, not who the guests on them might be. The next thing I know, he's yelling at me because I'm so incompetent, a slut both in bed and out, a crappy cook in the kitchen, and in the bedroom, forget it, he doesn't like the way I fuck, once he did but now he doesn't. He yelled that I was all fucked out when we met and he should have known better because once a drug-addled loser like me is worn out from too much bad fucking, it was no wonder that things just went all to fuck.

He would talk like that occasionally, but usually about someone or something else, as in: "Those people? They call themselves writers? Bunch of fucked-up fuckwads if you ask me, fucked their brain cells all to fuck back when they were all going to be the next Hemingway." Or: "I just can't stand that jerk-off fuckwad principal anymore. Do you hear how he *talks*?" (The children were by then in high school, and Jacob and I went to various back-to-school and meet-the-teacher nights.) "He ought to be arrested for talking like that, fuck." Or: "My ex was the world's biggest bitch, that cunt." But mainly, as in the first example above, he reserved his worst and most inarticulate venom for other writers, most of them more successful than he was. Though Jacob, holed up there in his study as I dealt with the children, eventually learning not only how to cook and clean and do the laundry but also to navigate the school system and various doctors and dentists, met with enough success to keep him at it. A pilot for a sitcom; a screenplay that was almost produced; a series of articles for *Los Angeles Magazine* about L.A.'s supposed hidden neighborhoods, which really meant the neighborhoods of L.A. that the readership of *Los Angeles Magazine* wouldn't be caught dead in. It was a better time for print journalism then.

What I later learned to call verbal abuse wasn't something entirely new between us, but usually, when he went at me—sometimes in a voice pitched so low that I had to lean in to hear him, other times with great and dramatic fury, big gobs of spit coming out of his mouth, red-faced—I, who had been trained to not react or even respond, did him one better. I didn't say a word. I didn't move a muscle. I was impassive, calm, utterly still.

Until, one day, not long after Ava's call, he slapped me. And I went crazy on him, berserk, throwing things at him—books, vases, paperweights, my fists, my feet. Oh, how he cowered.

I didn't leave right away. I had nowhere else to go. Also, by then I'd been settled in, there in Jacob's parents' lovely bungalow in lovely, leafy Hancock Park, for ten years and counting. I was the only mother-older-sister-mash-up-substitute that the children had ever had, and while I can't say that I ever grew to truly love either of them, loving them in the sense that a real mother might be capable of, from some place so deep down that the bond becomes something beyond you, something mysterious, with glimmers of both holiness and pornography, I had a strong affection for both of them. We were closer in age to each other than I was to their father, and, in many ways, I had more in common with them than with Jacob, who was becoming both more driven and more disappointed, his thoughts and conversations whirling around the one thing he thought he both needed and deserved but that never materialized; or, if it did, seemed to elude him, slipping through his grasp. If only the series for *Los Angeles Magazine* was turned into a book, and from there, perhaps, a TV series. If only that dickwad asswipe Larry Shieber or Striver or Scheurer hadn't been chosen as head writer for *Too Close for Comfort* or *Webster* or *The Facts of Life*, then he might have had a shot at joining the team. A TV writing job here; an almost script there. But money wasn't the issue. Along with the bungalow, he'd inherited his parents' retirement savings, the money that his lawyer dad and schoolteacher mom had socked away, year after year, as they dreamed of the trips they'd take to Mexico, to France, to see the pyramids in Egypt and the Parthenon in Greece.

So there I was, perhaps no longer as beaten down or ugly or unkempt as when I'd hitchhiked to L.A., but not exactly ready to take on the world, either. I liked nice things, clean sheets, a car that started without coughing, cash in my wallet, unopened packs of soap in their neat, rectangular boxes.

I read the want ads. I read the rentals. I went on interviews and finally took the only job offered to me, to be the companion to a young woman named Liza who was dying of cancer in her parents' house in the Hollywood Hills. She didn't want her parents hovering over her, wiping up her spills and vomit and worrying over her every cough and sneeze. She didn't want a nurse, either: she didn't need one; not yet, anyway. She just needed someone who wouldn't be too grossed out by her wildly uncontrollable body in all its uncontrolled self-destruction, and whose company she could stand. We were almost exactly the same age, and her parents—pre-heartbroken by their youngest daughter's imminent death—didn't seem to mind that my only previous work experience wasn't work experience at all, or at least not in the usual sense. When I told them my story (the edited version, at least), they seemed to accept that things were different now than in their day and took me at my word when I described how in the end I'd had to flee that nonhome with its nonhusband and those nonchildren of mine, and that no, I had no family of my own, what they called "family of childhood," who could help me or to whom I could turn for comfort.

Mainly what I did was read aloud. Liza liked Jane Austen, Charles Dickens, Trollope (whom until then I'd never heard of), George Eliot, and E. M. Forster, pretty much all the great British novelists, but she loved muscle-bound midcentury American fiction, too, Philip Roth and John Updike and Toni Morrison. I read aloud, speeding along in a kind of childhood wonder, a reawakened passion, akin to religious fervor, of simply finding out what happens next. But more and more often I had to slow down so Liza, whose own attention span was waning, could track. Sometimes I'd stop reading entirely so we could discuss whatever it was we were reading, but more often we'd stop and talk about other things: boyfriends (she'd only had two, one toward the end of high school with whom she'd broken up when she went to college and the other the year after college, the year she was diagnosed); sex (not enough of it, not for her, anyway); fashion and hair (which she no longer had much of, most of it having fallen out during her endless, but now mercifully stopped, chemotherapy treatments). She didn't talk much about the chemo or about the things I thought someone in her position would talk about—the Meaning of Life, death, consciousness, God. At one point, she told me, she had wanted to be an interior designer and had even thought about enrolling in art school to get some kind of graduate interior design degree, but she hadn't been able to take more than a couple of continuing ed classes before her illness came to define her life. I held her hand. I wiped the spittle and vomit off her mouth; I wiped her bottom, front and back, and her armpits, and the places behind her ears that tended to get damp or collect stray bits of fluff, of Kleenex, or stuffed animal fur from the family of stuffed rabbits, remnants of Liza's childhood, that sat on the bed beside her. It wasn't hard, this work, or even, for me, particularly sad. In fact, it was something of the opposite, as I came to a place of joy, or near joy, as I sat, day after day, reading aloud to Liza in her sunny, girly room in her parents' large and lovely house, with people coming and going—her parents; her two, much-older sisters (both of them flying in and out from their own homes, in San Francisco and Saint Louis, respectively); and the occasional visiting nurse, who took Liza's vital signs, checked her meds, made notes. Also her friends—she had many from high school who'd remained in L.A. There was one friend in particular, Ellie, whom I liked. I still remember her: Ellie with the wild red hair and the wild freckles, her birdlike hands flailing in the air as she talked, as she joked, as she cracked us up with stories about her own bad boyfriends and bad jobs and bad bosses and, she insisted, bad hair—even though it was as clear as tap water that Ellie's hair, like her whole demeanor, was excellent, beautiful, radiant. It was her idea that I dye my own hair, and cut it, too. After some weeks of Ellie's insistence, I did just that, going to one of the chain hair salons that were only then popping up in the malls in Los Angeles to have my hair cut super short like a boy's and dyed a bright blond. When I came out into the parking lot, into the sun, I felt myself to be radiant, too.

When I finally told Liza about my own past, my sister and brother, my mother and father, my years as a teenage slut, and then my years with Jacob, she fell asleep just before I got to the part where Jacob slapped me and I began to fall back down the tunnel that I'd thought I'd escaped when, years earlier, I'd left home. She did that all the time, though—fall asleep while I was talking to her or reading aloud. I watched her sleep for a while, then got up to stretch, to use the bathroom, to look out the window. When I returned to her room she was still sleeping but when I went over to her bed to gaze at her face, to make sure that she wasn't wincing in pain or balled up in a nightmare, she opened her eyes, then closed them, then died.

And it wasn't until nearly twenty years later, when I was telling a new friend about how I'd met my husband, that I remembered what Liza's face had looked like during that one last moment of life—a moment so fleeting that the best poetry couldn't begin to catch its elegant vanishing—and burst into gulping sobs. By then I hadn't really thought about Liza in years: not deeply, anyhow. I'd been too busy getting on with my own life, something that happened as if by a miracle, as if Liza herself were directing things, lining them up for me in heaven.

Because what happened was that, after Liza died, her parents begged me to attend her funeral, something they knew I didn't really want to do, as it was all too much for me, too sad, too terrible. I went, though, and there, at the funeral, was a man with thick black hair and a wide, slightly chubby face, a broad nose, and black eyes. He was neither handsome nor its opposite, neither arresting nor particularly passive. After Liza's coffin was lowered into the ground and everyone returned to Liza's house to eat, he and I began talking, and we talked into the evening, returning to my studio in mid-Wilshire where we sat on the floor eating takeout, and all the next day, stopping only to nap—me on the bed, he on pillows on the floor—and finally, after two days of talking like that, we agreed to be married. But only, he said, if I went back to school first. And then, he said, we'd travel. And then we'd return to wherever we wanted to return to, to live our lives, to have children of our own. That's what he said. He was Liza's first cousin, the second son of Liza's mother's only brother, and his name was Paul, and that's what we did, most of it, anyway. Our firstborn child, a girl, we named Liza. The two that followed I named after my parents, both dead, and the fourth we named Angel, as she was the child of our middle age, and utterly unexpected.

THE NIECE

Gordon is just coming off the elevator, stepping out into the hushed and over-heated parquet lobby, still all tingly from sex, when he sees his wife's niece, the one who's so pretty if kind of dumb, or at least that's what his wife says: Nice house, no one home. Or: She'll do fine, it's just that she's not exactly the sharpest knife in the drawer, now is she? Not that that has stopped him from glancing her way now and then—just taking one of those side-long avuncular glances that any older man might allow himself towards his wife's teenage niece, just noticing, for example, how shiny her black curls are or, to take another example, how graceful, how nicely rounded, her body has become. There's no doubt about it, actually: she's a looker, ridiculously so, particularly given what a homely gene pool the girl comes from, at least on her father's side. His own wife, Sylvia, is a product of that same gene-pool, and she's anything but a looker, although at one point he must have found her attractive, because if he hadn't, then why had he bothered marrying her? And it wasn't as if hers was the easiest family in the world to marry into, either, what with their general sense of superiority coupled with their specifically Jewish sense of superiority that had translated, at the time of his marriage, into his having to have a full Jewish wedding—the chuppah, the Hebrew, the whole ball of wax—and here his elderly Methodist parents were sitting in the front row of the goddamned Jewish country club surrounded by the rich Jewish friends of Sylvia's rich Jewish parents, not knowing what the hell was going on and furthermore worried that their clothes, that they'd driven into Wichita to buy, weren't quite up to snuff. His mother in particular had fretted, and he had to admit that—as well as he could remember it, which wasn't well—she had looked neither particularly comfortable nor particularly happy on his wedding day, and her dress, a bright green sheaf with a large bow on the bodice, had given her the appearance of an overstuffed, overgrown baby.

"Amy," he says.

A mistake perhaps, because now she sees him, whereas before there may have been a chance that, lost in a teenage reverie, or, better yet, stoned, she might have missed him. Too late for such considerations: trapped, Gordon sees her interpreting the evidence of her eyes, scrolling through the facts of his presence in front of her: his big old pot belly hanging over the waist-band of his wide-whaled corduroys; his flannel shirt; his high, perspiring, and no doubt flushing forehead. (That smooth pink dome that his mother always insisted held an unusually large brain.) No doubt about it: it's too late for either of them to pretend that they aren't there. Not that Amy has any need to do so, unless she, like him, is conducting an extra-marital affair, which isn't likely, given that she is a girl of seventeen, a child still living at home. Still, it's odd, her being in this big old Connecticut Avenue building at four in the afternoon when she should be home in the Virginia suburbs watching TV and stuffing her face with Ho-Hos and Diet Coke, like his own kids, who unfortunately take after their mother. Not that Gordon is himself such a looker, such a stud. He has no illusions on that point. Just for starters, would a stud have married Sylvia? Would a stud have allowed his father-in-law-to-be to shove an Orthodox Jewish wedding ceremony down his throat? Would a stud be standing in the lobby of the Grange, as the building is called, blushing and stammering like a boy on his first date?

"So, Amy, what brings you here?" he says, while Amy, blinking like a deer, fiddles with something on her sleeve.

"Doctor's appointment."

"Doctor's appointment. Ah, yes. There are several in the building, I believe."

She stands there looking at him—staring at him, actually, her great big liquid-looking eyes like big bowls of green Jello—and then says: 'Whatever." Her eyes are slightly swollen, pink around the edges, the black centers shiny like ice. Perhaps his first guess was right after all: she is taking drugs and moreover had just taken some, perhaps with an older boyfriend or a whole gang of exactly the kind of teenagers—daring, irreverent, worldly-wise—who had made Gordon's own adolescence such a torment. Perhaps that accounts for the way she stands there, fidgeting, her downcast eyes sliding back and forth like search lights.

Gordon considers his options: he can offer her a lift and during the ride discreetly ask her if she's "experimenting' with drugs, and if she indicates that perhaps she is, talk to her parents; he can stand there making small talk, again with the aim of seeing if he can catch her out; or he can pretend that the current meeting isn't happening at all.

Opting for the third, he says, "Bye now," then turns and walks briskly across the echoing lobby towards the waning light of the cold gray day.

As he pulls out of the parking lot, pointing his car north towards Baltimore, he once again contemplates his position. First: that he hadn't meant to have an affair, that he isn't, in fact, the affair kind—any more than, as a kid, he'd been the reefer-smoking, Grateful Dead concert-going, lose-your-virginity-with-a-really-pretty-girl kind. He doesn't intend to get caught; nor does he intend that his wife ever find out. He has covered his tracks, both with stealth and with carefully-considered lies. Still, in his line of work, affairs are practically *de rigeur*, and the only surprising thing about his own is how long it had taken him to finally conduct it. He is a professor of English at the University of Maryland: at one point he'd worn turtlenecks, his lecture rooms had been packed, and when people he'd just met asked him what he did, they tended to be more impressed than not when he told them that he specialized in James Joyce and had done his dissertation on *Finnegans Wake*, and yes, it was a difficult book, but not impossible, and quite breath-taking, quite thrilling, the deeper you dug. He'd done his fair share of publishing since then, too, you know what they say, publish or forget about tenure, well it's as true today as ever. And so okay, maybe the U. of Maryland isn't Hopkins (where he got his doctorate) or even G.W., but it isn't as if he's a high-school social studies teacher, either, which is how his in-laws sometimes treat him, even though his getting the job at Maryland allowed his wife to stay among her enormous and controlling extended family in Baltimore.

Not that there's anything wrong with being a high school social studies teacher, if that's what you want to do. But that was most certainly what Gordon did not want to do: he'd seen enough of high school when he was in high school—the damp cheesy smell of the cafeteria, the girls who giggled when he tried to talk to them, the persistent sense of deep damp shame that overcame him in gym class every time, it didn't matter if it was basketball or track or baseball or simple calisthenics. He had no wind. He was asthmatic, had been ever since the birth of his sister, Mary, when he was five. No: high school was something that he'd rather forget. And, too, his father had been a high school teacher, or at least, he'd started that way. He'd taught Geometry and Algebra to boys and girls who didn't need to know any math beyond what it took to calculate crop yields and keep payments up, and then had been bumped up to the front office, where he'd served as Vice Principal for just about as long as anyone could remember. Not principal, mind you—that was Dickie Chase—but the vice principal, the second-in-command, the one who stood in the hallway and said, "The bell rang minutes ago," and "Do you have a hall pass?" When Gordon was in high school, his father was known as "the Rover," for his habit of wandering the halls in a daze, whistling to himself, or leaning against a row of lockers staring out at nothing with an expression of almost pure longing on his face. Once, when Gordon's P.E. class was ordered outside to do laps around the football field, they'd come across his father walking under the bleachers, whistling "The First Noel." After more than thirty years he retired, and the faculty threw him a farewell dinner at the Sheraton. He'd never understood his only son's dreamy quest for something else. When Gordon had chosen to forgo the University of Kansas for Swarthmore, his father said: "They sure do charge a heck of a lot of money for the exact same stuff we have right here."

But the point is, the point is . . . what is the point, anyway? His train of thought zig-zags around, first to his lover (and to imagine that he, Gordon Harris, fifty one years old and sporting a paunch as big as Nebraska, has a lover) lying recumbent (yes, that's how she lay, recumbent, such a wonderful, such a redolent word) in his arms; then to an uncomfortable conversation he'd had with his eldest son, Josh, yesterday, on the subject of religion, and whether or not God exists (Gordon was pretty damn sure that He was no more than a giant projection of the condition of the human intellect); and finally back to his wife's niece: her green green eyes, her sassy "whatever," as if she knew, and had for some time, that her father's sister's husband was sneaking around Washington with a woman who was most certainly not his wife. Laura is her name—and though she is most certainly not Sylvia, she is also most certainly not a graduate student, or even close. She is a mature lady, a year or two older than Gordon, in fact, and only recently started working at the university as some sort of special assistant to the dean of students. In any event, that was her title: "Special Assistant, Office of the Dean." She called herself a secretary. He likes that in her, her modesty. He also likes the fact that even at her age she shows no compunction about going down on him and sucking him and that while she's doing it, her own hind parts, more often than not, are dangling somewhere in the vicinity of his nose. Laura is divorced, and her one child, a girl, is in college somewhere in the South.

But he didn't—as he tells himself as he maneuvers his beat-up car through silver-lit Washington—get into it for the sex. Laura isn't a knockout by anyone's standards. She's sturdy and has frizzy hair, and the flesh of her belly is loose with stretchmarks, and she tends to wear mannish clothes: dark trousers with a matching jacket; skirt-suits that look as if they'd been taken off a corpse. He'd been drawn to her anyway. Which just shows (as he tells Sylvia in his mind as he swings his car into the hideously angry traffic on the Beltway) that he is a man of discerning tastes; a man, indeed, who, perhaps like all men, just wants a little sweetness in his life.

Amy too has a secret, though nothing nearly as secretive as her uncle's affair. She is seeing a psychiatrist. She is seeing a psychiatrist because only a few months ago, in July, during a bout of somewhat self-conscious self-hatred coupled with what has always been, for her, a talent for self-dramatization, she'd taken just enough of her mother's sleeping pills to send her into a sleep so deep that neither her younger brother's drumming nor her father's lawn-mowing shook her from it, and had her mother not called her downstairs for supper several times, and then, in a bout of exasperation, gone upstairs to haul her out of her room, she might not have woken at all. She hadn't left a note, but it wasn't necessary, as the girl's beautiful face with its wide planks of cheekbones and thick lashes, set in an expression of deep surrender and mottled with yellow, told all. She was rushed to Fairfax Hospital, where her stomach was pumped and where she subsequently spent a week in the psychiatric ward, mainly watching TV, while her worried mother called everyone she knew who at one time or another had had to consult what Amy's father still called a "head shrinker," a species that he himself manifestly didn't believe in.

There was no note, but there was a diary, filled mainly with fragments of her poetry, doodles, and drawings of the family English Setter, Kennedy. Kennedy was of course named after the President, whom Amy's father remembers from television. "I remember the day he was shot," he often says. "I remember my mother crying." The cat, who didn't appear in any of Amy's drawings, was named Eleanor. One poem in particular interested her psychiatrist:

Black sheep
Dig deep
Big creep
Creeping up the hall —
Black bird
Absurd
I heard
you creeping up the hall—
Black black
On your back
Life's a rack
as I answer Your call.

Dr. Pinker was particularly interested in this poem because it seemed to indicate that Amy had been violated somehow—if not physically, then emotionally: a deep narcissistic wound of some kind, a mauling of her interior integrity. Amy herself knew what the poem was about: it was about trying to find enough rhymes to fulfill an assignment she'd had in her Creative Writing elective to do an a/a/a/b poem using as few verbs as possible. It was also about how her father used to wake her up early on Saturday mornings to go to synagogue with him, which she hated. Her teacher had given her an "A minus" and written, "dark, but powerful!" on the top of the paper.

Amy loves Dr. Pinker. She loves his bald shining head and the way his bright blue eyes twinkle; she loves his certainty; his deep voice; the clean, minty way he smells; the line drawings in his office. But mainly she loves being able to just lie there, staring out the window—for Dr. Pinker is a Freudian of the old school—and talk, and talk and talk and talk and talk, without anyone interrupting her or calling her stupid or rolling their eyes. She loves saying, "I hate my father," and bursting into sobs so deep that she nearly throws up; she loves telling him her dreams, which are complicated and unending. She goes to Dr. Pinker's office in Northwest Washington four times a week, driving herself there from her house in Alexandria in the secondhand Jeep that her parents had bought for her older brother, David, when he started dating.

She has a second secret as well, one that she's not told anyone about, not even Dr. Pinker. His name is Billy Rosen, and just about every night, after dinner, she gets a telephone call from him, but when she picks up the phone, she hears nothing but the sound of his breathing. These phone calls started during the second semester of her junior year—some months before her suicide attempt—but as far as she's concerned, they have nothing to do with anything. Right away, though, she knew it was Billy Rosen, both because she knew the sound of his breathing from a year of sitting just in front of him in French class and also because her family had caller I.D. Not once, however, has she told him that she knows who he is, or that he's a pathetic, miserable loser, which is how she thinks of him when she does think of him, which isn't often. Instead, when he calls, she places the receiver to her ear, and he breathes and breathes, sometimes for five or even ten minutes, until at last he hangs up.

When Gordon gets home to Baltimore, the house, predictably, is silent. Or rather, not silent, but rather silent—oblivious—to him. There are no fond greetings from either wife or children; no barking dog, its tail wagging, its tongue out. Nor are there any delicious aromas wafting his way from the kitchen at the back of the house, like there would have been once upon a time in the early years of his marriage. Instead there is the sound of "The Simpsons" on TV (Emily and Steven, his two younger children), overlaid with loud, thumping music coming from upstairs (Josh, his eldest, listening to something vulgar from the land of homicidal rap stars).

He announces himself in the empty foyer and then, rounding the corner into the TV room, says: "Hello, couch potatoes." The children glance up at him from their places on the sofa and return immediately to the screen.

When his own father—the assistant principal of Shelby High School—came home, Gordon, Mary, and their mother would gather around him as if he were a returning hero. It was one of the few ironclad rules in their house. When your father gets home, children, you get up to greet him. The other rules involved saying Grace before dinner, getting home by curfew, and making your bed. But Gordon's own kids took their cues from Sylvia, and Sylvia, almost from the start, had not been the fawning sort. Oh, all sorts of other people had fawned on him (including, especially, attractive graduate students), but Sylvia positively refused to fawn or even show much affection at all. That she reserved for her own family members—her younger brother in particular, the hot-shot lawyer in Washington who, according to Sylvia, made more money than God—and, once she herself became a mother, her children. In fact, in any dispute—any dispute at all—that involved Gordon and the kids, she invariably took the child's point of view, arguing it with a zeal that at one point had convinced Gordon that the woman ought to seek professional help: either that or enroll in law school, where her apparent hunger for justice might be better channeled.

"Where might your mother be located?" he says to the back of his children's heads. Both of them, in unison, shrug. In the kitchen, he makes himself a drink. Then he goes upstairs, where Sylvia is seated at the desk in what's supposed to have been his office but has increasingly become a spill-over room for the rest of them, paying bills.

"You're home," she says, her eyes never leaving her work.

"That I am."

"Josh needs some help with his homework."

"And also he's having some kind of conflict with his soccer coach."

"A conflict."

"Uh-huh," Sylvia says, bending over her desk. It's her one area of competence: the books, which she keeps with a vigor that never fails to take Gordon by surprise. True, she was once a generous and creative cook, a cook who enjoyed making fattening and delicious meals and sharing them with friends and family, but her interest in the kitchen (like her interest in the bedroom) had in recent years waned. She never did get over marrying a man who didn't make much money, even though she'd done it with her eyes wide open, and—at the time at least—eagerly, which is perhaps, Gordon thinks, why she goes at the check book with such alarming concentration, as if to prove what she'd known all along: ergo, that her husband does not bring home much in the way of bacon. Never did. Never will. The only question that remains for Gordon is why her over-protective and clannish family had allowed her to marry him in the first place, if they thought he was such shoddy goods, and a goy, at that. But he knows the answer to this one, too. Sylvia had been a hard job to sell. She walked with a pronounced limp caused by unevenly-long legs, had sinus trouble, and tended to be heavy. Nor had she been (unlike her brothers) much of a student, but then again, unlike her evenly-legged brothers, she'd never had much of a chance to go to school full-time, her education having been interrupted over and over by a series of painful operations that left her shorter leg dimpled and scarred, the flesh loose and hanging like an old garment bag. He'd met her when he was a graduate assistant, and she had eyes as deep and dark as nighttime lakes.

"I just got off the phone with Julie," she says, still not looking up.

"Julie?"

"Your sister-in-law? The wife of my brother?"

"Ah, yes."

"I called her, as always because she never calls me, to sort out Thanksgiving plans. She said that Amy ran into you today. At some building in downtown Washington? Apparently Amy had a doctor's appointment. What were you doing in downtown Washington, Gordon?"

"Amy had a doctor's appointment?"

"Girls do that sometimes. Go to doctors."

"I suppose they do," he says after a pause.

The room, he suddenly notices, is in greater disarray than usual, the desk cluttered with receipts and catalogues, the trash can overflowing. Even the sofa (purchased so he could read late into the night without disturbing anyone) is askew, as if its pillows weren't properly fitted. His guts twisting, he realizes that his wife suspects something and has been hunting down evidence: a receipt, a lipstick stain, a fervid, fervent love note perhaps tucked away in jacket pocket. But he'd been careful to a fault, conducting his affair only on his lover's territory and forbidding her to ever contact him at the house. Sylvia sighs loudly. "Nothing's wrong, I hope," Gordon says.

"Wrong? What do you mean, wrong?"

"With Amy. She isn't sick, is she?"

"How the hell should I how, Gordon? You think Julie ever tells me anything?"

"She told you that Amy saw me in Washington."

"That's what I just said," Sylvia says, finally straightening up from her bookkeeping and bill-paying and looking her husband full in the face. Under her dark eyes, the skin is shiny, as if she'd just applied Vaseline.

"Yes, it so happens that I did run into her," he says. " I was going to tell you about it. Because it was odd. Amy didn't look quite right. And she would barely speak to me. She looked—or maybe it was just the light—like she'd been crying. Or perhaps that she'd been taking drugs of some sort. That's what I thought, anyhow. She looked, I don't know, rather waxy. That's why I thought something might be wrong."

"Uh-huh," his wife says.

"She's a pretty little thing," he continues. But still he just stands there, the second time today that he feels called-upon to account for his presence. Unfortunately, all he can think of is how difficult it has been for him to come up with a title for his most recent article *on Finnegans Wake*. Modernism and the Modern Filter? The Fragmentation of the Self? Contextuality As Code? The *Finnegans Wake* Notebooks and Radical Philology?

Finally, unable to control herself, Sylvia says: "For Christ's sake, Gordon. What were you doing in a building in downtown Washington in the middle of the afternoon? Didn't you have classes to teach or something? Just please don't tell me that you've decided to have an affair with some smitten graduate student with perky boobs. At your age. That would just be too much, and I'm just not sure I could stand being in such a ridiculous position."

With that word, "affair," Gordon feels his palms sprout sweat, but fortunately, Sylvia has taken off her glasses and probably can't see him all that well. Fortunately, also, Gordon has long since prepared all manner of stories to cover just such an eventuality, though frankly, he hadn't anticipated needing to trot any of them out, ever, let alone so soon. He'd only just met Laura last spring and only started going to bed with her at the start of the fall semester, and now it was only November—which would make it just over two months that he'd been going to her place every Thursday afternoon after classes got out and screwing his brains out.

"Well that's just it," he says. "I didn't have classes to teach. So I went to see Allan Parker, instead."

"Allan Parker?"

"Surely you remember him?"

His wife just stared at him, her black eyes two hard dots, like checkers pieces. "He retired five, six years ago. The man is losing his eyesight, Sylvia. It's a tragedy, really, a brilliant man like him, and now he can barely read. I visit him from time to time, is all."

Sylvia just stares at him and then, as if bowled over by too much information, shrugs and says: "Can you believe this phone bill? Who have you been talking to, Gordon?"

"No one," he says, which is, for once, the truth. He does most of his talking at the office, and even then, it's almost always with other English professors.

Amy fiddles with the radio dial, hoping to find something to blot out her encounter with her uncle. She's never really liked him and finds him vaguely creepy. But as much as she dislikes Gordon, her feelings for him pale in comparison to her feelings for her father, whom she hates so much that the mere thought of his long, narrow impassive face looking at her over the dining room table fills her with anxious fury. He looks at her as if she were dirt under his fingernails; toe grit; poison ivy; or worse, nothing at all. Her father, the important lawyer, the big Jew: sitting there in his Orthodox synagogue with all the other men with their bad breath and fragrantly shaved faces, praying away to Adonai as if he had a direct line. *Baruch* this, *baruch* that. He looks at her as if he can look straight into her insides and see that she's all twisted up, broken. She spent most of her therapy session with Dr. Pinker telling him how much she hated him and then heaping all kinds of abuse on herself as well—I'm bad. I'm just so bad. I'm corrupt inside. No wonder he hates me.

She used to beg God to help her out, but these days even God doesn't give a shit, perhaps because He too has figured out that she's irredeemable. Her dreams are wild—wild: big fat slimy slithering snakes swimming in the back yard swimming pool; she herself dancing naked on a table, while her father and brothers watch; Jesus beckoning her and then turning into a monster whose shape and form she cannot detect or describe; making out with her best friend Lizzie Norman and then deciding to get married to her. And on and on, every night, these weird, bizarre, twisted, sick dreams of hers. Every morning she wakes, relieved and drenched in sweat.

Had he been following her around?

But no: she's being paranoid. Uncle Gordon might not be her favorite person, she reasons, but he's not a total weirdo, one of those creepy drooling psychopaths who follow young girls around, bonk them on the head, rape them, and then stash their dead bodies in abandoned mines. Nor is he some crazed teenage moron like Billy Rosen, who her mother seems to think is her boyfriend. Usually, when he calls, Amy herself picks up, but sometimes her mother does instead. Amy can hear her mother saying, "Hold the line just a sec," and then her voice, hopeful, saying, "It's for you, Amy, that boy!"

She doesn't know why she hasn't yet told him that she knows who he is, or told her mother or a teacher or even Dr. Pinker about him. It just doesn't seem worth it. One day, perhaps, while he's breathing into the phone, she'll say, "Cut it out Billy, I know it's you, and it's really pathetic," but until that day comes, she'll simply let him breathe. She wonders if perhaps Uncle Gordon had started out that way too: as one of those kids so nerdy, so geeky, so relentlessly weird that the best he could do was breathe heavily into the phone of girls he had crushes on, or hole himself up in his room with dirty magazines. But despite his baffling and sweaty appearance this afternoon, she doesn't think Uncle Gordon is truly psycho or even that much of a loser. He's just sort of vaguely distasteful. She doesn't like how white his skin is or the way he giggles, all up in his nose. But he's no pedophile; he doesn't diddle his kids; he probably doesn't even do it with his wife. He just looks. During all those endless Thanksgivings and Seders at her grandparents' house in Baltimore, he stares at her in this sideways way like he's pretending to be looking at something behind her.

"He can't help himself," is what her mother's always said about him. "He's a professional intellectual. They can be like that." But then she'd be off and running about her own experiences with the various eggheads and brain trusts whom she herself had dated when she herself was a graduate student in history at Harvard and blah blah blah blah—Amy has heard the stories so many times that she could recite them backwards. The boyfriend who whispered lines of poetry in his sleep (she had to hear about this?); the one who spoke five modern languages and a couple of ancient ones besides but who, on their one date, was so nervous that he could barely get two words out; and on and on and on, culminating with the blind date Amy's mother had had with Amy's father during the year she was writing her dissertation (on women's health during the American Colonial period), which led pretty quickly to their marriage and re-location to Washington, where Amy's father was clerking at the Supreme Court, which was a very big deal, the biggest deal there is for someone just out of law school. "Yup," Amy's mother would say, "he was the one." Unfortunately, Amy's mother always added, that blind date also led to her never having completed her dissertation. "What can I say?" she'd finish a flourish. "I got knocked up. We would have gotten married eventually anyway. But I must say that your older brother's arrival did kind of put a crimp in my academic career."

It's dark out, the suburban street where they live draped in purplish shadow, the trees all naked and spindly. Their dog, Kennedy, is waiting for her in the window of what her mother calls the "book room." Both her parents, but her father in particular, adore the dog, heaping praise on him as if he were the messiah.

"How was therapy, honey?" her mother says, as Amy lets herself in. Her mother is just fifty, trim, small, with dark sparkly eyes and a body kept hard and athletic from yoga. She works four days a week for a women's health organization writing grant proposals. Sometimes she goes to conferences in distant Third World countries—Zaire, Peru—and comes home with stories of women dying in pregnancy and the spread of AIDS. She takes her job seriously. But she usually manages to be home before Amy gets back from Dr. Pinker's.

"Well?" she says when Amy doesn't reply.

"Okay, I guess."

"Okay, you guess?"

Amy shrugs. She doesn't much like it when her mother presses her like this, pressing her to reveal what (Dr. Pinker has told her) is completely confidential, something for only the two of them. On the other hand, given the choice between her mother, who at least cares, and her father, who adamantly doesn't give a flying fuck, Amy much prefers her mother, who was, after all, the one who found her lying on her bed last summer lost in a numbed trance and sinking towards death, and who later sat by her hospital bed, saying, "I love you so much, Amy. Your father and I both do. I love you so much. I love you so much." She'd felt guilty, then: guilty for putting her mother, whom she loves with the same open-hearted and wet love that she'd felt for her since infancy, through so much worry. But more than that, she'd felt relief: wave after wave of relief, mingled at the edges with pleasure. Even her father had seemed upset. He'd been just outside her room, pacing the halls, and every now and then she'd look up from her sedated state and see him sitting in the chair in the comer.

> Blue black,
> Take it back!
> Big Mac
> — —on a stick
> Suck dick
> You prick

"When I was leaving, I saw Uncle Gordon."

"What do you mean?"

"Just what I said. He was getting out of the elevator."

"That's odd."

"He looked at me funny, like maybe he knew. Did you and Dad tell Sylvia about me?"

"What do you mean?"

It's useless. She will never—never ever, not if she lives to be a thousand years old—get away from her cloying, impossible, extended family: When I was doing my graduate work at Hopkins—The year I went out for Law Review—More pot roast, you're too thin—My thesis advisor—As if she, Amy, could ever get into Hopkins or Harvard or any of those places. But does her mother have to go blabbing about her private business to people like Aunt Sylvia, who isn't, Amy knows, her mother's favorite to begin with. Does that mean that her aunt and uncle in Cincinnati know too? Her grandparents? Her mother's friends at work?

"You did," Amy says. "You told Sylvia. And Sylvia's gone and told Gordon. And now the whole world knows about me." She's about to cry now; she can feel it sneaking up on her, the constricted throat, the. smarting eyes. "And the worst part is, you don't even like her!"

"Like who?" her mother says.

"Aunt Sylvia!"

The two of them just stand there, Amy and her mother, lost to each other. Her mother's wearing black slacks and a black turtleneck and black shoes, like some latterday modern dancer, like Audrey Hepburn in *Funny Face*. She turns to Amy and says:

"Honey, I'm just not following."

"My God! You just don't get it, do you Mom?"

At last the tears are flowing, flowing as Amy knew they would, coursing down her cheeks and spotting her sweater. Kennedy rubs up against her, wanting to be petted.

She bends down and hugs the dog to her chest; delighted, he licks her face, licking away her tears.

"Come on, sweetie," her mother says. "It's all right. It will all be all right. I swear. I promise. It will all be all right." Her mother lowers herself to the floor and sits beside her, stroking her back, murmuring. Amy wishes she could go back to the hospital and lie in a medicated daze. Unfortunately, she has homework. She's in her Senior year. She wants to go to college somewhere out west, where there are deserts and mountains. She wants to be surrounded by pale pink light. ln all that pale pink light, she thinks, she feels better.

Holy fuck! Why had he told her that he was visiting Allan Parker, of all people—Allan, who in fact was among the few faculty members who, years ago, had opposed Gordon's being hired and who continued subsequently to treat Gordon as if Gordon's field of study were, if not obsolete, then too silly for words? Silly? You want silly? How about the young woman—straight out of Stanford no less—whose field was "Star Trek"? She taught a course called "Mr. Spock Studies," a huge hit with the students, and no wonder, given that their homework involved watching videos. Or the other recent hire, also out of one of the better universities, who did Broadway musicals? Please. Was a little familiarity with the Western canon really too much to ask? And though it was true that Allan had retired in part because he was (tragically, it was said, for someone whose life revolved around the written word) losing his eyesight, it was also true that on the day Allan packed up his books and headed on out of Susquehanna Hall for good, Gordon had come home and told Sylvia that if it had been up to him, he would have spared Allan his eyesight and instead given him one of those strokes that leave its victims unable to speak. "I don't care if he reads, or even writes," Gordon had said. "Just let him keep his stupid yap shut."

But Sylvia's mention of the word "affair" had sent him into a panic, and he'd crossed his stories, or rather, taken one bit of one story and slapped it on top of another. Which is what happens, he's thinking, when you spend your life immersed in the words of Joyce, those dazzling flights of imagination! The iconoclastic—even now iconoclastic—manipulation not just of language but the very sense, the very essence, of language, of what it means to be a species dependent on language, a species swimming, breathing in language and as unaware of its potency as a fish is of the ocean. But there is hope, in the form of Sylvia's profound lack of interest in Gordon's career. What were the chances, after all, that Sylvia was paying attention that day years ago when Gordon had come home to pronounce that the English Department had now been exorcised and was free at last of Satan? And even if she had been, it's entirely probable that she wouldn't remember the first thing about Gordon's on-again, off-again battle with Allan Parker, whose own field was the Romantic Poets— Tennyson, Landor, Byron, Shelley, Keats, all that lot: The world is too much with us, late and soon, etc. etc. A big bore—a field so raked over that it was as dry as dust. And yet how Allan had clung to his beloved Romantic Poets and, more to the point, clung to his belief that somehow he, Allan Parker, had been put on earth to explain not just the Romantic poets, but indeed all poetry, all written language. "When writers wrote things that people actually wanted to read," he'd say. 'When poetry was important." As if Joyce—the single most towering figure of the twentieth century—had written ad copy, jingles for McDonald's perhaps, or the kind of poetry that appears in Hallmark cards.

Allan Parker! Allan bloody Parker! On the bright side, the man in fact lives in Washington—if Gordon recalled correctly, in one of those grand old apartments on Connecticut Avenue, funded, no doubt, by his wife's money. Or at least Gordon thinks he does. He pulls out his faculty directory, paws to the back where the emeriti are listed, and finds Allan's address: he'd remembered right. thank God. Thank God in heaven.

Although, on the other hand, maybe it wouldn't be the worst thing in the world if Sylvia found out. Then maybe she'd realize that she hadn't done so very badly, after all. Maybe she'd realize that she cared. God almighty. Why had he married her?

There is breathing on the phone. Not so heavy, but steady and damp. Inhale, exhale. Odd, too, that her mother still hasn't caught on to any of this, this boy who calls all the time, asks (apparently in a polite voice) to speak to Amy, and then breathes. Odd that her mother has never said, "Who's that nice boy who keeps calling here?" or dropped hints about whether Amy has a boyfriend. (She doesn't. She's still a bit afraid of boys, scared of their gawkiness and how desperate they all seem to be, the way they lean in when they're talking to you.) She is almost entirely unaware of the effect she has on boys, and girls too: almost entirely unaware of how pretty she is, though she's told all the time, both by her mother and her best friend Lizzie, who is the only other person— other than her mother and father, that is—who knows about Dr. Pinker. Amy knows she isn't ugly; she knows, too, that she has a good figure; what she doesn't know is that her particular face—with that thick curly black hair and wide-spaced green eyes—is rather exotic, mysterious, the kind of face that, later, men will read all kinds of depths into, all kinds of romance. They will see the Mysteries of the East! They see Esther and Rachel and Rebecca—the Unfolding of the Generations! But as far as Amy herself is concerned, she is just one more Jewish girl with curly hair and pale skin; a dime a dozen; a type: smallish boobs, biggish nose, a house filled with books, parents who were once, sort of, hippies. (Not her father, though, not really. She could never imagine her serious, hard-driving father a hippie, even though the photo albums that her mother keeps stacked in the living room are filled with pictures of her father sporting a little ponytail and wearing bell-bottoms.)

She thinks about saying, "What do you want?" and then about saying, 'You are such a fucking asshole, Billy," but as usual she says nothing and bides her time, sitting on her bed in the privacy of her bedroom, listening. It's a beautiful bedroom, she thinks: she's always liked it. At the back of the house, it's partially hidden under dormers and has the feel of a hideaway. In it are two old wrought-iron beds that her mother bought at some antique store somewhere, each of them covered with a white quilt, and on the floor is a Persian rug of deep swirling vine reds. The whole house, in fact, is beautiful: like something you'd see in a magazine. When Amy brings friends over for the first time, they're invariably impressed and say things like 'You live here?" as if they themselves are poor, which they aren't. No one in Alexandria is. Not even the Black people. "You live here?" Like it's her fault that her father makes a lot of money.

While Billy Rosen breathes, she thinks about her future. Perhaps she'll be a poet, or perhaps a teacher, or perhaps—well, the truth is she doesn't know. She's never known. That's part of the problem. Her brother David, a sophomore at Dartmouth, is studying philosophy and already talking about going to law school. He doesn't want to be a lawyer, though; he wants to be a law professor. When he comes home on vacation he sits at the dining room table and argues concepts like "truth" and "reality" with their father, until at last their father puts up his hands and says: "Enough, enough, you may be wrong, but you still have more energy than I do." Hardy har har, a big joke all around, how much David resembles his argumentative, brilliant father. Her mother's known what she wanted to do with her life ("anything but stay home and bake brownies") since she was about six years old. Even Lizzie knows what she wants to do with her life: she wants to join the Peace Corps, and after that, do something Peace Corps-like, something to do with feeding people or getting them medicine. Her mother, naturally, loves Lizzie. "That girl reminds me of me," she sometimes says. "Idealistic."

Is Amy also idealistic? She doesn't think so. She doesn't think she's anti-idealistic, either. She just thinks that it's really weird that Billy Rosen calls her just about every night and then doesn't say anything.

On the morning of the afternoon that she decided to see what it would be like to kill herself, Amy had gotten a telephone call from a boy she actually liked, albeit in a nervous, skittish way. His name was Eric Bibb, and she thought he had a graceful, almost British way about him: his fingers were long and tapering. In the spring and fall, he rode his ten-speed to school; in winter he wore woolen scarves. Apparently he was very interested in bicycling: he'd once confessed in front of the entire Honors English class that his hero was Lance Armstrong. He called to ask her if she'd like to go downtown with him one day to see an exhibit at the National Gallery. "Any time, really, is okay with me," he'd said, and she hadn't known whether that was pathetic or endearing. "We could even bicycle there." They talked for a little while more and made a date to bicycle down to the Mall on the next Sunday, and then Amy had looked out the window and seen her father mowing the lawn, gone into the bathroom, and swallowed the sleeping pills.

From the downstairs region, there is noise: her father letting himself in the front door, her mother going to greet him, and their hurried, murmured conversation: they are talking about her. Her father sighs. Their voices are pitched on an almost identical low note, and so the sound of their talking together is soothing, like cows lowing in a distant field.

Upstairs in her beautiful bedroom, Amy gently hangs up the phone.

Sylvia calls in for pizza and they eat it in front of the television, even though, on his side, Gordon hates television: always has. It gives him a headache, the sound of it; the way everything is so predictable, so forced. He watches what it does to his own kids: their stares glassy; their faces impassive, like rubber dolls. Sometimes he thinks his children have become just that: rubber toys, some kind of gadget. Which isn't how he'd pictured fatherhood at all, not when he and Sylvia had first gotten into the game, and then again with each subsequent birth: each time he'd felt a distinct inner rushing, like wings beating, or rising bubbles, inside his veins, and his chest was filled with a warm liquidy goo that he only later was able to identify as love. His wife exhausted and pale, a baby in her arms; and the little squalling thing itself, all damp-red and helpless.

Later, after the children have been banished to their rooms and the two younger ones are asleep, Sylvia says, "So I guess we have to talk, you and I."

They are in their bedroom, where, as usual, she's beaten him to bed. This has been a pattern in their marriage ever since the last of their children was born, at which point she claimed that she was just too damn tired to do much of anything after dinner other than wash the dishes and get herself into bed, activities which excluded even the remotest possibility of sex. He'd been understanding, too: after all, she was home with three young children all day, and even after all those operations, she still had trouble walking. At times the weight of the children in her arms aggravated her condition, such that her limp would become more pronounced, and she'd complain about shooting pains. She'd often rub Tiger Balm into her left hip, and the whole house would smell like menthol. But even after the youngest of their children attained an age of reasonable independence—dressing and bathing himself and able to play with the other kids on the street without adult supervision—Sylvia remained in what seemed like a state of permanent exhaustion. Every now and then, at her urging, he'd take her out for dinner, and have some wine, and then, maybe, he'd get lucky. But it was strictly touch and go with her, had been for years. (Another reason for his seeking solace elsewhere. What else was a man to do?)

He turns to her. She is looking up at him with those accusing eyes again; those eyes sunk in what look like miniature satin pillows. More and more, her face resembles a photograph of someone long dead. It's as if her looks—big face, square forehead, bulbous nose—had gone out of style, or merely gone out of the gene pool, sometime in the nineteenth century, and yet here they were, on her. Had she ever been pretty? She looks at him, waiting. He wills himself to be calm.

"What do you want to talk about, dear?"

"Thanksgiving. "

"Thanksgiving?"

"The one when we all get together and eat turkey and sweet potatoes, and one of the kids spills wine on the table, and everyone talks about his or her graduate degree? You know: Thanksgiving."

"What about Thanksgiving, dear?"

He's trying so hard to be sensitive, to indicate, in word and gesture, that he's being attentive. But his attempt at what he thinks of as old-fashioned courtliness seems to have backfired. Sylvia is sitting up in bed now, red in the face.

"For Christ's sake, Gordon, do you really have to talk to me like I'm an idiot? I can read and write, you know, even if I'm not some brilliant graduate student. You how, some of us were lucky just to get to college. I could barely walk during my teen years. Do you know what it's like to spend half your teenage years in hospitals and the other half literally sitting it out, sitting on the sidelines, or the benches, or stuck at home on the sofa, while everyone else is partying their heads off, or playing football, or getting laid?"

"I know, dear." An old story, alas: his wife's difficult childhood.

"And it's not like I went to finishing school, either. I worked for my degree."

He continues to listen: his role during these occasional tirades of his wife's. He knows that she just has to let off steam every now and then; the pressure builds up in her, and if she doesn't explode, it only gets worse. Not that he particularly enjoys her tirades; they are, he knows, simply something he has to bear. And at least this tirade—thank God—is about the usual stuff, and nothing to do with her niece, or his being where he wasn't supposed to be, or any suspicions she might have about him. She rambles, jumping from subject to subject, with no connective tissue, no common theme other than her own sense of outrage, her own sense of having been left out.

"It's just" she's now saying, "that I really don't much like Thanksgiving, or at least I don't anymore. I like the concept of it, even if God knows every year, year in and year out, I do most of the cooking, which actually I don't mind. I just wish people would thank me for it now and then. After all, Mom's really getting to be a bit too old to get round the kitchen well, and I'm a better cook than she is anyway."

There's a pause, and he realizes that he may be being called upon to say something.

"What is it, then?" he says.

"Oh God, Gordon, don't you understand anything?" she wails. "I mean, really. You simply can't be this stupid."

"I'm not particularly stupid, dear."

"Who ever said you were?"

"You did."

"It's just that, oh God, sometimes I just hate Julie! Haven't you ever noticed how superior she can be? As if you and I are nothing but peasants, and she and my brother are the king and queen of England! I mean, I'm just sick of it. Sure, he's had a successful career, but wouldn't you think that by the time a man was in his fifties everyone would stop talking about how well he'd done in fucking Harvard Law School, for Christ's fucking sake. And then there's Julie, and her big important job, and her perfect family, and she's just so goddamn smug sometimes that I can't stand it! 'Amy ran into Gordon today,' as if there's something I ought to know about. But with her it's always 'Amy this and Amy that,' and for God's sake I know the girl is pretty but who isn't at seventeen?" She's crying now, though thank God not noisily, or even particularly messily. At the same time, she seems to have come to a full stop, verbally. The only sign that she's upset are the tears that are spilling onto her cheeks.

He lowers himself onto the bed next to her. "Come here," he says, and a moment later, she is in his arms, her wet face pressed into his armpit, her whole solid body warm and grieving, though for what, he can not say.

She'd never been all that pretty, but then again, he'd never been very handsome. But what she'd had was a kind of fierce determination, an inner strength, like an animal's. Her hair had been pretty, too: thick and glossy, and he'd thought her body generous, like a figure from Titian, or Raphael. Her one short leg never bothered him. He remembers that now, or at least he remembers the memory of it. He remembers remembering how much he'd once admired her, and his memory fills him with unaccustomed longing.

After she's hung up the phone on Billy Rosen, Amy decides that maybe tomorrow she'll tell him to fuck off. Or maybe not. She'll figure it out later. In the meantime, she picks up her notebook, and writes:

> Breath—like death,
> a metaphor—
> inhalation
> exhilaration
> manifestation
> less of more—

She reads it once, twice, and a third time, wondering whether it's any good, and at last deciding that it is. She won't show it to anyone, though. It's hers, to keep.

THE MAN WHO LOVED HIS WIFE

A month before she died, Julia Glass accepted Jesus as her personal savior, which was both odd and unexpected, as Julia had never before expressed much interest one way or another in either the God of Abraham, Isaac, and Jacob whom she'd learned about in Sunday school, or in religion in general. Nor was her husband, Martin, any kind of Christian, though he had been raised as one, at least nominally, and once in a while, particularly after sex, he felt the presence of something composed of pure goodness that he couldn't name. Husband and wife both inhabited that land of in-between, embracing the abstract notion of a benign and loving God who acted like a kind of disgruntled superintendent in the universe, fixing things or not depending on whether He was sleeping off a hangover or otherwise engaged, while actively shunning identification with one religious group or another. Judaism, Christianity, Buddhism, Islam— it was all one and the same to them, which was to say, both mystifying and boring, kind of like sitting in pre-calculus class in high school when you knew full well that you didn't have a clue what was going on and would probably end up an art history or English major in college.

But Julia had other ideas. One day she rolled over in bed, fumbled for her pain killers, and, clutching her husband's hand, said, "Jesus came to me." It was early summer, hot and dense with humidity; in their garden, a jungle was growing, filled with lizards who climbed up their windows at night, showing their white, damp bellies and their suction-like feet. The news was filled with dire predictions about global warming, the Gulf of Mexico roiling with oil slicks, and hurricanes. It was so hot that even their dog, Johnson, refused to go out except when he had to.

"Sweetheart?"

"In a dream," she said. Her blue eyes were bright with drugs and fever. What was left of her short blonde hair was plastered to her skull by sweat. He could see the scars, a livid red, where the doctors had opened up her cranium two years earlier. To him, she was still the most gorgeous creature he'd ever laid eyes on. He wanted to put her inside him—shrink her down to the size of a mini-weenie and swallow her whole—and keep her there, tucked warmly and safely within. It had never ceased to amaze him that she married him.

"Only it wasn't like a *dream* dream. It was more like a . . . I don't know. It was more like a vision. Except that I was asleep. But I didn't feel like I was asleep. I felt like I was sitting there very comfortably, watching a movie. Or. I don't know." Since she'd entered the last stage of her illness—or what Martin had been told was the last stage of her illness—she often rambled on like this. Sometimes she was incoherent, but usually she was just a bit off, a bit confused, as if the words, once such reliable and stalwart allies, had lost interest in the cause and had to be rallied anew with each attempt at speech. "Am I making sense?"

Martin nodded. He squeezed her hand. Julia was a full ten years younger than he was, and even now, with her face creased and wrinkled from illness and everything shrinking and collapsing inwards, she looked like a teenager. Outside, it was beginning to thunder. He hoped it would be a whopper— the kind of storm that shook the rafters with its winds, pounded against the windows, and turned the sky into a dark, smoky gray. He hoped it would be the kind of storm that people would remember for years. He hoped that the scientists were right. Let the entire state be washed into the sea. What good was it?

"And I knew it was Jesus. Actually, he looked kind of like my grandfather. On my father's side—Grandpa Harry? You never met him, but Grandpa Harry was…." she began to cry. "I loved Grandpa Harry," she finally said.

"I know you did."

"And anyway, it was weird, because he was wearing a *tallit*. You know, a prayer shawl? And a funny old-fashioned men's hat, with a brim. Only it wasn't Grandpa Harry. It was Jesus. He was looking at me and I was looking at him and suddenly I just *knew*." She sat up, smoothing the covers, and then lay back down again. "I'm thirsty," she said. "Do we have any root beer?"

"What did you know, honey?"

"Do we?"

"Honey?"

"Have root beer?"

He got up, went down the hall to their little kitchen, and poured her a root beer. On the way back he stopped and petted Johnson. Returning to the bedroom, he said: "What did Grandpa Harry say?"

"But that's just it," she said, and now she looked exhausted again, like her entire face was about to cave into itself or melt into the sheets. "It wasn't Grandpa Harry. It was Jesus. And he came to me. To tell me that everything was okay. Oh God."

"Julia?"

But she had fallen back into her drugged, damp sleep.

She'd already been sick when he married her, but he married her anyway because what else could he do? He'd been married once before, but that had been years ago, when he himself was fresh out of Tulane and didn't know his ass from his elbow, and anyhow, the marriage had only lasted two years. But Julia was different. He was head over heels in love with her, loving her as if she were the sun and the moon and the rest of the cosmos combined, only no matter what metaphor he reached for, nothing quite got at how he felt about her, how she wasn't his wife, but, more pertinently, *him* himself. Yes: that was more like it: Julia *was* Martin. She was the very spirit that animated his form.

She'd had a brain tumor, the bad kind that starts as a throbbing inside your head and then grows tentacles that swallow up everything that had once been you, leaving nothing in its place but confusion and despair and panic and pain. It was tragic, of course. That's what people said. "Such a tragedy."

The first time he met Julia's mother, Julia had already been diagnosed; the clock was already ticking: *tick, tick, tick*. Her family didn't understand why Martin wanted to marry her and didn't care that he wasn't Jewish. They themselves hadn't set foot in a synagogue in decades. In fact, as far as Martin could tell, the only Jewish thing they still did was use the occasional Jewish expression, the "oi veys" and "messhuggenehs" and "shmucks" that had traveled over from Europe and melted into ordinary American English. Especially "shmuck," which according to Wikipedia meant "head of the penis."

"This president of ours, what a *shmuck.*"

"You should have met some of Julia's other boyfriends. What *shmucks.*"

Martin, though, wasn't a *shmuck*. Julia's parents were happy when she married him. They gave the newlywed couple a complete set of antique porcelain dishes covered with rose blossoms that Julia's mother had bought at an auction on Magazine Street. "I just couldn't resist," she'd said, handing them box after box of the stuff. "I just had to get it."

The first time he met his mother-in-law, though, there were no porcelain dishes or *mazel tovs*, but rather, a story. "When Julia was in high school," Julia's mother told him while Julia was out back, helping her father in the garden. "Our good friends' only son, Ben, suddenly got very very Jewish. He was a brilliant boy, just brilliant. He had just graduated from Tulane and was planning to go on to law school. Yale. He was one of those kids—he'd gotten in everywhere, but he had his heart set on Yale. But instead of going directly to law school, he decided to take a year off and go and work on a kibbutz in Israel. His mom wasn't crazy about the idea, but he was grown and anyway, that's what he did. He went to live on some kibbutz. When he was there, he fell in love with an Israeli girl who had grown up on the kibbutz, only now she was studying to be a nurse. Of course, she barely spoke a word of English, but they got by."

From somewhere a few streets over, Martin could hear construction sounds. Inside, it was over-conditioned, the windows beading with condensation.

"After the year in Israel was over," Julia's mother continued, "Ben came back to New Haven and started law school, and he and the kibbutz girl kept in touch and then he started having these terrible bouts of nausea." She stopped and looked out the steamed-up kitchen windows. Three blocks to the north, Lake Pontchartrain spread out for miles but from here, in the house, all you saw was the flat green lawns of other one-story brick houses. Martin knew what was coming next, because when Julia's mother said "nausea," her eyes misted over. "And anyway, long story short, he had a cancer. Cancer of the bowel, and by the time they caught it, it was too late. So anyway, the Israeli girl, her name was Penina, she came to the United States and the two of them got married, and she married him even though she barely knew English and she couldn't work as a nurse in America even though she was a nurse in Israel, and the only thing she *could* do was clean houses so that's what she did. While Ben went to law school, she cleaned houses, and then, a year or so later, he died."

"That's terrible," Martin said. "I'm so sorry."

"And his parents were….well, you can only imagine. They were devastated. Plus he was their only child. But here's the thing: everyone assumed that Penina would go back to Israel. She was a lovely girl, too—just lovely, with long beautiful dark hair. Very Israeli, if you know what I mean. Dark eyes. And here she was, stuck in New Haven, knowing no one and working as a maid, and her in-laws were all the way down here in New Orleans, and her own family was on their kibbutz growing oranges. But she had ideas of her own, and long story short she managed to start working as a nurse again. She got a job at the New Haven hospital, and the next thing we know she's engaged to be married to a nice Jewish doctor."

"Oh," Martin said. He didn't know why Julia's mother was telling him this story.

"Her family flies over from Israel for the wedding, and the groom's family is of course there too. But guess who else was invited to the wedding?"

"I don't know," Martin said.

"Ben's family."

"Oh," Martin said.

"And let me tell you. I can't tell this story without crying because even though I wasn't there I felt like I was, it meant so much to them. Ben's mom and dad went to Penina's wedding and danced and everything, because of course everyone was so happy that Penina had remarried, and to such a nice young man. Everyone was happy, and everyone was crying because it was so sad and so happy at the same time. That was twenty years ago."

Now Julia's mother really was crying, the tears spilling out over her cheeks. "I'm sorry," she said, "I just can't help it. Every time I think of our friends, still in mourning but at the same time they're dancing at Penina's second wedding, and Penina in a white wedding gown, and their own son just two years in the grave. Well, it gets to me. But thank God. Thank God that Penina was able to go on with her life like that."

"Yes," Martin said. "Well."

"Our girl is very very sick," Marian said, wiping her tears with the back of her hand. "I just don't understand a thing."

"I know," Martin said, but he didn't. All he knew was that he loved Julia, though he wasn't sure he was comfortable with Julia's mother. Something about her made him wary. She had thick reddish-blond hair, obviously colored, and the same bright blue eyes as her daughter. Her hands were covered in rings. He liked Julia's father, Sid, better. Sid was quiet, an accountant. According to his daughter, he loved nothing better than working in the garden. "It's his way of getting away from Mom," she told him.

People died all the time, of course. Martin himself would die. His best friend from high school had died of a drug overdose the summer before college. Another friend had committed suicide. His own parents had both died on the early side, one of cancer, the other of a whole combination of miseries. Martin himself wasn't young: forty-six when he first met Julia, forty-nine when she entered the last phase of her illness. Still, he'd clung on to the belief that, somehow, this one person, this person who meant so much to him, wouldn't succumb to the tumor that was already cannibalizing her body. He was in denial. Except that he wasn't, not really, because the whole time that he clung to his hope he knew he was in denial, which effectively canceled his denial and put him quite firmly in the realm of the expected, the clinical, the real. Julia had a brain tumor. He saw it on the sonogram.

"You know what you're getting into, son," his new father-in-law had said on the morning of the day that he took Julia down to city hall and married her.

"Of course I do."

Sid had squeezed his elbow.

Still, there was hope: he'd heard of a nun in Baton Rouge, a certain Sister Maria, who was reputed to have miraculous healing powers. Martin himself had a deep distrust of the Church as an institution and Christianity as a concept, and, of course, Julia was Jewish, but he got Sister Maria's telephone number anyway and made an appointment for Julia to see her, and only then, after he'd made the appointment, did he tell Julia about it, asking her if she'd be willing to make the trip to Baton Rouge to see a nun.

"You're kidding me, right?" she said.

"I thought it would be worth a try. I thought that at the very least, it couldn't hurt."

"I hate Baton Rouge," Julia said, which he already knew. Julia had hated Baton Rouge ever since her parents, claiming financial prudence, had made her go to LSU even though she'd gotten into a whole bunch of good colleges up north. "It's small and parochial and Bible-thumping."

"Sister Maria is really supposed to have a gift," he said.

"I'll probably go running, screaming, out of her office," she said. "If anything, she'll probably make my tumor *worse.*"

He didn't know why he held out such hope for Sister Maria, particularly as he generally held faith-healers and others like them—spiritualists, hands-on-healers, energy-channelers, aura-readers—in utter and complete contempt. In his opinion, they were all playing the same game as the white girls from Gentilly and Metarie who wrapped themselves in scarves from the Walmart and read the fortunes of the gullible in the French Quarter for ten bucks a reading.

"I mean it, Martin," Julia said.

"Gotcha."

He made a day out of it anyway, making plans for the two of them to have lunch downtown and then go to the LSU art museum. Julia liked that kind of thing. When he'd first met her, before she got too sick to do much more of anything than lie around the house watching videos, they'd go wandering down Magazine Street, looking in the galleries and junk shops, talking about how strange it was, when you really thought about it, that you spent a whole life time collecting stuff, and it was your stuff, and then you died, and your stuff got scattered to the four winds. And consider: how much raw *stuff* there was in the world, how many dishes and planters and forks and knives, napkins and chairs and rugs and boxes of stationary and CDs and pens and filing cabinets and pillows and curtains, not to mention the new stuff that was manufactured in China and shipped to the United States every minute of every hour of every day of the year. "I mean," Julia would say, "what happens to it all? You'd think there wouldn't be any need for a single new *anything* to ever be made, what with all the stuff we already have. And yet."

"And yet," he'd say. It always amazed him that she was a lawyer by profession. She'd still been working when he met her. He himself wrote an on-line music column for which he was paid little and did fancy interior painting, *faux* finishes and sponge-painting and stencils and rag rolling, for which he was paid a lot. Enough to live comfortably in a roomy apartment on the second floor of a ratty old building on the edge of the *Marigny,* okay, on the far edge, on the wrong side, headed down-river towards St. Bernard Parish, but he liked it, and he still had enough, after he'd paid his mortgage and electric bill, to go out to dinner and travel. Not like Julia, who, every morning, put on a well-cut expensive suit, grabbed her briefcase, and headed off to a well-appointed office filled with the hush of a first-rate air-conditioning system.

She loved it, though; she loved stuff. She loved buying old, faded linens—square of muslin printed with red geraniums or too-blue bluebells—and crooked lamps. She loved antique silver jewelry, too, though she usually bought it for someone else, a friend or a cousin. She had lots of friends, all of them women, from the different stages of her life: grammar school and high school and college, and then law school and then the year she'd clerked for a judge in Shreveport and then the year that she'd saved up all her money and gone and worked on a presidential campaign, plus friends from her neighborhood on the bad side of the Irish Channel and friends from work and friends of friends, people she'd met at yoga or through one of her cousins. She kept up with all of them.

It turned out that Julia had no intention of doing anything in Baton Rouge other than seeing Sister Maria. "Then we're going straight home," she said. "Promise me. Promise me you'll take me straight home."

"I promise," he said.

Amazingly, Julia liked Sister Maria. She came out of Sister Maria's office with her face white from crying and in the car, going back home, told Martin that Sister Maria hadn't tried to convert her and hadn't talked to her about Jesus and hadn't even prayed, but rather, sat and listened, and, when Julia was done talking, finishing her story, told her that she didn't possess any special powers at all, but rather, was working with a gift like any other gift.

"I've got a brain tumor," Julia said she had said. "My doctor has given me maybe two years, but that's at the outside."

Then, Julia said, Sister Maria put her hands on either side of Julia's head and held them there for a while, and while she held them, Julia felt an enormous sense of warmth, and had suddenly remembered that, when she was eighteen, she'd promised her friend Meg that, if neither one of them was married by the time they were forty, they'd run away to Europe together. Meg had gotten married when she was twenty-four but was divorced at thirty and never had children or remarried. "Her husband was a real dickhead," Julia explained now, in the car heading back to New Orleans. "So what I was thinking was that, if I hadn't met you, Meg and I would be living somewhere in Paris or Milan or London, and everyone would think we were a couple of old dykes."

"Do you wish you'd gone off with Meg instead?" Martin said. "Do you wish you were living in Paris or Milan?"

"It's an unholy mess," Julia said. "But I've always loved New Orleans."

"So, do you want to go back and see her again?"

"What do you mean?"

"Sister Maria? Do you want to see her again?"

"I don't think so," Julia said.

Martin thought about that. Then he thought that maybe he, Martin, should make an appointment to see Sister Maria himself. He drove Julia straight back to their building on the far side of the *Faubourg* before either one of them spoke again.

Johnson came into their lives because Martin had read somewhere that pets gave people a reason to live, but the dog became his dog, and he spent almost as much time walking him as he did fussing over Julia. Then he heard that there was an on-line "community" of people with cancer, but when he went on-line and read what people posted on the site, he grew heart sick, almost nauseous with grief. Then he learned that there was a woman in Baton Rouge who was dying of melanoma and writing a weekly column about it in the *Baton Rouge Advocate,* where she had a following. "End of life" is what dying was called now. It wasn't a euphemism, exactly, but still seemed blurry, a deliberate making-nice something that wasn't nice at all. Thinking it might help him come to grips, he went on-line to read the dying woman's column in *The Advocate* for himself, but soon gave up.

When Julia first told him that Jesus had come to her, Martin didn't know what she meant and passed her story off as one of many odd bits of information and bursts of narrative that had characterized her conversation for some months already. But when she told him a second time, and this time said that it really was him, it was Jesus himself, and he had come to her, personally, to tell her that it was all right, that everything was going to be fine and not to worry, and that everyone would be okay, even Martin, even her mother and father who were going crazy with worry and helplessness and tended to come over unannounced with pitchers full of iced tea and trays of muffins and cookies and baked lasagna and other things that Julia didn't want, they'd be okay too—well, the second time she told him, he believed her.

"And?" he said. It was another terrible day, hot and humid, with no air. Johnson lay on the floor by the bed at his feet, panting. He was a medium-sized black mutt with white forelegs. When he heard thunder he cowered in the corner and gave off a terrible odor of doggie-anxiety combined with hormonal effluvium, a canine musk.

"And I want to be buried as a Christian," she said.

"What?"

"Promise me," she said. "Promise me that I'll be buried as a Christian."

He didn't even know what that meant, but he promised her anyway, and later, when she asked to speak to her friend Margo's priest, he went and got him. After the priest it was a preacher she wanted, preferably black, and again Martin complied. On the appointed day the man showed up, wearing an old-fashioned men's straw hat, his short-sleeved shirt neatly tucked into his Dockers, and he sat in the bedroom with Julia, while at the other end of the house, Martin patted Johnson's belly and wondered if there was anything good on HBO that night.

He could hear them talking, their voices murmuring together.

When in early August she died, it was after she'd sent him away, saying, "That dog is driving me crazy. Go take him on a walk." It was true, too: Johnson, lying as usual under his feet, had been scratching at the floor, a sure sign that he needed to move his bowels. There weren't that many dogs in the *Faubourg*, at least not in Martin and Julia's scruffy end of it. Julia hadn't wanted to give up her own house at first, but Martin's place was bigger and had the added advantage of being closer to downtown, so close that on nice days she could walk to work. Not that she did much walking. Then she could barely walk at all. So he'd left her alone: she was zonked out, without pain—but the hospice nurse had already come and gone for the afternoon, so when he took Johnson out, there was no one else in the apartment with her. No one except Jesus, that is, only Martin, unlike his Jewish wife, didn't have much respect or need for Jesus, and certainly no love.

When he and Johnson came back, she was dead. He knew it even before he stepped into the room. He knew it even before he finished turning his key in the lock. He just knew it. Later, he got angry——how could she go and do such a thing to him, sending him out of the house like that, banishing him from her presence during her last journey?—but at the time all he felt was a great and terrible misery.

When, years earlier, his mother had finally died—passing away in her sleep—there had been practical things to attend to, and each of them, in his way, had attended to them. Cell phones were utilized; relatives were informed; the funeral home was contacted; and then her body was carted away, and he went to the funeral home to choose a casket. Followed by the funeral, the graveside burial, and the requisite nosh. But now, with his own wife lying still and white before him, without breath, without animation, without presence or consciousness or *being*, he was clueless. He needed to make some telephone calls, but to whom? Julia's parents? His own brothers? Hospice? That priest, what was his name—Father Clem?

He made himself call every single one of them—in-laws and family, his friends and clients, her former colleagues and her sisters and their children and all her old girlfriends, the ones from summer camp and day school and college and summer jobs, the ones she'd been a bridesmaid for and the ones who hadn't asked her and the ones who'd moved away to places like Chicago and St. Louis and the ones who lived in the suburbs with their kids and pets and husbands, and he called Julia's old law firm and the black minister, too, and then Hospice, and then he thought about calling a rabbi as well, only he didn't know any, personally, and couldn't remember the name of the temple on St. Charles Avenue that his in-laws once belonged to, and then he put a call into Sister Maria, in Baton Rouge, and then he sat down and cried.

And then—and then—

There were so many *and thens*—

Her parents were furious. They felt betrayed. They felt that he'd hoodwinked them, suspected him of doing some white-bread post-Christian goy voodoo on her, a kind of black magic mind-control. When he tried to explain, they became more and more hysterical, shouting at him, yelling, going red in the face. Even Sid, usually so calm, usually so reasonable, was beyond the bend, cursing at him, muttering, accusing him of helping Hitler.

"Helping Hitler?"

"What Hitler couldn't do—getting rid of the Jews."

"She made me promise," he said over and over. "I promised her. I promised her that I'd bury her as a Christian."

"But what does that mean?" her mother said. "What does that even *mean?* That if she isn't sprinkled with holy water or whatever she doesn't get to go to heaven? And what about *us?*"

"I'm sorry."

"What about sitting *shiva?*"

Martin didn't really know what *shiva* was until later, when he looked the term up on Google, but didn't say anything. He knew, however, that when Grandpa Harry died, no one sat *shiva* for him. They plunked him in the ground, said a few prayers, and that was that. He knew because Julia had told him so. Back when—back when they were in the first flush of their love for each other, and he knew he would marry her, and she was filling him up with stories, she told him. "Grandpa Harry was the last person in my family who actually cared about all that stuff," she'd said. "You know: the Hebrew, the Sabbath, going to synagogue. But even he wasn't all that into it. In his own way, he was an agnostic. When he died, Mom and Dad didn't even do a full Jewish funeral. They said that the only person they would have done it for was Grandpa Harry, but seeing that he was dead already, there wasn't any real reason to do it. Which in its own twisted way makes sense."

"I'm sorry," he said to his in-laws, to the undertaker, and, finally, to both the minister and the rabbi who would be conducting Julia's funeral, which is what he'd finally decided on—a compromise that he hoped would soothe his raging in-laws. The rabbi was young, right out of rabbinical school, and apparently didn't mind sharing the stage with a minister. The minister was a friend of his brother's, in Jackson, and according to his brother, "very cool." Martin didn't care. He wanted to cremate her. He wanted to cremate her body and scatter her ashes in the jungle of their backyard, where he could think of her sprouting up along with the elephant ears and the iron plants, feeding off mosquitoes, turning to moss and lichen and tangled, thorny vines.

They didn't talk to him after that. They left him on his own.

He was cracked. He was mad. He was raging. He was lonely. He was a madman, living on microwavable pizza and the occasional bottle of chilled Chardonnay, so when the voice came into his head telling him that he was a Jew, he didn't much pay it any mind. The second time he heard it he stopped and listened but then went about his business—he was paying the bills—and the third time it happened he took Johnson on a walk. It was past supper time, and the streets were taking on a lovely, hazy, blurred tone. When he returned home with Johnson, he heard it again, so he sat down on the sofa and said: "Okay. So I'm a Jew. Now what?"

The dog began to howl.

Jesus was a Jew, the voice said, to which he replied: "Duh." Actually, the voice that said *Jesus was a Jew* wasn't the same voice that had just told him that he himself was a Jew. The voice that said *Jesus was a Jew* was, distinctly, his own voice coming from inside his own head, from the place near the bridge of his nose where it felt like all his random thoughts came from.

But it made a weird kind of sense anyway. *Of course* Jesus was a Jew. Everyone knew that. But as he sat there, Johnson walking in increasingly smaller and smaller circles on the living room rug, it struck him as a revelation: *Jesus was a Jew.*

Uncle Harry was a Jew, too. Maybe Jesus and Uncle Harry were even related, in the way that everyone was related, particularly if you were Jewish. So-and-So begat So-and-So and so forth and so on for forever and ever. He remembered that from the two years of Bible Study that his mother had made him take when he was in grade school. Ergo: Jesus and Julia were actually related. Distant cousins, many many times removed. Which meant that he, Martin, was a Jew too: everyone, in fact, was a Jew. Even Africans. Even Chinese. They just didn't know it.

He got in the car and drove straight to the home of his in-laws in Lakeview. He knocked at the kitchen door. Sid answered it. "Oh," he said. "Martin. What do you want?"

What *did* he want? Forgiveness? Understanding? Love?

"I want my wife back," is what he said.

"We all want Julia back."

"No," he said. "You took her from me."

"She died of a massive metastasized tumor."

"Look Sid," he finally said. "I have to tell you something."

Sid just stood there, his arms crossed over his chest.

"I'm a Jew," he said.

"Ha!"

"I am. So was Jesus. Jesus was a Jew."

"So I've been told."

"I'm a Jew, too," he said.

Sid told him good night.

"All of us are Jewish," Martin said. "That's the point. The whole world is Jewish. I miss her, Sid."

"I do too."

"I loved her more than I loved my own life."

"Look, Martin," Sid said, but he didn't say anything else. Instead, his pale green eyes began to water, and when the tears came, he didn't wipe them away or attempt to inhale them back into his eyes like most men would, but just let them be. Finally, his arms still crossed over his chest, he said: "Okay."

"Okay?"

"You're a Jew. Mazel tov."

A few months later, the hurricane came, washing everything away, drowning the young and the old alike, sweeping the whole city away under the swarming brown filthy waters, filling peoples' refrigerators and medicine cabinets and bedside tables with muck, coating family photographs and silver wedding anniversary presents with toxic waste, soaking heirloom carpets and antique oil portraits and hand-sewn quilts and hand-painted porcelain—but as whole worlds of memory disappeared, Martin, the Jew, walked through the waters all the way to Baton Rouge.

THE TEACHER

It didn't start percolating out until years—decades—later, and by that time even the youngest of what we'd soon be calling "the victims" were in their early fifties, with husbands and children and grandchildren of their own, or not, with houses, careers, garages stuffed to the gills with lifetimes' worth of patio furniture and forgotten Halloween costumes and broken lamps and tools. Someone saw someone who knew someone, who'd remembered someone, and again the stories were abroad, the whisperings, only this time it was with heavy sighs of regret and anxious handwringing: How could we not have known better? How could our parents not have known?

And if they, the parents, had known—and surely some of them had—they were too busy themselves and perhaps too ashamed, too abashed to see it for what it was and, after all, busy and perplexed with their own lives, their own divorces or philandering husbands or careers that felt like prison, with alcoholism and dying parents, with inheritances and bright futures withered to nothing. All those bright promises of their bright and perfect childhoods curling like so many brown November leaves.

His name was Mr. Bryce—Evan Bryce, as we later came to call him— and he was among the most popular, perhaps *the* most popular, of the upper- school teachers, with a yearly following of students lucky enough not only to have been enrolled in one of his classes, but allowed, as if by virtue of their own charmed stars, their own charming uniqueness, to lean against his desk during free time, or joke around with him as he walked, his battered book bag in hand, toward the lunchroom. He taught history and geography; his classroom was the first on the left as you rounded the corner from the art room to the open-air corridor that the upper school classrooms abutted. Beyond that strip of covered poured white concrete was a kind of rough lawn, made patchy by years of boys tackling each other there or throwing a Frisbee around, and beyond that, on the other side of a narrow gravel road used only, as far as we could tell, by the school's groundskeepers whose names, despite their ubiquitous presence, we didn't know, was the first of the playing fields, used for hockey and soccer. Beyond the playing field was a covered sports arena with a huge swooping roof like the wing of a swan and beyond that, hills covered with mowed green grass—perfect for tumbling down on bright spring days—and others still wooded, watered with streams and crisscrossed with trails. We knew the trails of course—some of our natural science classes took place in the woods—and we knew each of the hills and fields as well, each tree, each row of boxwoods or pines, until finally, out there, beyond the school grounds, was where the residents of the town lived in red-brick development houses of two and sometimes one-and-a-half floors, in modified colonials and California-style split-levels, each with its own small patch of lawn and a garage. We felt sorry for the people who lived in those developments (we always called them developments, never *neighborhoods*, which is where we lived), but we rarely wondered what their lives might be like, or where their children, if they had them, might go to school.

Our houses weren't like that, of course. Susie Bluestone's house was old, tall and thin, in a neighborhood of other old, tall, thin houses, with Oriental carpets running up the stairways and a laundry chute that the children were forbidden to play in and played in anyway. My best friend Nan Jones lived in a farmhouse on the top of a hill and wasn't allowed to use the guestroom bathroom, even though her room was right next to it; her mother kept horses, and her father had once been some kind of fencing champion. There were black-and-white pictures of him, in black frames, on the walls of the little room where they watched TV. Daphne McKenzie's French mother had filled her house with bright flowery fabrics and hung porcelain dinner plates on the wall for decoration, and every time my mother picked me up from there, she said that in a million years she wouldn't have thought of anything so charming, even though, like most of the mothers, my mother gave our own house— which a famous architect had designed—something verging on obsessional attention, perhaps because our father, like all the fathers, wasn't around much. He wasn't around much because he was working, downtown, with all the other fathers, and like all the other fathers, he came home after dark, just in time for dinner, really, and had a cocktail while he scanned first the *Washington Post*, and then the *Wall Street Journal*. Every now and then our mother joined him, she with her bourbon sour and he with a whiskey, but usually by then she was in the kitchen, putting the finishing touches on dinner.

But all that—the obsessional interest in things like American antiques on the one hand and politics on the other—was their world, not ours, not once the school bus came and collected us in the morning and took us to our real lives, our *lived* lives, where everything important or exciting or terrible or hurtful or damaging or embarrassing or thrilling happened, where everyone knew who the slutty older girls were and who were the boys worth wrestling with there on the tufted grass, there where everyone could see him pull your hair if he was mean or merely pull the Frisbee out of your clutched arms if he wasn't, if he were smart and popular, with straight thick hair and clear skin and good grades and the right answers. That was important, being smart, because eventually we'd all go to either day school or prep school, if your family did that, and then to college, preferably one of the Ivies, and we all knew which were the better ones, and if you weren't smart enough or talented enough to go to one of the Ivies, you might go to one of the good small colleges in New England or the Midwest that, though they didn't *quite* have the shine of a Princeton or a Harvard still kept you well within the confines, the known and comfortable bounds, of where we belonged.

Mr. Bryce had gone to Harvard. We knew this not only because his educational background was listed, along with all the other teachers', in the school handbook, but also because he talked about it: "When I was tackled one day by my so-called best pal in Harvard Yard. . . . I rowed at Harvard, but the truth is I was lucky to make the team. . . . Damn, if my first winter in Cambridge wasn't as cold as a witch's. . . . Oh, sorry, I didn't say that!" We loved it, of course, when he did that: when he swore, or almost swore. It was just one of the things that made him so attractive, so popular, so *cool.* Before Harvard he was at Choate. And the fact that he stuck to the costume of his youth—the bow tie, the pastel pink or blue or fraying white shirt, the somewhat scuffed up dock-siders or loafers, and the somewhat baggy or worn khakis (if it was warm) or corduroys (if it was cold) made us love him all the more. He was what he was: the real deal. And that he'd chosen to go into teaching, rather than law or banking or government, like most of our fathers had done, made him all the more interesting. He was our own future, incarnate, or if we were girls, he was our future husband, or boyfriend, or lover. And he was funny, too. So funny, the way he talked about George Washington's men freezing their asses off, or how he referenced the spread of what he called "creeping mediocrity" and "calculated androgyny," which we had to look up when we got home. Out there, in the world that one day we'd have to join—but not until later, until after, until then—the world was going to hell in a handbasket; there were protests in the street—and those protests were important, too, right, just, even noble. But what did any of it have to do with us, with the chalk dust we inhaled in Mr. Bryce's room, with the way the sunlight slanted in through the windows and the trees rimming the far side of the playing fields swayed in the wind? What did the world that made our fathers grumble and our mothers sigh have to do with who had started to wear a bra or whose parents were getting a divorce?

At first it seemed that he only chose blondes, and even if they weren't blonde, they all possessed a kind of rough-and-tumble quality that we associated with blondes, the quality of girls who spent summers sailing in Maine and roughhousing with older brothers. Names were mentioned: Beatrice Sutherland, who'd already graduated and gone on to Madeira; Leslie Peters and Leslie Chase, the two Leslies they were called; Martha Ann Vosberg, who ever since middle school had been known as Andy. But the first one I knew of for sure was Polly Jones, Nan Jones's older sister, who wasn't blonde, or tomboyish, or even remotely rough-and-tumble. There was no sense of her hair ever having been whipped about by sea winds or her lips having been chapped by too much time spent outdoors on a cold day. Instead, she was somewhat heavy-set, slightly plodding with a big bottom and a round, smooth, white face, like the face of a beach ball, and perfect, perfectly spaced, small elegant features. Her hair was dark and fine, almost as dark and fine as Lia Chang's, our one Chinese student, except we weren't really sure if she was Chinese or something else, and in any event it didn't matter because not only was her English perfect but also because before she'd moved to America she'd lived in London. Polly's hair was cut straight across at her shoulders, straight like the bottom of a curtain, and at school she tended to be quiet. But at home—at that farmhouse at the top of the hill with its endless driveway and horse barn—she could be both loud and mean. Or at least she was mean to Nan and me, three years her juniors and still caught up with reading *Mad* magazine and riding horses, Nan's mother's horses, which she let us ride but only if we promised to be back by a certain hour, which we almost never were, which meant that, if I were sleeping over, an earlier-than-usual bedtime or perhaps no dessert. She was very strict, Nan and Polly's mother, stricter than my own mother, with her love of what she called "antiquing" and equal love of Broadway musicals, the musicals of her girlhood in faraway New York, where my grandmother lived, in an apartment.

Nan told me that one day Mr. Bryce had asked Polly to stay behind after class, and when she did he pushed her into a corner and put his hands on her chest. "Are you sure?" I said after a while, because while I knew that something wasn't right about this I wasn't really quite sure what it was. "I heard her telling Mom," Nan said. "And then he did it to her again, but this time he yanked her shirt up, and put his hands right *there,* under her bra."

"Right *there*?" I echoed, still not sure exactly what to think or what area of Polly's anatomy, precisely, Nan was referring to.

"*Right* there," Nan said.

But it didn't seem all *that* bad to me, not when Mr. Bryce was Mr. Bryce, and he hadn't done anything all that different from what the older boys and girls were said to do, there at their parties, in basements, or back rooms, or even during the day, leaning against trees on the nature trail at school, so when Nan was silent for a little while and I still didn't know how I was supposed to react, I said, "Are you sure?"

"I'm sure," Nan said. Then she clutched me: "Don't tell anyone. It's a secret."

Of course it was a secret, and after she made me promise not to tell, Nan made me promise not to mention it again, or ask her anything else about it, because if her mother knew that she'd told me, or even knew that Nan herself knew about it, she'd be punished for sure, big time. She was already in trouble, in the crap-box, she said (*crap* then being the worst word we felt entitled to use) because of something else she'd done, something else she wouldn't tell me about but which I thought might have involved going down to the horse barn a few weeks earlier with one of her cousins, a cousin from Vermont who had come to visit with his family—or maybe he wasn't a cousin, but more like a cousin-of-a-cousin or perhaps the son of an old family friend. No, strike that. He was a cousin, and his name was Roger, and he had his own BB gun, which he used in Vermont to shoot squirrels. Also, he was already such a good skier he could do the black diamond trails.

So there was that nasty business, whatever it was, and then the astonishing news about Polly Jones, who, when I saw her at Nan's house or at school didn't seem any different than she'd ever been, with her plodding sort of walk and sturdy pinkish legs, her hem line carefully hemmed by her mother (my mother sent my uniforms out to be done) in small careful stitches. Like always when I went to Nan's, Polly slammed her door on us and called us "brats," or sulked when she had to take out the trash or feed the dogs, and one day, when I found myself alone with her in the basement rec-room where Mrs. Jones made us change out of our clothes if they were muddy or smelled too much like horses, she pulled me aside and said, "You're probably a lesbian and don't even know it."

"What?" I said.

"I see the way you stare at me. So just cut it out. Now. Lesbian freak Jew."

Which, of course, was the other thing that I, and for that matter my older sister, was—Jewish—making us, like Lia Chang, slightly outside, slightly apart from the run of things. Only unlike Lia, who was in fact one of the smartest and most popular girls at school, a girl envied both for her smooth darting legs under her hockey pinnies and her smooth blue-black hair, we were ordinary, with skin and hair like everyone else, except not really, because both my sister and I had wild curls that looped and frizzed like electricity when it got hot, and our house, though nothing like the development houses that surrounded the school grounds on the other side of the woods, was modern; a modern glass rectangle with slate floors and a long drafty front hall, filled not with inherited furniture and well-worn Oriental rugs or treasures brought back from living abroad, but an odd combination of sleek white-blonde furniture and the oversized and deeply shined period pieces and china closets that our mother hauled back from her forays into the Virginia or Maryland countryside. She'd grown up in New York City, and, while the idea of the countryside intrigued her and she practically swooned every time she dropped me off or picked me up from Nan's farmhouse, she herself couldn't live any farther out of town than where we did live—on a patch of land that had once belonged to the boxy Victorian next door, its grounds now whittled down to its own garden and two stately weeping willow trees. Our house, where the original carriage house had apparently once stood, gazed off in the other direction, toward the street.

But I'm off track now and need to return to the fact of my—of our—Jewishness: a thing, a condition that set my sister and me just slightly apart from our friends and classmates and endowed upon the both of us a combined sense of superiority and inferiority, which, though we barely sensed it, we knew in our bones. Not for either one of us were the attentions of the most admired and sought-after girls or boys, and certainly not the attentions, or even recognition, of Mr. Bryce. For better or for worse, and it wasn't at all sure which was which, neither one of us would find his gaze, or his attention, on us. And in my own case, which I'll come to shortly, the chances were made even slimmer by the fact that I was never assigned to sit in any of his classes. In any event, at school I was neither fish nor fowl, neither despised like the chunky, pink-legged Susie Stewart, with her pink hair ribbons and constantly runny nose, nor envied like Virginia Hoff, who not only was beautiful, with the rare and shining beauty that bespoke generations of excellence—flying hair, taut body, bitten-down nails, and eyes as blue as the bluest lake—but also daring, fearless, fierce. How she pounced on the ball when we played free-for-all dodge ball and ran headlong down the hills! How she huddled near the row of crabapple trees, surrounded by other girls of her ilk, to plan her next move! Ever since the fifth grade she'd been going back and forth between Gary Spaulding and Gray Dyer, never able to make up her mind between them. And who could blame her? Gary was the more handsome, with dimples and reddish-brownish hair, but Gray, who had a sharp face and close-set, brilliantly black eyes under bushy eyebrows, was slated for greatness, for a career in the State Department or even in electoral politics. He would tell anyone who asked him that he preferred Yale to Harvard and planned to go there—to New Haven, as he referred to it—when the time came.

My sister, however, she was her own and different story. *Katerina.* She'd been named for a character in either a ballet that Mom had loved as a girl or a Russian novel, only every time my parents told the story of her name, they told it differently, so I could never be sure. Katerina was like our father, which is to say intense, green-eyed, stubborn, outspoken, occasionally rude, and extremely, almost frighteningly smart. Only no one knew all those things about her then—no one, that is, other than our own family—because in school she tended to read spy novels during class, hiding them behind her textbooks so no one could see, or design houses. Her notebooks were filled with floor plans, exterior dimensions, placement of furniture and windows. She *was* enrolled in one of Mr. Bryce's classes, English history, where she, predictably, scraped by with low Cs and didn't call attention to herself except when Mr. Bryce called on her, and then she would stammer out the wrong answer and turn a mottled yellow-red. In middle school, she'd been the butt of some of the mean boys' jokes, but now they mainly left her alone. Nan said it was because the boys' parents had been called in to meet with the head, who said that our school was trying very hard to open its doors to people of all different kinds of backgrounds, not just Jews and Asians, but blacks, too. And after that the worst of the teasing had stopped, and Katerina was allowed to sink back into the oblivion that was her natural habitat. Also, by upper school, when she was in Mr. Bryce's English history class, her nose began to take on a distinctly Semitic slant, curving at the bridge and broadening at the nostrils, giving her the distracted look of someone who'd only recently woken up and was still half-way caught up in their morning dream, but it also gave her an expression of wary ferocity. In any event, the torture she'd endured at the hands of the popular boys in her grade had ceased, and she was more or less left alone, a party of one huddled with her books and her pencils and disturbingly alive hair: a girl who threw tantrums when our parents told her that she wasn't working up to her potential and who disappeared for hours on end in order to avoid going to *Rosh Ha Shana* services or visiting our father's parents in Baltimore or anything else she found trite or boring or a waste of time, only to return home with scratches on her legs or small bruises on her upper arms. To get away from us, she'd spend the entire day in Rock Creek Park, just looking at things: at the sunlight on the rippling water, at leaves, at squirrels. She was an angry girl, a sullen, headstrong, rude girl quite capable of kicking the furniture or deciding that from now on our family dog would sleep with her, in her bed, and she didn't care about her allergies or about all the extra work our mother would have to do. She was the last person in the world who Mr. Bryce would so much as notice. I, too, would be camouflaged and made invisible, as much by my Jewishness as by my rank in the pecking order, but unlike my sister, I was rather daintily made, with the high cheekbones and long thin limbs of the dancer our mother had once dreamed of being, with the same wide-spaced mud-brown eyes of our mother and all our mother's family.

And in any event our parents knew nothing of Mr. Bryce and what he and his favorites did or didn't do, or, for that matter, about Polly Jones, whose past with Mr. Bryce, whatever it had entailed, was just that—*past*. Polly had gone on to Holton Arms, because even though her parents had divorced and Mrs. Jones had remarried, selling the old farmhouse on the hill and moving in with her new husband so that Mrs. Jones was no longer Mrs. Jones at all but Mrs. Wenners, Polly had resolutely refused to go away to boarding school, and in the end her mother had agreed. "Polly's always been such a handful," my mother would say. "And she took that divorce hard. At least this way she can transition more easily."

I didn't really know what my mother meant but I, too, was happy that Nan's mother and father were no longer married and that Nan and her family had moved in with her stepfather, because now not only was Nan living much closer to me—just on the other side of Connecticut Avenue, in fact—but also because Nan's real father seemed in general to find me distasteful. I think a part of it was that I ate so much, much more than either Nan or Polly Jones, and I wasn't a very polite or neat eater, either, completely unlike Nan with her small careful bites. Also, because I was Jewish I didn't eat bacon, except sometimes I did anyway, and on those occasions, I'd find Mr. Jones peering at me as if I were covered in some repulsive substance, like blood, or boogers. Of course after Mrs. Jones married Mr. Wenners, it didn't matter as much anymore what Mr. Jones thought or didn't think about me, and as for Polly

Jones, the one time, years later, that Nan mentioned Mr. Bryce's interest in Polly, his assault of her, his hands on her, it was only to say that Polly's college boyfriend, to whom, Nan said, Polly had "lost her cherry," looked a little bit like him. Then she rolled her eyes.

Then we were in upper school, and it seemed that there was a whole crew of them, a whole club, a sorority to which I would never be initiated, never be tapped—all those freckled or flat-chested or sporty girls, most of them, Polly Jones aside, blonde or dirty blonde, all of them thrilled, at least at first, to be chosen, to be called out as special. One girl had been invited to Mr. Bryce's backyard swimming pool—he'd since married and had a couple of small children—where Mr. Bryce had pulled off her top and fondled her under the chlorinated shimmering blue coldness; another had found herself caught in his hot embrace in the boiler room at school; a third had been bending over to retrieve her books after school, and had suddenly felt herself to be exposed and naked and then the sharp pain, the sharp thrust, and the squirt—spurt—the wetness, the drip, drip, drip in her underpants all the way home on the late bus. Eventually, it was said, some parents had gone to the school head, and Mr. Bryce had to go to counseling. No one even knew if he was still teaching or not. We were busy with our own lives, our own boyfriends, our own college friends, and first jobs and apartments and eventually weddings and children of our own.

As our parents had always known, Katerina—despite her stubbornness and lack of manners, her headstrong sense of rightness and inability to be corrected—was slated for excellence. An imposing woman in beautiful, tailored, tight-fitting suits and excellent high heels, she'd gone first to Harvard and then to Harvard Law School before being asked back to Harvard, this time to teach—outshining Mr. Bryce in his own back yard—even as I, the little sister, the one who'd been blessed with ordinary prettiness and impenetrable invisibility, struggled to keep up, to maintain my own bit of breathing room. But at least I was still up and moving forward, checking off all the boxes on the life-long to-do list: college, check; job, check; boyfriend, husband, children, house, car, mortgage, minivan, varicose veins, good sex, bad sex, no sex, bewildering sex, noisy children, sick children, growing children, endless boredom, endless soccer games, endless longing, check check check. Which was better than we could say about so many of our former classmates, our former tormenters and best friends and playmates and school yard adversaries. Polly Jones grew plump and then plumper and finally so fat that she wheezed; both of the two Leslies became addicted to prescription pain medication, or perhaps one of them was addicted to something else; Daphne McKenzie had moved to France with her French mother, leaving the sunny house in Chevy Chase behind for what my mother—who still kept in touch with her mother—said was a disastrous marriage to a Belgian psychiatrist. And then the news, conveyed at first in phone calls and then in email exchanges, all of us connected again, connected through that shared memory, that memory of something unmentionable, something terrible and titillating and thrilling all at the same time, until at last someone—no one knew exactly which of the girls it was—saw him again, saw Mr. Bryce, now well into his seventies, getting out of his car in front of the Hillsbury School, a school that had been founded as an alternative school for children of parents we didn't know— parents who grew their own vegetables, perhaps, or read Freud, and had long since become an equal of our own children—and there he was, gathering his things, a battered book bag that looked just like the one he'd carried back then, a pile of papers, a raincoat slung under one arm, headed across the lawn. She wasn't sure it was the same Mr. Bryce who had raped her in his swimming pool, pulling down her bikini bottoms and entering her from behind, telling her that no one would believe her, but that it didn't matter because he loved her and that he'd chosen her out of all the other girls, chosen her for her beauty and sophistication, for her astonishing vibrancy, her star on the rise; and would she remember him years later when she was famous and living in Paris or London or Milan or even Istanbul because that's the kind of special amazing magical girl she was, not like all those other girls, ordinary girls, drab and plain girls, headed into dull lives and dull marriages. Because, although this man sported the same kind of jaunty bow tie that Mr. Bryce had worn, and his small feet, like Mr. Bryce's, were shod in loafers, he was jowly, with a face neither oval nor round but somehow square, and the eyes, which had been merry, were all wrong: downcast, dark, rimmed, puffy. It had been such a long time.

So it wasn't until it was in all the newspapers, all the details save the name of the one brave woman who had recognized Mr. Bryce getting out of his car in front of Hillsbury School and then followed up with phone calls and a meeting with school administrators and finally with other girls from school, girls she tracked down on Facebook and through the alumni office; until there was a full-blown investigation, and an arrest, and a trial, and they were all there, in front of the courthouse in suburban Virginia, talking to the reporters, making their statements, saying that the day of justice had at last come, that the memories had come flooding back, crippling them in some cases and emboldening them in others, and all of us watching it live on TV or streaming through our laptops. It wasn't until all this that my sister, calling me on the phone while I was making dinner, said, "Did he ever do anything to you?"

"No," I said. "I never even had him as a teacher, thank God."

"You were always lucky that way," my sister said. "You always lucked out."

"It amazes me that it took so long, is all," I said, unsure of myself, of my words. There was something old and vicious in my sister's tone.

"Considering that everyone knew it."

"Not everyone," Katerina said.

"Most people."

"Not Mom," she said. "Not Dad." She was speaking overly loudly now, as if into a phone on speaker.

"Why would they?" I said. "Nothing happened to us. I mean, other than your bad grades. And none of my friends were his favorites, either. And you barely had any friends." It was a joke but it fell flat.

"You didn't know either, though, did you?" she said.

"I didn't know that there were so many," I said, thinking of the crowd of women standing straight and tall on the TV news, telling bits of their stories, refusing to cry, including fat Polly Jones and pretty Alexa Parker. The onions I'd sliced and put on the stove were cooking too quickly, smoking and turning black at their edges.

"I knew it," she said. "No one knew. No one in the whole world."

Which is when it all came together, everything that had happened that year, the year Katerina had been in Mr. Bryce's classroom, her bad grades, her tantrums at home, her disappearances, and then the beginning of what would become her dazzling, dazzling career, her endless successes, her beautifully tailored, expensive clothes and her perfect home and elegant bearing. She was everything they'd hoped her to be, everything they knew her to be, smarter than those waspy blue bloods, made of better stuff.

She said that when he'd met her in Rock Creek Park, at the zoo, and later beside their own special trees or near large slabs of ancient rock face, he'd been gentle, so very gentle, so gentle and tender and loving, taking her again and again as she'd stared straight up at the leaves and behind them the endless wash of blue or gray or white sky, knowing, as she finally did, that hers, and hers alone, was the power to comply.

Do This Together

They were the four middle-aged children of their just-widowed father, riding together in their father's ancient Mercedes. There was a fifth sibling, too, the long-deceased first-born, who would have been fifty-four, had she not died at two weeks of some mysterious ailment that neither their mother nor their father would ever talk about. Crib death? Failure to thrive? What else could sweep away an otherwise healthy infant—unless the child, whose name had been Emily, hadn't been healthy at all but born with any number of hidden problems: heart, lungs, musculature, blood. Who knew? The family never talked about that first, brief life: not at the kitchen table; not during the seemingly endless trips to the beach; not on the even more endless excursions to see the kosher summer camp in upstate New York that their father had attended; not at night, when their parents came to their rooms to tuck them in and plant kisses on their foreheads. It was as if that one child had never existed, and, in her nonexistence, was everything. Everything! How else to explain their father's strange silence, the silence that outlasted their extended, combined childhoods, their mother's illness, and even now threatened to take over the car's interior, sneaking into the synapses of each of them, as if to stifle dissent? How else to explain their mother's crying, her bitter moods, the times—sometimes lasting weeks—that she'd lie in bed in her darkened bedroom, listening to opera? Or the fact that both sisters struggled with depression? The boys had felt it, too. The older of the two brothers, Dan, was on his third wife; and Joe, the so-called "surprise package" of their parents' own middle age, couldn't manage to get married at all, though God alone knew that he was attractive enough. (Those green eyes! That devilishly curling, salt-and-pepper hair! And his wit—for all his other faults, Joe could make each of his siblings laugh until tears rolled down their cheeks.) The siblings weren't sure if he was still with his latest love interest, a lovely, lively woman named Julie who was also, unfortunately, the mother of a retarded teenage daughter.

Their father's car, a 1991 sedan, was snug. Inside, their thighs rested up against each others', and their combined exhales filled the atmosphere with a peculiarly familiar oxygen: part longing, part licorice, part something else that none of them could define, yet each of them recognized as belonging with ultimate definition to them and them alone. It might have been funny— how alike this situation was to the countless carpools and road trips of their childhoods— except none of them could find the right words to make a joke of it. Not that they didn't try. Eleanor, the eldest, said: "I dibs the front seat." Joe said: "Dad, tell Dan to stop *breathing* on me."

"Move over some." This from Joe to Eleanor, who, rather than claiming the front seat as she had joked, wedged in between her brothers in back. She barely had room for her own thighs. Moreover, and each of her siblings knew it, she'd gotten the worst spot in the car: the axle seat, with its padded bump. It was Becky, the younger of the two sisters, who sat up front.

"You move over," she said.

Starting with Eleanor and ending with Joe, their father had for years driven his brood to school and then gone on to his office in downtown Washington, before returning in time for cocktails with their mother. The school was called St. Stevens, and the four of them, in turn, had been the sole Jewish child in his or her class. An odd choice, sending them to a school that, though it wasn't technically affiliated with the Episcopal Church, still drew from the mainly well-heeled offspring of Washington's traditional Anglo-Saxon elite, children who were taught that, though it isn't polite to say so, Jews were just not quite like the rest of us, not that anything was wrong with them, they had their own ways, is all. . . .

Because the children had been sensitive to this— aware that socially they seemed to carry a taint—there was anxiety in the car, which invariably led to fights. Their father, meanwhile, liked simply to sing—loudly and rather hideously off-key. His favorites were from musicals: "Somewhere Over the Rainbow." "If I Were a Rich Man." He also, occasionally, started to sing some ancient Hebrew ditty from the old days, back in Jersey, when Jews were really Jews, not like now, kids, when even the Orthodox drive on *Shabbos*. "*Ahavat olam, bet Yisroel* . . ." The whole deal—their father's entire shtick—was a great but painful joke: first because the family rarely attended synagogue, and, when it did, only because someone or another was having his *bar mitzvah*; second because though their father claimed that he kept kosher, he fixed himself a Reuben sandwich every chance he got; and finally, and more to the point, their father's name (and theirs) was Singer. A Singer who couldn't sing to save his life. A Singer who sucked all the joy out of song, who mangled it, contorted it, twisted it of all liveliness and left it in bloody shards on the floor. Singer also smoked Havana cigars, which the children hated. He rolled down the windows in the winter, claiming that cold air was good for the lungs.

Now the windows were closed, and their father no longer smoked. He'd given it up when their mother was first diagnosed with cancer, years earlier. Outside, the ground had begun to thaw, giving off a premature smell of spring.

Their mother had died in the late afternoon of the previous day. She'd died in what had once been Becky's room, wearing her favorite nightgown, the one that said, "Who Loves Grandma?" in bright red letters. Their father hadn't liked the nightgown—he'd always been uncomfortable with silliness— but had been proud of how their mother faced her death, with none of the dramatic emotional swings that characterized her middle decades. Only moments after she took her last breath, he'd looked up from where her body lay on the bed and, gazing at a spot on the wall behind Eleanor, said, "She had such dignity, didn't she?" It wasn't a question. Other than the housekeeper, who'd been hovering in the hall outside the bedroom, no one had cried. Later, he announced that he wanted all four of them to go with him the next day, first to the undertaker's, on the other side of the Beltway, and then, afterward, to the synagogue, the one their mother had liked, to discuss with the young rabbi there (a new one) what should and should not be said, and who should or should not say it. The cemetery plots had been purchased long ago, but there was a lingering question about that, too.

"Eleanor, Dan, Becky, Joe. We're going to do this together. We're going to do this as a family," is how he'd put it, knowing that the rest of the package—the sons-and daughters-in-law, Joe's friend if he had one, grand-children, various family friends and distant cousins and retired household help and the friends his wife had made in chemotherapy—would start arriving soon.

He had light blue-gray eyes under a wide forehead, springy, thin, bright silver hair, and a wide, affirmative nose. His lips were narrow and un-giving. His chin was unremarkable. Clean-shaven, he was neither short nor tall, heavyset nor slender, athletic nor delicate. All in all, though, he was a handsome man, vigorous and coiled, and women noticed him. Even now (as his daughters knew) women noticed him. He wore beautiful, expensive, tailored suits of soft, dark grays, and pastel ties. In the summer, he played tennis. He was a lawyer by training but hadn't practiced law since the last of his children went to college. He still worked, though what exactly he did remained a bit of a mystery, even to Becky, who herself was a lawyer and often consulted with him on legal affairs. Something to do with leveraged buyouts. Or was it divestiture that they specialized in? He and his partners had an office on M Street. The sign on the door said OVERVIEW STRATEGIES. Whenever any of his children visited him there, they came away with the feeling that, compared to their competent, energetic, elderly father, they themselves were as insubstantial as mist.

Swinging the Mercedes onto the Beltway, their father began to sing. He sang "Over the River and Through the Woods." In the backseat Joe wept quietly, and Eleanor, hearing him, patted his knee and wondered whether he and Julie were still sleeping together.

The funeral home was filled with dark wood furnishings and dark wine-colored rugs, but the man who met them was plump and friendly and boyish, with a round face and puffy hands. He smelled like talcum powder and kept swinging up onto his tip-toes. He ushered them down a paneled hallway and showed them into a small private room, furnished with a table and chairs. "This is better, I think," he said. "Please, make yourselves comfortable." Leaving them to themselves, he went out of the room, returning a moment later with bottles of Perrier water. "Now, let's see, you said you wanted simple?" he began.

Their father nodded. "Because we can do simple. But how simple? Simple as in elegant but no frills or simple as in simple-simple."

"Simple as in Jewish," their father said.

"I thought we'd already told him that," Dan, who since last night hadn't spoken more than two words, mumbled in the general direction of his brother. Alone among the Singers, he'd been affirmatively handsome as a teenager, but that handsomeness had given out to a certain blandness: he had straight sandy hair, a straight nose, black eyebrows jutting above his eyes.

"Simple as in plain pine box," Becky said, adding, just in case the man hadn't quite heard them the first or second or third time, "We're Jewish. The cheapest you have. No lining. No silk. No brass handles. A box."

"I see."

"A box. Simple. Pine. Cheap."

"We're Jewish," Becky again said.

"Not to put too fine a point on it," Joe whispered, while their father, growing annoyed, took on a grayish cast, as if he'd forgotten to shave.

"Fine then," the cheerful undertaker said.

Last night, two men from the funeral home had come to take their mother's body away, first wrapping her in a sheet, then placing her inside a kind of pouch (blue, made of some kind of strong synthetic), zipping her up, and carrying her, carefully, into the back of the waiting van. The sound her body made when it was placed inside the doors was similar to the sound of groceries being put away, final and unremarkable and earnest. The arrangements had been made months earlier—it was only a matter of making the phone call. Both girls had insisted on helping carry their mother's body, but the brothers had been busy elsewhere: Joe on the phone with Julie (whom he in fact wished to marry, despite the difficulties in raising a retarded step-daughter); and Dan on his BlackBerry, where he was sending emails to his partners in Hong Kong and Vietnam and Los Angeles about the deal he was trying to put together with a start-up telecommunications firm, which, now, would have to be delayed by a few days, and would that cause any undo inconvenience? He hoped not, and felt both foolish and miserable for being on his BlackBerry, talking about opening up cell-phone markets in Indochina when his mother's body lay, in the next room, and his third wife, in West Hartford, frantically hoped that the infertility treatments she'd been taking for more than a year would finally produce results. She was not yet forty: there was time. Dan already had two children by his first wife, but they were already in college, almost grown. He missed them. He hoped that when they arrived, they'd let him hug them.

"Let's just take a look-see, shall we?" the man continued, rubbing his hands together. "Or, if you prefer, we might just glance at the catalogue." He reached for a binder on the table, and, flipping it open, said, "We have quite a few that I think would suit."

All four of them, along with their father, stayed exactly where they were, some seated, others standing around the table. There was a pause until finally Becky said: "No. Just show us the cheapest, simplest one you've got," and the man, realizing, perhaps, that there was no use resisting, got up and led them to a room filled with coffins.

"Mom always did love a good shopping trip," Eleanor said.

She had been pointed, their mother, about exactly what she did and did not want for what she insisted on calling her "send-off party." A shroud, she'd said, was out-of-the-question—and she didn't care how Jewish their father decided he wanted to be now that his own years were dwindling, and he was feeling all sentimental about his own long-dead father. Who were they kidding? Once Dan had had his *bar mitzvah*—a nod to the grandparents on both sides—they'd barely managed to drag themselves to synagogue at all, forgetting entirely about the second, younger son, who in any case had no interest in mastering so much as the Hebrew alphabet—soccer games and therapy appointments and all the rest of it gobbling up time when the kids were younger, and, well, once they had grown, why bother?—and then, suddenly, in the wake of her illness, the man threatens to go all Jewish on her, talking about the old *shul* in the old neighborhood back in Newark *(Newark!)* in the good old days when the town was almost exclusively Jewish and Irish and Polish and Italian, and the high school graduated nothing but geniuses, not like now, a tragedy what's happened to Newark, a tragedy for white and black alike . . . and now he's talking about sitting *shiva* for her and rending his garments and God knows what else, and she's sorry, I'm sorry, but *no shroud and I really mean it do you understand me? A plain coffin I don't care about, let him save his money, it's stupid how people spend thousands of dollars on fancy coffins, and anyway, I'll be dead, but I want to be buried wearing something with a little more style than a shroud, thank you very much.*

Sitting together in the back of their father's car (Joe having taken the front seat this time), the sisters conferred in low tones.

"The thing is, she's gotten so fat," Eleanor said. "I don't know that she can fit into any of her dresses."

"It doesn't matter. They can slit the back, like they did with Grandma. And anyway, no one's going to see her."

"But we'll know."

Both brothers stared out the windows at the passing, familiar, predictable, dreary landscape: hideously expensive condos with orange-brick facing; winter trees with their skeletal branches; low-rise office buildings surrounded by other low-rise office buildings, all of them with bands of windows glinting in the sun. Who knew what took place in such buildings, anyway. Sales? Investments? Microchip development? How could it even be possible that there was such demand for the kind of professions that were practiced in such dwellings to have produced such a wildly improbable sprouting of them in the first place? It was a mystery—the kind of mystery that Dan had been fascinated with years earlier when he first went to college, first started thinking, seriously, about what he might want to do with his life. *Do people actually want to become accountants? Or does it just sort of happen to them? Does anyone say, When I grow up, I want to be an actuary and live in Cincinnati?* Now look at him: opening up fiber-optic networks in Vietnam, with partners named Ying Chang and Nguyen Thi Quynh Anh.

"And she'll know that we know," Becky added.

"Okay, fine. What about just putting her in a black skirt with one of her silk blouses? The yellow one with the black polka dots. She'd like that. Festive, but not over-the-top."

"Shoes?"

"Black pumps."

"Will they fit?"

"Why wouldn't they?"

"Don't your extremities begin to swell up or something?"

"How would I know?"

Eleanor was wondering if she'd packed enough anti-anxiety meds to make it through the six or seven days that she knew she'd have to spend in her parents' house—now her father's—the same house that she'd grown up in. The house was large enough, with six bedrooms, a small room off the kitchen where the maid used to sleep in the days when people had live-in maids, and various comfortable, worn sofas covered with their mother's needlepoint pillows. She felt a shiver of electricity moving up her neck and knew that she could start screaming any second, if only from the sheer discomfort of being among her entire family. Things would be better when her husband and children arrived.

They were driving down from New Jersey, waiting until after the girls' classes before leaving. The older of the two girls was in her senior year—her crunch year—and bent on getting into Brown. The younger was in tenth grade and more interested in swimming (she competed in both butterfly and freestyle) than in her grades. Eleanor herself had a lump in her left breast and was waiting to get the pathology report back on the needle incision that a breast specialist at Mount Sinai had made earlier in the week. Her mother had died of cancer, of course, and Eleanor didn't particularly want to follow. That, she thought, would be just so like her, to do as her mother did, right down to the end.

Her mother, who had once dreamed of becoming a musician—she played both cello and piano—had instead gone to Mt. Holyoke and become a first-grade teacher before retiring to stay home with her children. Eleanor had wanted to be a dancer, but instead had studied Eastern European languages at Vassar and become a translator at the U.N., and then stopped doing that, when she learned, in her mid-thirties, that she was going to have a baby. Now, with those forthright, middle-aged hips of hers, not to mention her ample breasts . . . had she ever fit into leotards?

"I thought you knew everything," Becky now said—a reference to their birth order, with a zillion memories of Eleanor's alleged superior attainments attached to it. Eleanor smiled. Becky smiled. In the front seat, their father started humming "*Aveenu Malkaanu*" and the brothers smiled, too, even Joe, who wasn't at all sure that, even now, he could quite get by in the world without his mother's constant vigil.

Northern Virginia had changed. Even well into the '70s, the suburbs— houses, sidewalks, playgrounds, stores— didn't spread, but stopped, and just like that, you were in the country: picket fences, barns, trees, cows, horses.

"Horsy people," they had collectively called the wasps of their childhood, those elegant devil-may-care children, all of them (in their imaginings) with straight light hair and straight short noses, who had houses in Martha's Vineyard or farms in Loudon County. They played tennis; skied; rode horses, and named them, too: *Lightning, Cherokee, Apple Dumpling*. Whereas the Singer children merely had dogs—packs of them really—and the occasional hamster or parakeet. The girls in particular suffered from the comparison with their non-Jewish classmates—and both, in fact, were destined to grow up to look exactly like what they were: the dark and fiercely intelligent daughters of generations of scholars, their light brown eyes set slightly too close together on either side of their slightly crooked noses, and hair that, left to itself, formed halos of curls around their faces. The boys, who took after their father, blended in better, and in any case, being boys, didn't think so much about their looks. They played sports, thought about cars, masturbated, got high to the sounds of the Rolling Stones or the Grateful Dead in endless parties in endless basement rec-rooms.

By the time they arrived at Temple Beth El, Eleanor had decided that, if the news from Mt. Sinai was really bad, she'd just go ahead and get a double mastectomy, ridding herself not only of any stray specks of cancer, but also of her too-big bosom—something she'd thought about doing anyway. In Montclair, where she and her husband lived, plastic surgery was generally considered a no-no— something for vain, shallow women who had nothing better to do than go to aerobics classes and meet each other at trendy restaurants for lunch.

But her bosom had been a hindrance to her almost from the first, when, as a teenager, she'd dreamed of leaping across a lit stage, only to be mocked by her own ampleness.

At Temple Beth El, they were informed that the rabbi was momentarily detained. Would they mind waiting in the synagogue library? Would they care for anything? Coffee?

No, they wouldn't, though it was long past lunchtime, and in truth both brothers, as well as their father, were famished. The sisters were, too, but were disconnected from their hunger, unaware that the gurgles and chortlings in their bellies were hunger pangs. They merely felt tired—vastly, vastly tired— and unsure, and strange. Becky thought about her college roommate, who had lost her own mother at the age of eleven. Whereas Becky was in her forties, the mother of twins, a boy who looked like her and a girl who looked like her mother-in-law. A big surprise, learning that she was carrying twins, and an unpleasant pregnancy. Her mother had driven all the way from Virginia with two ice-chests filled with bland frozen food: chicken-and-dumplings; turkey meatloaf; chicken soup. God, she'd been sick! But now the twins were almost eleven, and in fifth grade: she wasn't at their beck and call like before. She couldn't even remember the nausea. Twins: God's little practical joke on her. She lived in Vermont, where she practiced family law out of the barn in her backyard. Her husband, an architect, had converted the barn into open office space. In the winter, for P. E., the twins went cross-county skiing. There was a mountain out her bedroom window. She hated Washington.

"I hate Washington," she whispered to Joe, who sat beside her and looked more miserable than she ever remembered him looking. He was thinking about his future. He was thinking: so the girl is retarded, what of it? That didn't mean that he couldn't love her. That didn't mean that she couldn't love him back. Her name was Martha. She was fifteen and small for her age, and she called him "Jojo."

"I hate this synagogue, too," Becky continued quietly. This time Joe said: "And therefore?"

"Well," she said, out loud, "I do. Remember the time they refused to let Mom teach in the Sunday School just because she'd admitted that she wasn't sure she believed in God?"

"Ancient history," their father said.

"Mom volunteered to teach in the Sunday School?" Eleanor said.

"Yeah—it was when she, herself, was thinking about going back to teaching and wanted to kind of get her feet wet before she took the plunge. She thought it would be a good test, you know, to see if she still liked kids."

"They wouldn't *let* her? That's crazy."

"It wasn't that they wouldn't let her. It was that the woman who had been teaching the class had had a heart attack and wasn't going to come back, but then it turned out that she was fine and so Mom wasn't needed, after all."

"You're rewriting history," Becky said.

"And anyway. That was how many rabbis ago? Two? Three? It was when Metz was here, I think." Their father crossed his arms over his chest.

Metz was the rabbi Dan had studied with for his *bar mitzvah*. Neither girl had bothered, and by the time Joe came along, everyone seemed to have forgotten what all the fuss was about.

"Mom didn't believe in God?" Dan now said.

"She was on the fence about it."

"She told me she knew that she was going someplace, you know, afterward," Eleanor said. "That she wasn't scared."

"She told me that she kept having these dreams, but they were more like visions, visions of peaceful beings," Joe said.

"Whatever she said, or believed, or thought," their father said, "she was never prevented from teaching in the Sunday school because of her private cosmology."

Everyone was quiet. They could hear the sound of approaching footsteps. As the rabbi—the new one, or rather, the new-new one—entered the room, Becky said: "That's not what Mom said," and the rest of them looked at the rabbi, whose *kippah* was held on by two bobby-pins and covered with pictures of *Sesame Street* figures: Big Bird, Elmo, Bert, and Ernie. "A Father's Day present," he explained, pointing to his head. "I'm Rabbi Kerner."

He was young. Thirty-one? Thirty-two? He wore blue jeans and a turtleneck sweater and high-topped sneakers. He had a black beard and full pink lips. "Please accept my condolences," he now said, seating himself among them, his legs spread wide. "I didn't personally know Alma—not well, anyway—but I know she was beloved. A truly beloved woman, capable of both receiving and giving love."

"Yes, she was," Dan finally said, but that was only after the rabbi had swung his knees in and out, like a nervous child, and cleared his throat a couple of times. The rest of them just sat there, miserable with knowing that already things were off to a bad start, that, if he didn't watch himself, the young rabbi would find himself embarrassed, and what's more, that each of the four Singer children was ready and willing to do the job—to put him in his place, to point out that he didn't belong among them, to inch him, inch by inch, into the mouth of the lion. He was fidgety, too, this rabbi: his legs swinging in and out, his fingers fluttering back and forth to the ridiculous beanie. What right did he have to have any part in their private affairs? How dare he come galloping in here, with his rabbinical-school insights, his naïve good will?

"May her name be for a blessing," the rabbi said, while Joe, coughing, pulled out his cell phone.

"*Baruch ha Shem.*"

Maybe, Joe thought, he should ask her to marry him now, *before* the funeral, as soon as she arrived. Why wait? He knew there were all kinds of rules governing death and mourning, but why put off what his heart knew to be true? She herself had told him that she had too many responsibilities to indulge in romantic fairy tales. She herself had said that, while she loved being with him, her daughter came first, and more than anything, her daughter needed stability. The ex-husband had abandoned her when it was discovered that their daughter's slowness of speech was, in fact, a profound disability. She referred to him as "the dickhead." Too bad his mother had died, he thought: it would have made her happy to know he was finally going to take the plunge.

"Let's take a moment, if you will, to unpack some of this," the rabbi was saying. "I often find it helps—for me, for the family, yourselves—to talk. To talk about our grief. To talk about our love. To talk about death, itself, its meaning, its finality. To talk, really, about anything you want to talk about."

"No," their father said.

"Excuse me?"

"With all due respect, rabbi."

"All right then," the rabbi said, trying again, and trying, quite obviously, to recover from the rebuff. "What in particular would you like me to know about, about Alma? Her strengths, her weaknesses, her favorite books, what she liked to do. For the eulogy."

It was getting worse and worse. For one thing, what was with the first-naming business? *Alma, Alma.* What right did he have to put her name in his mouth? There, he did it again—*I understand that Alma struggled with her illness for many years.* He should be stopped, and soon. Their father had the pinched, pained look on his face that meant that he was about to either walk out or say something so cutting that there would be blood.

"You are her family," the rabbi said. "Tell me about her."

"She liked to read," Dan said.

"What did she like?"

"Everything."

"Everything?"

Dan glanced at Becky, who said: "Chaucer. Shakespeare. Biography. Poetry. History. She reread *The Great Gatsby* during her last round of chemo. Bellow. Tolstoy. Elliot, George *and* T. S. Philip Roth. Toni Morrison. Thomas Mann. Balzac. Trollope. Dickens. John Updike, John Cheever, Alice Munro, Alice Adams, *Alice in Wonderland*."

"She loved *Alice in Wonderland*," Dan said.

"Read it over and over. To us. When we were kids," Joe said.

"Freud, Ford Maddox Ford, *Sophie's Choice*, *The Makioka Sisters*, Sylvia Plath," Becky, who once had literary ambitions of her own, said.

"She was an avid reader, then, your mother?" the rabbi said, writing on a small lined pad. "Any particular favorites? An author who spoke—to her soul?"

"John Dos Passos, George Orwell, John Steinbeck, James Wilcox, Joseph Conrad, Flannery O'Connor."

"Wonderful."

The Singers glanced at each other. Writing furiously, the rabbi licked his teeth.

Finally the father, himself, spoke. "With all due respect, rabbi, I think we can handle this."

"Excuse me?"

"She wouldn't have wanted a eulogy," he said.

"She really wasn't very religious," Becky added.

"Her friends are going to speak."

"People who knew her."

"If you could help us, rabbi, and just stick to the prayers?"

The rabbi—Cohen? Kaplan? Karlin?—suddenly none of them could remember his name—looked from one face to the other and then rubbed his hands together and then sat back in his chair, smiling mildly.

"My wife—" their father said.

She didn't actually like to read: not that much, anyway. It was their father who read—their father and his two ravenously smart daughters. Becky didn't know why she'd said what she'd said, except that she knew that each of her siblings had wanted to impress the wet-behind-the-ears rabbi with a sense of his own immaturity. What their mother had mainly read, especially in her later years, was popular novels, self-help, memoir, and magazines. She especially liked decorating magazines and could spend hours lying under blankets in the sunroom, gazing at their glossy pages. "Would you ever," she'd say, admiring some particularly high-end living room or set of curtains. "You call this taste?"

By the time, at the end, she was on morphine, she preferred watching TV. Every night she had a double (having switched from wine, which made her nauseated, to bourbon, her own mother's choice, some time during her first go-around with chemotherapy) and watched reruns of *The Rockford Files* on cable.

What she'd really liked to do was go to lunch with her friends, and fuss around the house, and go to the movies, and look at china patterns, and take her daughters out. She used to play the piano for fun, but around the time the last of her children went off to college she'd stopped doing that, saying that she no longer had the concentration, the edge, the passion that had once made playing the piano such a joy. She'd always liked children—particularly her own grandchildren—and dogs and flowers and chintz. She liked discussing the foibles of her children and her friends' children and their friends' friends, too. She liked saying: "If only Joe would get married, already, then maybe I can die." She also liked saying: "If Dan blows it this time, I'm personally going to have to kill him." Of her daughters she said, "They've always been stable, both of them, even with all the trouble they've had with their issues." She liked to refer to her daughters' bouts with depression as "issues." It sounded better than "depression," which smacked of suicide, despair, time-out in funny farms, women going mad in trashy novels. She thought a lot about the fact of her own impending death but didn't dwell much on the miseries of her own past. Her dead child, Emily, was no longer even a memory. Of her husband she said: "I give him two years, tops, before he's remarried."

The house would be filling up by now—with family, with friends, with friends-of-friends. With former teachers. With cousins and second cousins and their spouses. But their father still had one errand that he insisted on having them do with him. He wanted to check out the grave site—he referred to it as "the real estate"—and then he wanted to go to the river.

The river wasn't really a river. It was a stream-fed pond where, during cold winters, the Singer children had gone skating, racing crazily around the trees that grew enfolded by ice, the children, themselves, sweating under their layers; but when Dan was little, he'd insisted that it was a river, and the mistake had stuck. They'd walked through the woods to get there. Now the pond—a victim of the housing boom that never seemed to stop—had been choked to less than half its former size, filled in with mud and sludge and runoff, with downed limbs and churned-up dirt and the detritus of carpentry: sawdust, odd bits of pink, petroleum-based insulation, leftover wiring. The woods were gone, too, of course, replaced by brick town homes with paved patios, but the path that the children had taken through the scruffy woods had mysteriously— miraculously—survived. It wended its way behind a clump of weeping willow trees, behind homes, along what was left of the stream, and finally to the pond itself. But Mr. Morgan, on whose property that pond was, was gone, too; the people who had bought his house had ripped off the screened-in porch to build an addition.

"Remember when I used to take you fishing here?" their father said to no one in particular, as they gathered along the muddy, ice-encrusted bank.

"You never took us fishing here, Dad," Becky said. She wondered how long it would be until he started to date.

"I did. I took you all the time. I took all four of you."

The sisters eyed each other. "You took the boys, Dad. You never took us."

"You took me," Dan said. "But my line got tangled."

"We must have taken six fish home one day. Your mother didn't know what to do with them. She said that she didn't like the fish staring up at her."

"There were no fish in this pond, Dad," Dan said. "Just tadpoles and frogs. Nothing worth catching."

"You're wrong. Don't you remember? It was stocked. We'd go fishing here. Every summer. We'd talk."

Talk? His father never talked, or at least not so far as Dan could remember. It wasn't that he never emitted words, either, but that when he did indulge in conversation, he talked at you: he told you things. He told you, for example, about Europe between the two World Wars. Or about famous Jewish baseball players: Sandy Koufax; Hank Greenberg. Or about shoveling snow in Newark, how the ice crackled under his shovel; how, one winter, it was so cold the shovel broke.

The spot where their mother was to be buried was on a small rise, overlooking a vast expanse of newish-looking headstones, themselves circled by carefully tended evergreen trees. There was room for at least two more bodies, possibly three, because at the time that the Singers had bought the plots, they weren't at all sure that Becky would marry any time soon, and as for Joe—all bets were off. Of course, there was the added complication of where Singer's second wife would be laid to rest—but that was getting too subtle even for their mother, who loved to plan, and had planned both her daughters' weddings with such enthusiasm that their father had asked her to stop talking about the subject entirely. Flower arrangements? Bridesmaid dresses? All of it bored him to death, but his wife—she had loved making decisions about the most picayune of details, worrying over them and prying them apart until she lost sleep . . . but the choice of cemetery plots had come easily. Both of them had liked the quiet rise of the grass, and the way the wind sounded in the upper branches of the trees. It was strange though, because the first child, the tiny infant, was buried elsewhere: in Newark, in fact, with her father's grandparents. No one could quite remember, anymore, why she'd been put there.

"Dad?" Joe finally said.

"Yes, son?"

"Why exactly did you want to come here?"

"I'm not sure myself," the father said. "Didn't we go fishing here?"

"Maybe now and then."

The father stared off in the distance, his blue-gray eyes watering in the cold. "I thought I took you a lot. It was so pretty then. When your Mom and I first moved here, all this was country."

No one said anything: it was simply a fact.

"There was no one like your mother," he said. Again, no one replied, though Becky thought about it. She thought about saying that there was no one like him, their father, either, but stopped herself. For the second time in about five minutes, she let herself speculate about the woman, whomever she was, who would be her father's next wife: a widow like himself, or perhaps not. Perhaps next time he'd go for a divorcée, a woman with her own profession; her own office; her own expertise. Someone more like his own daughters, only different, older, calmer, grateful for second chances.

"I just don't want her to be lonely," he now said.

It was well into the afternoon, and the sky had taken on a metallic glint: snow. Or maybe not. Maybe it was just the combined projection of the Singers' wistfulness. None of the Singer children knew what to do—how to comfort their father, or whether he even wanted comfort.

From Dan's jacket came the sound of his BlackBerry ringing, and as he answered it, each of his siblings reached into their own pockets, bringing out their cell phones, dialing. Becky called her husband, who said that they were just outside of Baltimore, and should be arriving within the hour; Eleanor called her older daughter, who didn't answer, and then her younger daughter, who did; Joe called his girlfriend, and told her that he missed her. Dan said: "Actually, we haven't had lunch yet—could you pick up some bagels or something?"

Impossible, this death. She was gone! Gone. Their father stood on the side, gazing at his aging children with wonder.

MY COUSIN'S HEART

I have literally just finished doing the do with this joker I met yesterday at Barnes and Noble when the phone rings, and I pick it up hoping it's Jay, but of course it isn't. It's Mom, calling to tell me that my cousin, Michelle Blatt, is getting married. Aunt Shirley is just thrilled to death, Mom says. Then a whole lot of other junk about the ring and the guy (whom I sat next to during Seder, not that Mom remembers) and the guy's parents. Uh-huh, uh-huh, uh-huh, I say, but it's kind of hard to concentrate, because this guy Michael, who I met yesterday in the checkout line of Barnes and Noble, has a hard-on again, and he's sticking it in my back. Finally, Mom winds down and I promise to meet her soon for lunch.

Who was that? Michael says into my shoulder. Like he cares. He's pushing his thing against me and rubbing it around.

That was my mother, I say.

Oh?

Yeah, and she'll be here in about five minutes.

Because suddenly I don't like this guy Michael at all. He's got one of those faces that knows how handsome it is, with the kind of square jaw and thick black eyebrows that seem always to be considering themselves. He probably meets girls in the checkout line at Barnes and Noble all the time. Dostoyevsky—my absolute fave. Josephus—now that's what I call a historian with a story to tell.

Oh man, he says.

Actually, there's very little chance of my mother ever coming to visit me in my apartment, which she calls a slum dwelling. I stay up at night worrying about you, she says. I can't sleep, thinking about you in there, dead. But Ma, I say, I'm not dead. But you could be. What's wrong with you that you live in that hellhole with the rats and the homosexuals? But Ma, I say, everyone in New York is homosexual, even the Catholics, even the nuns. Whatever, she says, but you're not—are you? Do you think I'm a dyke, Ma? That's not what I said, and you know it, Laura.

Long pause. And then: But why do you have to have so many earring holes in your ear? Don't all those earrings hurt?

Long pause. Then: What do you want for your birthday, Laura?

Ma, my birthday isn't for another two months.

I just thought maybe we could go shopping together.

Michael calls. He says: Are you free? And when I say I'm not—even though really I'm sitting on my bed in my slum dwelling painting each of my toenails a different shade of red—he says: How about tomorrow? I tell him that's no good, either. I tell him I have to work. Take the day off, he says.

I have to admit, it's tempting—stay home to do the thang thing with Michael, which in turn would lead to spending the next day in bed watching reruns of ancient TV shows, which in turn would lead to getting temporarily fired again. Why don't you get a real job? Mom wants to know. Why don't you do something that utilizes your talents and skills? Say what? I majored in English, Ma. I don't have any skills. I mean your communications skills, Laura. Oh. That.

This raft that you ride . . . .

I run errands for a living. I'm the so-called production assistant at a production company that makes television commercials. And I got the job in the first place only because I know Peter, the owner of the company. Peter is the first grown-up man I ever slept with, and, also, he's my friend Liz's father. I'm still kind of half-in-love with Peter, and I think he's still kind of half-in-love with me. At the time he and I were screwing around, he had left his wife— his third—and I hadn't yet met Jay. It was pretty great: I'd been in love with Peter ever since he taught me how to do the Charleston when I was twelve years old, and now here I was, big, and Peter and I, having already spent countless hours on his crushed velvet sofa talking about the demise of standards in the art world and the rise of fundamentalism in the Middle East—not to mention the frightening turn toward the right in mainstream American politics, a trend that had turned both of us into born-again bleeding heart liberals— were already great pals. Every Friday night, he'd pick me up in a taxi, take me out to eat at a different restaurant where we'd both drink too much wine, and then we'd go back to his beautiful apartment with the view of the Hudson River all the way up to the George Washington Bridge.

Darling, Peter says when he sees me. Darling, do us a favor and run out and get coffee? Black for me, and—you know the rest. Take ten. No, better take twenty. Come to think of it, get some bagels, too. You all right, darling? You look tired. Jay ever call? That asshole. I'm sorry, but he is. Poor darling, give us a kiss.

As I said, I don't mind being Peter's errand boy. The man still wears the same jean jacket he embroidered himself when, in 1968, he decided to become a hippie, even though he was already too rich to really be one. The back of the jacket is covered with flowers and butterflies and plants in thick crayon colors.

The amazing thing is that Mom, when I finally meet her for lunch, doesn't utter a single word about my cousin Michelle Blatt until dessert—apple pie a la mode for me, Jello that she doesn't eat because it's too fattening for her. I know this effort has been killing her, but she's probably been consulting her best friend Miriam on the subject, who probably said something along the lines of, Laura is a grown woman and she'll settle down with the right fellow when she's good and ready and there's nothing you can say or do to change that.

So? Mom says.

Yeah?

So what's new?

I shrug.

So I just had to tell you, she says.

Yeah.

You have such pretty hair, Laura. When I was a girl, I begged God to give me hair like yours. Those curls. I wish you'd let me take you to see Richard. He'd give you the cutest cut. I know he would.

Forget it, Ma. I like my hair the way it is.

Fine then. Do you want to hear about the engagement party or not?

The waitress approaches, her skirt making itching noises. Everything all right with you ladies? she says.

Just fine.

Anything more I can get for you?

Just the check, please. And then, after the waitress has gone: How much do you think I have to tip her? She was awfully rude, don't you think?

Mom's hair, swept back from her high forehead, is tinted a beautiful silver-white. Her skin smells like baby powder. Her silk blouse is newly dry-cleaned. I love her so much that it hurts.

Of course you know that Aunt Shirley is just thrilled thrilled thrilled because not only is Michelle finally getting married, which of course is all Aunt Shirley's been talking about for years, but her fiance is such a catch, and of course I'm going to have to hear about how great he is until the day I die. Jewish, of course, that goes without saying, but as your father said, it's awfully ironic that here Michelle is, and she didn't give a fig for Judaism, she didn't even have a bat mitzvah, no surprise given the way her parents raised her.

But now apparently she's planning a traditional Jewish wedding, but guess what business her fiancé is in?

He sells Christmas tree ornaments.

My mother's eyes widen. How did you guess?

I didn't guess, Ma. You told me already. Plus I met him, remember?

And apparently the family is very comfortable. Aunt Shirley says that the house is just gorgeous, and the young man—

Rank.

His name is Frank.

Whatever.

He's a very nice young man.

He's boring.

He is not.

He is, Ma. I got stuck sitting next to him at Seder. Please pass the pepper was about the most interesting thing he said all night.

You and your smart mouth. He's a very nice young man, and his parents are going to give them an engagement party. At Sunningdale. At the end of the month. And Michelle is your cousin. Aren't you going to say something?

Like what, Ma?

I do hope you'll come, darling. It would break your cousin's heart if you didn't.

Why wouldn't I come, Ma?

I don't know, Laura. It's just that sometimes you get these funny ideas.

I don't have any funny ideas.

You need something decent to wear, she says.

My cousin Michelle was one of those girls other girls either wanted to be like or to sleep with, only of course they wouldn't tell themselves that they wanted to sleep with her. They told themselves that they wanted a pair of designer jeans like hers. It wasn't that she was so beautiful or anything. It was more her manner, this straightforward, boyish quality that boys liked and girls emulated. Button nose covered in freckles. Sparkly green eyes. Great legs. Plus she put out big time, but unlike the more unsavory girls, Michelle was not generally known as an easy lay, even though she boinked her way all the way through senior year and then, if she can be believed, all the way through Princeton, where she did her junior paper on the Kansas-Missouri border wars of the 1850s that occurred against the national debate over slavery and the admission into the nation of free-versus-slave-owning states. I, meanwhile, was less than her shadow. I was a pea. I was a fly.

This afternoon I steer clear of Barnes and Noble. I don't know why I bother going there, anyway, even to the Annex. Actually, that's a lie. I go to Barnes and Noble for the same reason everyone else goes: I go pretending to be looking for an actual book to read, but really I'm heading for the rack of magazines, where I stand with the jacking-off-under-their-raincoats computer nerd types, casually glancing around to make sure that no one I know sees me there. Then I go for the kill: Capricorn: With all the major planets in the high-achievement sector, this year will bring an embarrassment of riches. . . .

But as I said, this time I don't go anywhere near Barnes and Noble. Unfortunately, Shakespeare and Company is off-limits, too, because it was there, in New Titles, that I first met Jay, who was turning over a book of short stories about gay guys when he noticed me staring at him. So I head straight for the Strand, where, among the dust and dust mites and sweet staleness of decaying paper, the intense depression that had descended on me during lunch with Mom gradually dissipates, until, at last, I can breathe without feeling brain dead. I am deep into nineteenth-century poetry, even thinking about giving Caliban upon Setebos a whirl—only who am I kidding, I didn't get that stuff in college, why would I get it now?—when this guy bumps into me and mumbles excuse me, and when I turn around I see that it's this guy I once met at Liz's house.

Aren't you Liz's friend? I say.

No. I don't know any Liz.

The truth is he looks a little bit like Liz's friend, but Liz's friend, now that I remember, is better looking. This guy has that kind of pitted skin that's recently become fashionable among punk rockers who live in London and wear nothing but black, even though black is such a retro cliché it transcends itself. He's also got a severe crew, but his teeth are large and shiny-white, and his eyes are large and shiny-black.

You look like Liz's friend, I say. You even smell a little bit like him.

> Give me truths;
> For I am weary of the surfaces,
> And die of inanition—

He says, later, after we're shit-faced on vodka martinis. I memorized that bit, he says. Emerson, Ralph Waldo, he says. Then I say:

> When my devotions could not pierce
> Thy silent ears,
> Then was my heart broken, as was my verse;
> My breast was full of fears
> And disorder.

Only because I'm snookered it comes out: my breast was full of beers, and we both crack up.

Oh darling sweetheart, Peter says the next day when I show up like three hours late to work on this shoot he killed himself to get, a commercial for a new ice-cream sandwich made with all-natural ingredients. Oh darling, what have you gone and done now? Tell us about it.

Just one of the things I like about Peter—just one of the things that makes me half-in-love with him, even now that he's gone back to his third wife and I'm stuck on Jay in this really neurotic self-destructive way—is that he talks like a homo. Either that, or like an English decorator, one of those guys who, even though he's married and has affairs on the side, worships chintz.

Sweetheart? he says.

Do I look that bad?

Not bad, darling. Just worn-out. You aren't still sleeping with men you meet in bookstores, are you? Please tell me that you've given that habit up. Why? Am I giving off a scent?

He takes me aside, puts me under his arm. From my perch under his jean jacket, I can smell his soap: Irish Spring. Not to mention the half-dozen cups of coffee he's already swilled today. His mustache tickles the top of my head where he plants a kiss. Sometimes I wish I could just move in with Peter and his third wife, a plump, pretty woman named Jess, and watch TV all day. I can't bear to see you so miserable, Peter says. Tell me what I can do. Do you need time off? Do you need money? Just tell me.

Can you make me rich and famous?

Anything.

Actually, what had happened was that me and Ralph Waldo Emerson, only I called him Waldo for short, ended up having absolutely spectacular sex. This really came as a surprise, because, for one, I was really pretty stupid from vodka, and, for two, Waldo's thing is on the petite side. Not to mention that I just kept thinking and thinking about my life. Specifically, I was thinking about the time that this girl named Carla Castelli called me in my own apartment once, asking for Jay in this ditzy-girl-from-Jersey-what-me-have-big-tits? voice. And now Jay's gone and moved with Carla Castelli to Stamford, of all places, where they apparently have a garden apartment, which in itself is enough to make you puke, and, in the meantime, Waldo and I finished up, but afterwards he got mean and actually told me that I have a flabby butt, and he doesn't like girls with flabby butts. I tried to get him out of my apartment, but he got all fake-sweet and, thank God, he fell asleep. Then I called Liz. She told me to sleep with a knife under the bed, just in case. In the morning Waldo smiled and apologized and told me that he knew he'd been an asshole. Then he left. But by then I was pretty exhausted and had to sleep an extra three hours just to feel even halfway decent.

Michael is talking: So then I realized that I actually wanted to, you know, have a life. I know it's lame—

It's not lame.

Well, it is, but that's how it came to me. Here I was, only two months on the job, when it hit me. So when I went to get lunch that day, I kind of forgot to go back.

We are pretending to be looking at red peppers and pumpkin squash at the Union Square farmers' market, but all we're really doing is thinking about: will we or won't we do it? All those pretty fresh vegetables. All those pretty flowers. And Michael himself, with those thick eyebrows, that great leather bomber jacket. The sky heavy, wet, with heavy, moving clouds. It's enough to make you want to go out and buy a bunch of new clothes at the Gap and then get your picture taken on a beach with a couple of golden retrievers.

Michael was actually waiting for me on my front stoop when I got home, an especially neat trick given that I don't have a front stoop. The building I live in opens out directly onto the sidewalk. On one side of the door is a pizza parlor that makes only so-so pizza, good enough when you're starving at two in the morning, but not a place you'd take your dream girl to dinner on the first date. On the other side of the door is an abandoned building.

And now he's gone ahead and told me that before he became a would-be screenwriter, which, in my opinion, is even worse than being a would-be poet, he was, if only briefly, a lawyer. He worked for one of those giant downtown firms with five or six names where everyone makes a half million dollars a year and owns a summer house on Nantucket.

Anyway, he says. It's not like I'm some freak who goes around picking up girls at bookstores. The truth is, I haven't really been involved with anyone for, like, more or less my whole life.

Very hard to believe, given Michael's self-referential eyebrows. The way they flick up at the ends. The way they arch in the middle. It kind of comes from being Catholic, I think, he says.

Altar boy and all that stuff? I say.

No, not really. He picks up an apple, puts it down.

These are some of the reasons I adored my cousin Michelle Blatt, even after she became popular. First, she taught me, when I was only six or seven, how to scratch my mosquito bites just enough to make them bleed enough to take the worst of the itch off, but not enough to leave scars. When I was older she taught me how to spot girls who were wearing their first training bras. Later she showed me how to give a hand-job, demonstrating on a Tampax.

And now she's marrying Rank, pale-faced, blob-cheeked, well-groomed, tennis-playing graduate of the Wharton School of Business and seller of

Christmas ornaments, and she wants me to come to her engagement party, the one Rank's parents are throwing for the bridal couple at the Sunningdale Country Club—site of some of the worst public humiliations in my life, like the time I made pee-pee in the big pool, and the lifeguard spotted it and, blowing hysterically on her whistle, pulled me up, out, and away. The invitation came yesterday.

I'm trying on the dress that Mom went out and bought for me at Anne Taylor that she says is returnable if I don't like it when the buzzer buzzes, and I look down and it's Jay, standing on the sidewalk. My heart does this whole flip-flop number like in a bad novel and then my armpits sprout sweat and I'm sweating down the Anne Taylor dress, right down the raw silk that was stitched together by child slave-laborers in Pakistan. Two long oblongs of wetness, all the way down to my hips. The dress is pretty, dazzlingly so, like something you'd wear to Jay Gatsby's house. It makes me look even more flat-chested than I am, though; it makes me look like I'm playing dress-up. Laura? Are you up there?

Why are you wearing that? he says when I let him in. You going somewhere?

It's something my mother bought me. At Anne Taylor.

Nice, he says, though I can tell he doesn't think so.

We just stand there for a minute, Jay and I, and then Jay flops himself down on the fold-out sofa I bought at Conran's after he moved in with Carla Castelli.

New furniture, he says.

What do you want? I say, only it comes out wrong. It comes out pleading, when what I'd wanted was the tough, slightly flip, I-can-take-care-of-myself-thank-you-very-much affect of girl policemen on cop shows.

Look, he says. Then: Look, Laura.

Sure. In front of me is the oil painting that my friend Liz made for me when, in college, she went through a brief but passionate post-modernist, abstract-realism stage: intense red, intense blue, intense yellow. There is the dust on the edge of the frame, a velvet grayness. The wall itself is dingy, in need of a new coat of paint. And Jay. I know exactly what he looks like, every inch of him, from his too-big, intelligent nose to the eight hairs surrounding his right nipple and the nine surrounding his left, to the way he shivers at night when his dreams trap him.

Fuck, I say.

I know, I know, he says. I have no excuse, no excuse at all. I shouldn't be here. But shit, I feel like I'm suffocating, and I didn't know who to talk to, and I was worried that if I called you first you'd hang up on me, so here I am instead.

And he goes on and on like this while I sweat through my dress.

Blah blah blah blah and he misses me, he doesn't know what to do, Carla is so great, and besides which she wants to have a baby, only he's not ready, and can he just sit here a little while. Maybe can he just hold my hand. God, it's so pathetic. All those clichés, one after another. It hurts my ears, really it does.

But I let him hold my hand, and then I let him undress me, and my beautiful new dress is doubly ruined, lying on the floor by the bed.

Waldo had the nerve, that asshole, to telephone me. Not once, but twice, the first time of which he tells me that he'd like to take me out for a cup of coffee and then go back to my place for the main event, and the second time of which he tells me that as far as he's concerned I can go take a piss up a tree, whatever that means. Go away, I say into the mouthpiece, only it's too late because he's already hung up.

This puts me in such an evil mood that I seriously consider going out and doing something really stupid, like taking up exercise or learning how to meditate. But then, just as I'm getting ready to take a walk so I can punch the lights out of the next fat person who blocks me on thé sidewalk when I'm hurrying to cross the street, Michael calls. He says he wants to take me to Coney Island for a hot dog. I say I can't. He says, How about a slice? So I say okay and when he comes over we go downstairs and buy a couple of slices and then we go all the way up, past the doorway that says DO NOT ENTER DANGER to the roof, and we eat our pizza under the gray-purple sky.

At Michelle Blatt's engagement party there are old-fashioned paper lanterns strung across the trees and white candles in glass dishes on all the white-draped tables. Michelle is wearing a flowing flowery dress with kickpleats and her hair is piled on her head like Audrey Hepburn's in all those wonderful old Life magazine pictures and Aunt Shirley looks like she's gained about. forty pounds since the last time I saw her, two months ago. When Michelle sees me she comes over and gives me a big, perfumey kiss and introduces me to Rank, whom I have already met. She then says some non-thing along the lines of, Did you get yourself something to eat? Then her eyes widen and she says: You look pretty. I'm wearing an outfit that my friend Liz let me borrow: it's this swishy, dark blue pants thing that makes me look vaguely exotic in the standard Semitic way, like I probably know how to speak Italian and maybe I take modern dance classes, too, but I could tell the instant she picked me up at the train station that Mom was disappointed.

So you didn't like the dress, Mom says, later, after both she and I have had a drink. We are just outside the club house, looking across the lawn toward where the golf course stretches out toward a stand of weeping willows. It wasn't that I didn't like it, Ma—

You never like my presents.

I like your present, Ma.

Couldn't you at least pretend to be happy for your cousin Michelle?

I think Rank's about as interesting as a door.

His name is Frank.

I think she'll be bored to death with him. I think after maybe two years of marriage, she's going to want to blow her brains out.

How can you say that? He's a very nice young man. Handsome, successful, smart. Why do you always see the bad, never the good?

I don't think he's capable of uttering an intelligible sentence or opinion on any matter whatsoever.

When did you even meet him?

At Passover, Ma. Remember? I had to sit next to him, all night long.

So what? she says. You're not the one marrying him, your cousin Michelle is, and Michelle loves him.

Then, inexplicably, she begins to cry. The tears spill out of her eyes, taking black streaks of mascara with them. Oh Laura, she says, if only you knew how much your father and I love you, how much we always loved you, how we only want you to be happy, darling, don't you know that that's all we want, is for you to be happy?

And she's holding me to her and I'm saying, I know, Ma, I know.

THE STORY OF MY SOCKS

When I was nine, I lived for a year with my family in London. It was my father's sabbatical year from George Washington University, in Washington, DC, where he was a professor of economics. Before we left, my mother talked about what fun we'd have; all the places we'd see and visit; about the school she'd enrolled me and my brother in; about the funny, old-fashioned uniform we'd both be wearing; about learning to take the Underground—"the Tube," she called it laughingly, laughingly employing an English accent—which I pictured as a 19th century steam-engine pulling something like the inside of a tire. I couldn't help it. I was a dreamy, romantic boy, somewhat weak in the knees and ankles, with a tendency to get bad colds in the winter and allergies in the spring.

We flew to London, took a train into Paddington, piled into a taxi, and arrived at our new flat—all four of us already calling it that. Our mother seemed slightly dissatisfied with the size and arrangement of the kitchen: she said it was ill-equipped and she'd have to go out and buy some decent pots and pans, what a waste given that she'd have to leave them behind at the end of the year. Otherwise she seemed reasonably pleased, and if our mother was pleased then the rest of us were too. What did we males—our brooding, ambitious father; my messy, moody, adolescent older brother; and myself—know about houses, about the arrangement of furnishings or for that matter the arrangement of our very days? What did we know about finding places in which to put our clothes in that small and rather cramped flat—small for us, that is, compared with our ramshackle split-level in the suburbs? Versus the flat, where Mother said there weren't enough closets; moreover, the closets were shallow, almost miniature, as if built for a hobbit. The room that I shared with my brother was narrow, with twin beds and a single cupboard that was meant to serve as both closet and bureau, which he instantly claimed as his own. No matter: Mother made more space with some wine-cases she'd found in the alley, stacking them just so, making a place for my socks and sweaters, hanging my own jacket and pants besides my brother's in the cupboard. She upended an end table such that it served as a place to put my brother's sports equipment. She told him to stop putting his feet on my bed, something he did just to annoy me. And so on: she was the genius of the place.

Our father was spending the year as something between a scholar-at-leisure and a lecturer at the University of London. He was very proud of this, he couldn't stop marveling at it—how he, a middle-class Jewish boy from Huntington, Long Island, the son of a dentist and a piano teacher, a boy who hadn't distinguished himself in any way until halfway through college, at SUNY Stony Brook, had made it here, all the way to University College, London. One of the top-ranked universities in all of Britain, with students coming from all over, from India and Pakistan and Spain and Italy and even America—and he was a part of it! He'd been given an office, a computer, a new set of colleagues, and time. Time was what he craved more than anything else: time to think, to study, to read. Time to exchange ideas with other scholars. And most of all, time to write.

He was always working on a book or an article, mulling over the next idea—and how he hated it when one of us interrupted him when, at home, he sat writing at the dining room table, his papers and book spread out on the polished wood. It's not that he yelled or even scolded so much as that you could see it on him, how angry he was, how his whole face would tighten, the small muscles under his ears pulsing like a terrified fish's. Sometimes we'd hear him complaining to our mother: his days were spent teaching and sitting on committees and dealing with all kinds of academic business; he mowed the lawn, went to our soccer and baseball games (my brother's games really, as even then I was somewhat allergic to sports). Was it too much to ask that on occasion he have a little time to himself to get some work done? "But they're boys," she'd reply, as if he didn't already know it. But now that we were in London, things were different. His palms spread wide as if to take in the entire glory of Britannia and his face alight and smiling, he'd say that it was a miracle, his having all day long to do nothing but think.

So there he was, thinking his thoughts at the great and ancient university. That way, things hadn't changed much. What had changed was the quality of time itself.

Come September my brother and I went to a public (that is to say, a private) school not far from our flat in Maida Vale, where we ate hot lunches and wore scratchy woolen uniforms. At home we both went to the neighborhood schools, the rough-and-tumble public schools that we and all our friends attended, that we didn't think twice about, where we wore our own clothes and brought our own lunches. Our afternoons were either devoted to sports (my brother), or, for me, tending to my collection of unusual rocks or bicycling around looking for cast-off treasure. But London was a city, and once school was over, there was nothing to do. I was bored. I was miserable. I whined. I drove Mom crazy.

All that stopped when I discovered The Diary of Anne Frank jammed at the back of the closet. My brother had shoved all kinds of stuff there—school assignments, half-smoked cigarettes, candy, books he was supposed to read but didn't. I was already in the habit of stuffing my head with paperbacks—science fiction, detective stories, fantasy, thrillers, and most of all, horror, the more horrible the better. But The Diary was something new for me, giving me a glimpse of something so huge and awful that I couldn't resist its pull. Not that I lived in a cave. Like every other kid, I knew something about what had happened, about the valiant allies and the evil Germans as well as the camps.

But this was something new and different, something personal, and I had to know more. Thus I set out one day, with a house key and a map which my mother had drawn for the purpose, to the library. Equipped with my best manners, I asked the librarian where the World War Two books were. I was afraid to ask him directly to take me to the Holocaust section—what if he thought I was too young, or asked me where my parents were?—but it made no difference. I quickly found what I was looking for, an entire archive of the Holocaust, with maps, histories, and most of all, photographs: skeletal Jews in striped pajamas being liberated from the death camps; more skeletons, this time with dead eyes and mouths shaped into soundless screams; Germans saluting Hitler; Hitler himself, with his fat hips. Place names: Auschwitz. Belzec. Treblinka. Terezin. I collected other words, too: kapo, bloch, crematorium, SS, Judenrein, Fuhrer.

I was stunned. Why hadn't my parents, who went on and on about everything, debating the merits and demerits of books and movies and politics and basic finance, about home décor and core values, ever filled me in? All Mom and Dad had ever told us was that our own ancestors had immigrated long before the disaster, and were safe, in America. All my brother and I knew about them was that they'd come from Russia (on our mother's side) and on our father's, from Germany and Poland, maybe both, he wasn't sure. There were some old letters, some old ticket stubs, a few old sepia-toned photos which my mother had framed, and not much else. "They were poor, religious, God-fearing Jews," my mother would offer by way of explanation. "They kept their heads down."

I couldn't quite imagine any of that, what life would be like if you were poor and religious, and as for God-fearing: what did that even mean? We didn't even belong to a temple. God, the Torah, the Sabbath—that stuff was for other people, Jewish Jews who cared and talked endlessly about Israel and what did or did not constitute kosher, what you could and could not eat, and why.

I ate everything: fried pasties, donuts, hotdogs, ice cream. Food was important to me. At school the food was atrocious. We ate it anyway, ravenously. Both of us, my brother as well as myself, were always hungry.

"You boys are termites," my mother said. "You'd eat the walls if you could figure out how."

I wondered if you actually could eat a wall—something we might have to do if the Nazis started rounding us up—but even with my overheated and morbid imagination torturing me at night and my awful older brother torturing me by day, I managed to settle in well enough. Our father, when he came home from his office on campus, would grab a beer and tell us funny stories about his new colleagues, their accents, their bad teeth. Even the weather cooperated—days of cool sunshine and slowly turning leaves, not that it much mattered to me now that I spent most of my free time at the library. When I asked Mom if there were still Nazis in Europe, pointing out that London was in England which was part of Europe, she laughed and told me not to have such a morbid imagination.

I figured that if Mom was laughing, things were fine, we were safe, life would continue rolling on in its usual boring way, no one would check my penis to see if it was circumcised or brand numbers on my arm. Then disaster struck. When I got home from school, instead of Mom greeting me, there was a note from her saying that she was out and would be back soon. But when my brother came home an hour or so later, she was still gone. By then I'd started worrying: what if she'd been kidnapped, or rounded up, or—I didn't actually think that she'd have been put on a transport, but by then my mind was already playing horror movies, and called Dad, who didn't sound happy. Finally he told me that she'd had to have some medical tests done: no doubt, this being England, things had gotten backed up. It was dark when he got home, and I was starving. "What's for dinner?" I said. He glared at me like I was a demon, and said that if I was hungry I could make myself a sandwich.

When the phone finally rang, Dad picked it up immediately, but all we heard was him "Okay." When he got off the phone, he looked stunned. That's when we knew for sure that it was Mom who'd called, and knowing that, we begged him to tell us what was happening. He told us that she had been diagnosed with cancer.

"We'll know more as soon as she gets home."

It seemed like another week passed until we heard her fumbling at the door, but when she let herself in, I could see no difference in her. There was the same small neat face; dark curls; red lipstick; raincoat. But when she took her coat off, I noticed that her blouse was buttoned wrong and hung unevenly off her shoulders.

"How bad is it?" Dad said.

"They don't know yet."

She said that her cancer had been caught early, that though she'd have to have an operation, she'd only be in the hospital for a few days. After that, she said, we'd all just have to wait and see until the lab reports came back. "To see if I need chemotherapy or not." Chemotherapy. That was a word I was familiar with, and though I didn't know exactly what it meant, I knew it was bad, that it made you look like the corpses of Auschwitz with bald heads and skeletal bodies. With that image in my mind, I began to cry.

"Not now," Dad said.

"But I want to go home!" I wailed, diving into my mother's lap, while my father, his nostrils flaring, looked at me as if he'd never met me. But it didn't matter how much I—or anyone else—wanted to go home. We couldn't. My father's grant was time-bound, and to lose it would mean losing that year's income. And where would we go, anyway? Our house in Maryland had been rented out. And as it turned out, Mother insisted that she didn't want to go home anyway. She was adamant about it. She loved travel, adventure, wandering. She didn't want to give up our year in London, our magical year across the sea.

"I'll be fine," she said.

But she wasn't fine. After her surgery, she was in the hospital for a full week, with tubes sticking into her side and a funny sort of smell coming off her bed. When, later, she came home from her first chemotherapy treatment, she was both flushed and pale, and her hands shook. For the next two or three days, she slept a lot and whimpered, which I found confusing and terrifying and sad all at once, and even when I tried to comfort her, when I threw my head into her lap or brought a poem that I'd secretly written just for her, she was still sad. I could see it, feel it, how sad she was. "For God's sake, get a hold of yourself, you're scaring the boys," our father said some days after her first treatment when, at the dinner table, she began to weep. But then she felt better again, and started talking about all the things she wanted to do to take advantage of our year abroad, all the places she wanted to see, explaining that she could plan around when she knew she'd be feeling better.

Sometime later, she announced that during our winter break—which was a good deal longer than at home—we'd be taking a trip to Eastern Europe to see the countries that until recently were "behind the Iron Curtain." It was a once-in-a-lifetime opportunity, she said. When she herself was an undergraduate, studying abroad, such places were off-limits. You couldn't visit them unless you had special permission, and even then, it was difficult. Such places were police states, under the thumb of Communism, and in any event, why go there? But now things were different. The Berlin Wall had come down—did we remember seeing that on TV? (Not really.) You could book a hotel in advance, and walk around to see the sights, just like in any other country. Here were the homelands of Kafka, Freud, Klimt, Adolf (that name!) Loos, Otto Wagner, Max Lieberman! That's where we'd be heading—to the cradle of modernism, where Jewish civilization was once so magnificent that it outshone a million diamonds. This was all from my mother, who loved this stuff.

Our hotel in Budapest was old and elegant in a shabby, dusty sort of way, with faded flocked wallpaper, sea-green and pink, and employees who spoke perfect English with heavily Slavic tones. My brother and I had one room; my parents were down the hall. Neither room had a working television, which didn't bother my parents at all, though it was hard for my brother, who was not only addicted to sports and sporting events, but unused to entertaining himself, impatient when our parents tried to explain that the chances of there being anything on television that would interest him were slim to none. For the first day, he sulked around complaining of boredom as our parents trekked us through the Hungarian National Gallery and to various pastry-and-coffee shops and late Gothic churches, but during breakfast of our second morning, he met a girl—we both did—who was his age, thirteen. She too was on holiday from England—she lived in the north, in Manchester—and she had blonde curls and small hands and feet, and wore a heart-shaped silver pendant on a silver chair around her neck Her name was Liza, and she not only smiled at me, but told me things about herself: that she loved Toblerone chocolate, that she had a collection of teddy bears. I was instantly in love with her, loving her as only a dramatic and imaginative nine-year-old boy could do, with complete devotion, and an inner knowing that somehow, through the grace of fate and fortune, we were meant to be together.

"She thinks you're a freak, freak," said my brother. "She only talks to you because she's nice."

"Not true."

"She thinks you're weird, which you are. You've got boogers hanging out of your nose."

I went to wipe my nose on my sleeve, the only surface available for wiping, but as usual my brother was winding me up, running me up the flagpole, and when I challenged him on his booger-dripping assertion he told me that just because nothing had come out on my sleeve didn't mean that the offending matter wasn't there. Which of course meant that I had to explore by hand, putting my finger deeply into one nostril at a time, jiggling it around a little, searching with my fingernail for whatever bits of flakes or clotted snot might have found their way forward.

"She's watching you."

I yanked my entire body backwards against the chair, managing to fall over, and though unhurt, I felt stupid and angry at my brother for having tricked me again. At least Liza wasn't in the breakfast room or even in the hall outside the breakfast room. In fact, when I knocked on her door a few minutes later, she opened it, smiled vaguely at me, and told me that she and her parents were getting ready to go out but that I could come back later, after dinner but not too late, and we could talk then if I liked, adding that she'd never been to America and wanted to go and had I ever been to Disneyland?

I hadn't.

I hadn't been anywhere other than to Washington D.C. a few zillion times, the apartment building filled with old people in Baltimore where my grandparents lived, and to Florida, where my other grandmother lived. And

London, of course—I got that in too, hurriedly and slightly embarrassed, not wanting her to think I was stupid.

"See you, then," she said.

"We're going to the old Jewish quarter," our mother said.

"It's your mother's idea," our father said, his brow furrowing just enough to let us know that he was displeased. "There isn't really anything to see other than abandoned, decrepit buildings. The old ghetto, good God, who wants to see that? It's a ghost town."

But I couldn't think of anything better. A real live ghetto? I didn't know there were any left. In my mind's eye I could picture skinny terrified starving Jews crushed, twenty or thirty to a room, with no heat or running water, surviving on melted snow and the occasional crust of moldy bread.

"Don't forget the Grand Synagogue," our mother said.

"It's called the Great Synagogue and I doubt it will be open."

"The man at the front desk said it would be."

"The man at the front desk didn't even know what it was. He looked at you like you had horns growing out of your head."

I didn't know what that meant. Nor—despite my new obsession—could I have imagined that anyone, even Hitler, could believe that Jews were so bestial that we were actually beasts, with actual horns. (I learned all this much later.) I thought maybe Dad's comment had to do with how strange my mother looked now, with tufts of hair falling out from the edges of her silk scarf. But her head, unlike mine—which I regularly checked for signs of impending brain tumors— wasn't weirdly shaped at all. Wrapped as it was in a blue silk scarf, anyone could see that it was regular, a perfect, regular oval, like a blue balloon.

"In any case," she said. "This is our one opportunity to see it."

When we got to the Great Synagogue, our father went to open the massive doors and found out that he'd been right after all: the place was locked. No amount of banging on the doors changed that. "See?" he said, with a glint of victory. "I wish you'd listen to me. It's a matter of common sense."

"Well, we're here now anyway. So let's make the best of it."

So instead of going inside and seeing whatever there was to see there, we ended up trudging around the old Jewish quarter, now abandoned, as our father had predicted, one empty frozen courtyard surrounded by empty peeling apartment buildings after the next, all of us trudging through the slush. I still wanted to find the ghetto, the exact place where Jews had been herded together, but there weren't many signs and even if there had been, none of us knew Hungarian. But I persisted, asking question after question until at last my father, his hands balled into his pockets, exploded with annoyance. "This whole damn place was a ghetto. Is a ghetto. Look around. It's the old story. First they caged us in. Then they starved us. Then they drove us out. Finally, they murdered us. And for the coup de grace, communism destroyed the rest. Not to mention, who would live here?" He shook his head slowly, as if to indicate the obviousness of it all. "This whole city is no doubt still crawling with Jew haters."

That wasn't like my father, but the words had come out anyway, and with them, my heart was seized with fear. As we trudged on, I saw murderers and anti-Semites in every shadow, and ready to dart ahead at a moment's notice, ready to scream, to cry for help, I clutched my mother's hand. She chattered along about how, when we were older, my brother and I would have to read the great Yiddish novelists, how they'd captured the world we were walking through when it was still bustling with life. But it was clear that even she, with her endless capacity for exclamation, was disappointed.

After about ten minutes more of walking around like this, I stepped into an icy puddle. When I came out, my feet were soaked up past my ankles. I burst into tears, frantic that now I'd have to spend the rest of the already miserable day with cold wet feet, that I'd never be dry, that eventually I'd succumb to pneumonia, or worse, pleurisy.

"Retard," my brother said.

"Shut up, you're the retard, retard," I said.

Dad told both of us to hush.

"But I'm wet!" I wailed. "I'm freezing! My feet are soaked! I'm soaked through with ice! And it's December and I'm freezing and I'm already getting feverish!"

"You walked into a puddle," my father said. "It's not the end of the world."

"Ha ha," my brother said.

"My feet are going numb. I'll get frostbite!"

"That's enough," my father said.

"Take me back to the hotel!" I wailed, thinking of how nice it would be to get back inside my bed with my book—I was then reading Sherlock Holmes in a frenzy of obsession that wouldn't cease until years later—and how, when Liza returned from her own day of sightseeing and learned of my incident, she'd bring me hot chocolate and pet me and maybe some of the other things that I'd heard my brother and his friends brag about. Then I'd tell her everything that was in my heart, how my father, despite his intellectualism and fancy degree, was impatient and said things that made me feel bad, how Mother, though ill, had to placate him, and most of all, how ignorant, how brutish, and how mean my brother was. Then that thing that my brother was obsessed with would happen, and I'd tell her that someday, when I was grown, I'd love her with all my heart, and then we could be married. "Take me back now! Do you have any clue how uncomfortable it is to walk around with wet feet in winter? It's like I'm in the Holocaust!"

"Simmer down!" our father said while my brother snickered.

"I'm going to die, and you don't even care!"

"Good God, you're not going to die!" my father said, clenching and unclenching his fists the way he did when he was seriously, seriously angry. "Just enough! Enough! You're nine years old. Show some self-respect."

At least my mother had pity on me and, grabbing me by one of my mittened-hands, said: "We'll find a store, and I'll buy you a new pair of socks. That ought to do it."

"Where will you find an open store in Budapest on a Sunday?" our father said. "Everything is closed."

"It's Sunday, not Christmas. We'll find a place."

"But what if we don't?" I whimpered. Truly, I was miserable.

"We will," she said, leading me out of the courtyard we were in and into the next and then the next until we were on a busy boulevard in a busy neighborhood somewhere near the river. The blue Danube was brown and frothy, like icy hot chocolate, laced with large chunks of brown ice.

My father was right: the shops were closed. Even the one pharmacy we came across was closed. But by then we were in a district of shiny hotels, newer ones than where we were staying, big well-scrubbed places with a flurry of bright flags flying and lines of taxis out front. That's when Mother decided that, if nothing else, she'd take my socks and dry them out in the ladies' room, using the hot-air hand dryer.

"You can't do that," my father said. "You can't just march into a hotel where we're not staying and use the facilities."

"Why?"

"Because we haven't paid for it. It's not honest."

She did it anyway, marching straight into the grandest hotel of them all, and as I sat barefoot on a sofa in the hotel lobby, my brother sat on the other end, kicking his feet back and forth and humming under his breath in a way he knew annoyed me. He was doing it on purpose. Of course. At least he couldn't do more than that now, not in the hotel lobby with people around and our father pacing back and forth behind us breathing audibly.

Finally Mother emerged from the ladies' room, my still-wet socks in her hands. "At this rate, they'll never dry," she said.

Grabbing me by the hand and all but yanking me onto my feet, she pulled me into a group of German-speaking tourists who were only then checking in—I remember it was two couples, both of them middle aged, wearing beautiful heavy coats with beautiful leather gloves. She asked if any of them spoke English, and when one of the men acknowledged that he did, she asked him point blank if perhaps he had a pair of socks in his luggage that he wouldn't mind giving to me, her son.

"His socks, as you can see, are wet," she said, holding them out in her two palms like an offering.

"I only have men's socks, I doubt very much they would suit," the German man said.

"They'll be fine," my mother said.

"They're very high quality, I just bought them, pure wool, very fine," the man continued. "For hiking. We were hoping to get into the mountains."

"I understand, but my boy here—"

He opened his suitcase to show her, holding them in the palm of his hand. "You see? Very fine. For hiking."

"I'll pay you for them."

"You don't have to pay me, but I don't think they are suitable for a young boy." He squinted at me under heavy black eyebrows that reminded me of Hitler's mustache, those short thick black slashes that moved up and down when he fulminated from the stage, and as the tears rose afresh to the surface of my eyeballs, my mother took the socks, saying, "Thank you so much. Thank you."

"But— he said. "Please, Madame—"

"Thank you. Really. I really, really appreciate it."

As my mother returned with the socks, my father, red in the face with fury, said, "You just can't do that."

"Well, I did it anyway."

"Do you enjoy embarrassing yourself?"

"I'm not embarrassed."

"I am."

"First things first," she said, indicating me with a nod of her head. "He can't go around all day long in wet socks."

"Kids go around in wet socks all the time. It's part of being a boy. He needs to learn to suck it up and not be such a mamma's boy. At this rate—"

"At this rate, what?"

"He's already turning into a sissy."

I hated him then. I hated him with hot rage and cold bitterness. I hated him for being mean to Mom. I hated him for making me share a room with my brother, and for how helpless he was in the face of Mom's illness. I hated him for not understanding me. I hated him for subjecting me to the icy misery of Budapest, and for his own bitter certainty that the Great Synagogue would be closed—how snidely pleased he'd been to discover he was right!

A minute later, the German man's warm thick woolen socks were on my feet, and how wonderful they felt, they were so thick they all but blocked out the dampness of my shoes. But even the wonderful comfort of those thick German hiking socks couldn't neutralize the fear rising up from my belly to my brain when my father, his fists balled up at his sides, went at it again: "You can't behave like that, Jill. You can't just walk into a fancy hotel and ask a stranger to give you his socks, you can't do that, Jill, it's not done, you're embarrassing to be with. What's wrong with you? What's wrong with you? You don't think straight. Has the chemotherapy affected your brain?" He was so loud that other people, including the German man, were noticing, and when I saw the German man walking in our direction, I knew the game was up. The German man, with his thick, Hitler-mustache eyebrows and beautiful, elegant luggage, would come and get me, he'd come and get me and snatch the socks from my feet and the next thing I knew he'd summons all the Jew-haters to aid him and we'd be herded out of the hotel and headed for God knows where, headed for extinction, for extermination, and I fainted softly and slowly onto the soft, soft carpet of the hotel lobby.

When, a moment later (and it really was only a moment) I came to, my mother was hovering over me, and my father was standing far above both of us, his face looming like the moon. "Now look, he's fainted," he said. My mother, her own face gone yellow-white, remained just above me, as near to mine as a wish, and as her hair fell from the edges of her scarf and drifted in the air like snowflakes, I suddenly became wracked with curiosity, and reached up and plucked a piece for myself. How easily it came off in my hand! How filled with horror I was! I was nine years old, and my world was ending.

I'm Getting Married Tomorrow

(A) I'm not bad-looking, and (B) I've never had any trouble finding girls, so (C) what I did that night was not the act of a desperate self-deluded jerk. Only I know what you're thinking and that is: who the hell is this jerk? To which I'd have to say that I'm no more or less a jerk than anyone else my sister tells me about.

I love my sister, okay? But she's allowed herself to become a parody of herself, uptight to the point of implosion, thinks that everyone's looking at her as if they can hear her ovaries aging and that if she's not married by thirty-one, thirty-two, she's history, may as well hang up her skimpy underthings and retire to Tampa, take up shuffleboard. It's a hostile attitude. She's smart, too, way too smart to fall for that crap, but there's nothing I can tell her about my gendermates that will make her feel any different than she already does, which is: men are all scum, except for the ones, like the ones our parents are always pushing on her, who are wimps with unimpressive johnsons (her expression, not mine).

She tells me stories: the guy who sent roses to her every night for two weeks until she agreed to sleep with him, and then she sleeps with him, and it's great only guess what? He has to leave right afterward to go back to his place in case his girlfriend who lives in Jersey calls—oh, you mean I didn't mention my girlfriend? The lawyer who took her out to dinner and then, holding her hand, told her all about his psychotherapy, and actually began to cry. (It was disgusting, she said. His eyes got red and he kept dribbling all over his dinner napkin.) The investment banker with the proverbial neckties from Barney's and the platinum Am Ex card only he's built on the dainty side and he's finished in about three seconds flat. (Poof, she says. Then he's snoring.)

So I figure that, compared to these guys, I'm not so bad. But my sister says no, because I'm one, too, worse, in fact, than any jerk-off who's ever messed with her. But by now she's partisan, can't be trusted. She wanted her chance to stand in front of all those people and maybe get a chance to catch the bridal bouquet and God knows what else because the entire way that females think is alien to me, and if I were smart I'd join some silent monks in France or Indiana, if they'd have me, or if not then sign on with the Lubavitchers, marry some nice, terrified eighteen-year-old and maybe, if I'm lucky, drown myself in so much overcooked pot roast and Manischewitz that I can no longer remember what girls smell like.

This is what happened: what happened was that there was Robin, my fiancee, and then there was Emily, this girl I'd known in college who we used to call Free Love because once, in a poetry seminar when we were comparing the love sonnets of John Donne to those of Shakespeare, she said something along the lines of her believing in free love, and then while the rest of us snickered and looked at our feet she explained that what she'd meant had to do with the difference between formal patterns of sound versus the abandonment of traditional versification as in her favorite, Walt Whitman, the ultimate master of free verse—but as far as I could tell, the only person who was interested in this bullshit was the professor, a middle-aged lesbian who had the bad habit of playing with her middle-aged acne. Needless to say, this was back when I had poetic aspirations myself, long before I chucked my youthful idealism and adolescent passions for a law degree and, as of this writing, one-ten-a-year plus bonus, office on the 21st floor, great secretary, and an endless supply of free paper clips.

This girl, this Free Love, was something else, too: smart in that intense, overly animated way of a person with an inflated sense of the superiority of her own soul, plus a serious looker, with a body that wouldn't quit. She was so beautiful that every time I looked at her my tongue swelled up in my mouth and I became hyperconscious of how much saliva I was producing. But during her freshman year she kind of took on half the rugby team, and later got into women, or at least that's what the girlfriend I had during the first semester of my last year of college told me. She said: I know she's pretty if you like that slutty type but let's face it, Hal, she's probably got some kind of disease. Then she told me that, on a dare, Free Love had done it with a banana at some dance club in the East Village during spring break. All I had to do was think of this girl with a banana—her underpants around her ankles, her skirt hiked up—for my anatomy to come to attention like a West Point cadet.

This is what she looked like: she looked like a total fantasy from California or some place where they grow them like that—tall and shapely—and with this beautiful, heart-shaped face and these kind of slanty brown eyes and long dark wild hair that she raked her hands through as if she were auditioning for a shampoo commercial. Later, when I got to know her a little bit, people were always coming up to her and saying: you look just like that movie star, you know the one I mean, the one who was in. . . . But the totally most amazing thing about Free Love was that she wasn't from some exotic tribe of Asian-Swede-Afro-American-Sioux at all, but from Trenton, where her mother worked as secretary to the rabbi in the Reform temple where she'd been bat-mitzvahed, and her dad worked for Exxon, something to do with emission control. *Trenton*, which is almost as bad as being from Newark—or, for that matter, Ozone Park, which is where I'm from.

Okay, moron, is what I know you're saying. So you had a thing for this Jewish girl from Trenton. So what about it? Did you or did you not? And what about this other girl, this Robin, your fiancée? Where'd she come from? And who wants to hear about how horny you were in college which is such an old story that it makes me cry with boredom? Ever hear of Philip Roth, genius? Didn't he already do this one? Like maybe a half-dozen times? How big is your whizmaster, anyway? Why aren't you in therapy?

A few years after I finished law school I ran into Free Love—Emily—on Madison Avenue, between Forty-fifth and Forty-sixth. It was early March, cold and wet. She was hurrying past with that intense forward-looking expression that all women get once they've been in New York for more than a week, carrying a styrofoam take-out carton. Her hair was wet, slicked back, and her feet, on the sidewalk, made rat-tat-tat sounds. She walked right past me even though I called out her name, and then, when I turned around to catch up to her, she looked at me with no recognition at all.

It's Hal, I said, Hal Wolf, from school. We had a poetry class together. Sophomore year.

I'm sorry I don't remember.

I didn't talk much, I said. She looked at me as if I were a con-man or an insurance broker trying to sell her whole-life even though she's not yet thirty. So I went: not like you. With your free verse.

I'm going to be late for work, she said.

I'd like to say that I ran after her, calling her name and giving her additional hints about my identity—you know, I was the idiot who used to sit near the door and doze off; or, I knew you when you were Free Love, do you still do it with bananas?—but the truth is, I followed her. I followed her for six blocks, until I saw her disappear, along with a few dozen other great-looking women, into the Condé Nast building. Then I went back to my own office on Lexington, where I was working, if memory serves, on a case involving faulty ceiling-fan parts.

And from there it was easy, because I figured all I had to do was call the Condé Nast switchboard to get put through to her, and when I did I stammered all over myself and apologized and generally begged and she talked to me for a long time and it turned out that she worked for *Vogue. Vogue?* my sister said when I told her about it. So what? She's probably a secretary. Spends her days answering the phone. Either that or maybe she places advertisements. *Vogue.* Big deal.

What I'd said when I got her on the phone was: I had a crush on you for all four years of college will you please have lunch with me anyplace in the tri-state area?

But it didn't really matter, anyway, because by then I was seriously involved with Robin, a lovely girl, and I know I sound patronizing but I don't mean to be. My sister's like: you are a total pig how can you justify your scumbag existence get out of my face. Even my secretary—I share her with a junior partner—said as much, only of course she couldn't be quite so straightforward, verbally. She was more like: are you sure you know what you're doing? My best friend from high school, Sam, who's gone Hollywood, is the only male person I tell any of this stuff to and his opinion was, so what? Only, as my sister pointed out, Sam writes sit-coms, or at least he's trying to, so why should I trust his opinion on anything?

But Robin was lovely, as lovely as any girl I've ever known, as lovely and sweet and gentle as a person can be without becoming a devotee of Eastern mysticism. She was a lawyer like me. I met her in law school. Like me, she'd grown up local: in her case, Jamaica Estates. She was my height exactly, which is five-nine—she said it made her feel overgrown and excessive—and very very steady. Everything about her was steady: her quiet, steady, brown-eyed gaze; the slow, graceful motions of her fingers and hands as she chopped green beans or worked on her computer; her rise and fall under or over me. She and I spent countless hours drinking coffee and cramming for exams and going out for middle-of-the-night Chinese before it dawned on either of us to touch each other, and then when we started, neither one of us saw any reason to stop, and after that it was just a hop to being a kind of semipermanent couple, and my mother was going around telling all her friends that I had a very nice girlfriend who was—there is a God—Jewish.

What I told my sister about Emily, because it was true, is that even in college you could tell she was different. (Yeah, she was different, she said. She made it with bananas.) But I mean, even then, there were girls—guys, too— who already had the mark of middle age on them. I mean, you could tell, just by glancing at them, not only what they were going to look like ten or twenty years later but what they were going to do, and where they were going to live, and how they were going to decorate their living rooms and what books they'd have on their bookshelves, if any. You could take one look and see: future CPA two kids one basset hound split-level in Cherry Hill spends his weekends gardening. Or: frustrated concert pianist turned third-grade teacher with lots of tribal rugs and hardwood floors. Or: marries for money but denies it until she starts having affairs. You could *see* the trips to the dentist and the carpool rides in the minivan and the requisite weekends-away-from-the-kids where the sex is satisfying but not quite quite what it used to be oh well at least we're in a stable marriage which is more than I can say for some people. Or: spineless attorney who settles into a steady but dull marriage because he doesn't have the guts to do anything original, fools around in a desultory kind of way, ends up living in a condo in West Hole, New Jersey, sees his kids every other weekend, only they don't like him.

But with Emily, it was different. You could look at her, stare at her like I did, and come up with nothing. And it wasn't only that she was beautiful, because there were a lot of beautiful girls—my own sister's great-looking only she thinks she needs to lose ten pounds. She says: you are delusional.

The next part is tricky because it couldn't have happened at all without the bizarre timing of things. The background is: Robin and I are steady. But also, okay, I'm beginning to see Emily, first only for lunch, and then your occasional movie, your occasional Chinese, but all very casual, very low-key, because it isn't like we're dating or anything, we're just hanging out, because it turns out that Emily has a boyfriend, only the boyfriend isn't around much, because he is—get this—getting a combined Ph.D. and law degree from Yale. Meanwhile in her eyes the fact that I'm pulling down decent money means squat because I went to Brooklyn Law School, which is where you go if you don't even know where Yale is.

In the meantime, she tells me all kinds of crap about herself: how she still writes poetry, even though she knows it's hopeless; how she's bored to tears at *Vogue*, where her job involves editing the movie-star column and something to do with shoes, or maybe it was hats; how she's thinking about going back to school herself, maybe in linguistics, which she's very interested in, she's always had a knack for languages; how she believes in God; how she wants to get married and have a whole slew of kids. And I'm thinking: what about the *banana?*

One day Emily and I meet for lunch—it was one of those brilliant warm early October afternoons where all of a sudden people who usually look fat and pasty and sticky look, through your fevered, feverish eyes, merely achingly, tragically human. I remember it exactly: Emily's wearing white pants, a white blouse, a white sweater. And I mean everything is *white* white, like something a nurse would wear, only on her it looks fantastic. Her wild brown hair is doing its usual electrified number all over her head, and she has these big fat bangles on, and this bright red lipstick, and they say that men don't pick up on these things unless they're gay. I want to make love to her right then and there on the corner where we meet but instead we go to a deli and get sandwiches and eat on the steps of Saint Bart's. Where she says:

I've got good news.

It's been maybe seven months that we've been hanging and so by now I know quite a bit about her, including the name of her boyfriend, Richard, and how brilliant and sweet he is, and how he'll probably teach law himself one day, maybe even at Yale, blah blah blah blah. So I say:

New job?

And she says:

Jesus. Are you blind? And she flashes her hand in front of me and right there on it as big as Nebraska is a diamond ring.

He asked me this weekend, she says.

Then she chatters on about how happy and excited her mother is but how already she's fighting with her about the details of the wedding, the date of which isn't even set yet, but already her mom is insisting on having it at Beth Shalom synagogue where her mom has worked for forever, and she doesn't seem to notice that I'm choking on my roast-beef sub.

Which is how, in a roundabout way, Robin and I finally decide to get engaged. One day I'm telling Robin about this buddy of mine who's taking the Deep Plunge, and the next day Robin starts talking about making a commitment, and this goes on for a few weeks, maybe a few months, I don't know, because I'm sunk into this depression that has me up nights with this awful combination of the hots and the sweats and sometimes I swear to God I wake up and there's Robin sleeping right beside me but I have to go to the bathroom to take care of myself. And when I come out of the depression it's spring again and I look at myself one morning in the mirror and realize that I'm going gray at my temples and that the woman who has been sharing her body and soul with me for going on four years is as steady and decent and intelligent as they come. And that day I ask her to marry me.

In Hollywood, my friend Sam is like: congratulations. Only it sounds as if he's saying: I'm sorry to have to tell you that we've found a malignancy. My sister is going: well at least one of us is getting on with life it's so much easier for guys I wish I had a dick. My mom is ecstatic. My dad is going around the house humming "When the Red Red Robin Comes Bob Bob Bobbin' Along." The only person who doesn't react one way or another is Emily, because of course—and this is the part you're going to incinerate me for—I never exactly ever got around to telling Emily about Robin.

At first I didn't because I held out this slim hopeless hope that maybe Emily would let me go to bed with her. And then I didn't because it never exactly came up which is—okay I admit it—not exactly true either: Emily asked me all the time about my love life, and I told her, too, only I never exactly told her the truth because the girls I made up—girls like Sally O'Mally who did PR for the Giants and who had a mirror over her bed so she could watch herself while we went at it, or Jeannie Rubin the struggling folk singer who actually sang at the moment of highest pleasure—were a lot more interesting than Robin, and made her laugh. And when she laughed—big laughs coming out of her gut—her whole face turned red and her eyes watered and I felt like a million bucks, I know it sounds corny but it's true.

But Emily and I had been seeing less of each other, anyway, mainly because every time I called her, for lunch or a movie, she was busy: she was spending more and more time with her fiance in New Haven, and then she was promoted at *Vogue*, and on top of that she started taking graduate classes at Columbia in postmodernist semiotics or some other bullshit. But then what happens is: she's calling me one morning at work, crying into the phone, saying, oh God, I feel so stupid.

Do you want me to come over? I say. No, no, you're at work. I'll be fine. Are you sure? It's no trouble. No, really. Look, Emily, whatever it is, you shouldn't be alone. Well, okay.

This is my big moment. I'm like: it's an emergency, Susan, hold my calls. The crosstown traffic is murder, but when I finally get to Emily's apartment it's all worth it because there's Emily saying oh God I'm so sorry to do this to you but I just wanted a shoulder to cry on and when I say What? What happened? she says: Richard dumped me. And I'm like: you've got to be messing with me big time who would dump a babe like you but I'm making all these sweet shushing noises and telling her that I've been in love with her since the first time I saw her, in that poetry seminar in college. And God help me but I'm thinking about that banana at that nightclub or whatever it was in the East Village all those years ago, how drunk she must have been, or high, or both, or high on her own lust. And a minute later I'm all over this girl.

You get your rocks off you get your rocks off, is my sister's take on all things sexual, but then she likes to pretend that she's a cynic. But it was—I swear to God Himself—more than that happy little burp at the end of things, it was sex like sex is in the movies; the kind of sex that turns God into a voyeur; sex like heat and lightning and thunder and dew. It was afterward, during our post-coital bliss phase, that I blew it. And this is where I made one little error in judgment, because if I had just been a little bit *more* of a scumbag, rather than less of one, none of what was about to happen would have happened, or at least not in the same sordid way. This is where my man Sam is in total absolute incomprehension and my sister is about ready to hang herself for the prophylactic benefits thereof. But in this fit of *après-sex* arousal and desire, I'm not thinking clearly. Because instead of begging her right then and there to spend the rest of her life with me, and to forget about that faggot Richard with his fancy Ph.D. from Yale and his unappreciative jones, I say:

Is it true?

And she says: what?

The thing I heard. The thing, in college, with the banana.

And the next thing I know, she's the color of sand, and she's pulling her clothes on and telling me to get *out* of her house. What? What did I say? I'm saying. And: I heard a lot of stupid rumors in college not just about you but about other people too. Only she cuts me off and tells me that she never ever wants to see or hear from me again. Never. Not ever. And then I'm on my knees, literally down on the floor, begging her to relent, begging her to let me stay, let me hold her and make it up to her—whatever she did or didn't do, I don't care—and I'm spewing out all these words and in the middle of them I kind of throw in that I'm engaged to be married but it's all over now I've only loved her all this time I've been fooling myself I'm going to cut off my engagement and so forth and so on until she says, in this very quiet voice:

You're engaged?

Well. Yes. Sort of.

You never told me.

I'm telling you now.

Goodbye, she says.

And for the next several days and weeks, every time I called, she hung up, and on the two or three occasions I showed up at her office, the receptionist wouldn't let me back. You don't have an appointment, she said. Sorry.

I know what you're saying. You're saying: what about Robin? You did, as gently as possible, break things off with her, did you not? I mean, that would have been the only decent thing to do, given that you were in love with another woman, right? Well, the answer is: yes and no. I told her I was having second thoughts, and she said: I understand. And I told her that I was going through a bad time, trying to figure out what I really wanted in life—told her I was burned-out at work (true), and pulled in too many directions the rest of the time (not precisely true), and some other junk, too. And she said: I understand. And then, because Robin was so good and I felt so guilty, I told her that I'd met another girl but that nothing had happened (false) and that nothing would happen (true). And she said: what girl? And I gave her this whole line about this girl I'd met through work, only she was married. And Robin sat there in her tiny living room—on the dumpy light-blue loveseat that she'd reupholstered herself at night and on weekends—and cried. Then I started to see a therapist and then she started to see a therapist and slowly, slowly we got it back together—and bit by bit I was beginning to feel like I had blood in my veins instead of dead insect parts, and so we got re-engaged, and set a date, and chose china.

The night before our wedding, the guys give me a bachelor party which was just about the last thing in the world I wanted. Suffice it to say that the girl they got to perform performed a few unnatural acts but nothing to compare with the millions of times I'd imagined Emily with the banana, and when I got home that night—I was still living in the same studio on East Thirty-sixth Street that I got when I finished law school—I called Emily and I said:

I'm getting married tomorrow.

And she said: congratulations.

And I said: don't hang up.

And she said: why?

And I said: because I don't want you to think I'm some kind of pathetic schmuck, but before I do this, I just want to make sure. Because if you're still not married or involved or whatever, I would like you to marry me.

You're crazy.

I'm serious. What do you think?

Sounds good.

Do you mean it?

Sure I mean it.

And this part gets extremely complicated, so I'll cut it short. I got a taxi to Robin's parents' house in Jamaica Estates, where Robin was spending the night, and told her, and I kept expecting her to slug me or cry or yell, but she just stood there, staring at me. Then I took the same taxi all the way back to Manhattan, to Emily's building on the West Side.

What? her voice on the intercom-speaker says.

It's *me*. It's Hal. Let me in.

Then, while I'm waiting to hear the buzz and the click to let me in, there's this pause, and then her voice saying:

I thought I made it very clear that I never want to see you again as long as I live.

You said you'd marry me.

A joke, she says.

Oh Jesus, I'm saying. Oh Jesus.

Grow up, she says.

What I told my sister, because it's true, is that it wasn't the banana. It was Emily, all of Emily, her blood and her guts and her bones. I said that she wasn't just an excuse to get out of a marriage I wasn't really sure I wanted. I said that I knew that what I'd done was unforgivable. What do you want me to do, castrate myself?

That would be too good for you, she says.

What should I do, then?

But my sister just looks at me and shakes her head.

Sol's Visit

He didn't want to do it. God knows he didn't. But in the end, after two trips to the emergency room, a hairline fracture, and a series of long rambling conversations about meeting Hershel to go swimming in the pond that lay through the wood outside Mszcznow on the road to Zboiska, Sol knew it was time. His Mammala, his Mamuleńka—Yetta was her given name but in America she was called Yvette—had to go to a home.

It's a nice home, as far as such things go, or at least that's what the geriatric social worker who'd helped Sol find a suitable place for his mother had said: "None of them is exactly the Garden of Eden, but some are better than others, and some are much better than others." Devorah House, she insisted, was in the latter category.

You couldn't tell by how much his mother complained, though. She complained that she didn't get enough natural light in her unit. When she was moved to the other side of the building, she complained that it was too drafty. She complained that the food was terrible, which it wasn't, at least not for kosher, but what did she expect, given that she'd refused to go any place that wasn't kosher? She complained that the hot water wasn't hot enough and then scalded herself and then she complained that the attendant hadn't been attending her properly and threatened to sue. She complained that the bed was too hard, which was ridiculous, because it was the same bed that she had shared with Sol's father for thirty years and had continued to sleep in for the next sixteen. When Sol bought her a new mattress she complained about its smell. She said she couldn't abide the staff and insisted on having a private attendant, instead, and then she fired her.

"These shvartzes," she said. "Every last one of them is lazy and stupid."

"You can't say things like that here," Sol said.

"Why? Because they're afraid of hearing the truth?"

"Because it isn't nice," Sol said. "Also, the woman who runs this place is African-American."

"She's what? Albanian?"

"African-American."

"Is that what they're called these days?" his mother said.

"Yes."

"Why aren't you married, are you a poof?" she said.

"No."

"You sure?"

"I'm sure."

"It's not the end of the world, you know, if you are." she said. "Even in Poland, we had them. The Pedzio. The Paperios. Everyone knew what they were up to. Once, in Mszczonów, right in the synagogue, if you can believe it, the gabbai, he's putting things right, Shabbos is over and he's putting things away, you know, and there, right under the Holy Arc, right there where Moses rabenu can see them, these two little fegalas, Moishe and Zalman, sticking it in each other's arse holes."

"Nice story, Ma."

She shrugged. "Sometimes I think maybe even your father was one of them."

"You're dreaming."

"How he loved the opera, remember?"

"Loving the opera doesn't make you a homosexual," Sol said.

"He was a Verdi fanatic. He loved Rigoletto."

"So?"

"The prince in 'Rigoletto.' Didn't he have a thing for boys?"

"Not that I'm aware of."

"Well then, Verdi himself—a famous feygele. A famous Italian opera-loving homo."

"Wasn't Verdi married?"

"How would I know?" She momentarily looked defeated. "And even if he had a wife, what does that prove? They all got married, it didn't mean a thing."

"I see."

"You see nothing," she said. Which wasn't fair. It wasn't fair for any number of reasons, but towards the top was the fact that he was paying for her care. It was only a stroke of ridiculously good luck that had allowed him to afford it, not that his mother either knew or cared that his book had been made into a documentary, which in turn had launched him as the founder of a new psychological specialty, an under-the-radar niche in the field of mental and emotional health: adult child of survivors, or ACOS. Now there were ACOS groups in thirty-two states that met in synagogue basements and quiet corners of libraries to discuss the particular difficulties of being the adult child of a survivor. He'd been on NPR. President George W. Bush had called him in as a consultant regarding International Holocaust Remembrance Day. And there he was, Sol Zamesk, Mr. Jewish nobody from Hollis Hills and a graduate of Queens College, his mother a housewife, his father an air-conditioning unit delivery man, shaking hands with the President of the United States on the White House lawn.

They weren't from the same town, his parents. Both parents had grown up poor. Both had been swept up by the Nazis. Both had been sent to the camps. They'd met in New York.

"They died," his mother said.

"Who, Ma?"

"Moishe and Zalman. Why? Are you deaf too?"

"I'm not deaf, Ma."

"Is that why no one will marry you, because you don't hear so good?"

"I'm not deaf, Ma."

"Then why aren't you married?"

"I guess I just can't find a girl as good as you."

"Does your thing work?"

"Ma! Don't you think that you're maybe crossing a line here?"

"Because it happens," she said with another of her infuriating, exasperating, homicidal-impulse-inducing shrugs. "I was married to your father for a long time before he died, you know."

"Got it."

"You still working at that hoity-toity Yekke magazine?" she said. "What's it called again? Oh yeah: Commissary."

"You know I'm not," he said. "And it's called *Commentary*."

"So?"

"You do, Ma."

"I could care less," she said.

"I left a few years ago, Ma. I've got my own business going now."

"You? A businessman? Really?"

"I told you I met the President recently?" he said.

"You told me you met that putz from Texas, if that's what you mean," his mother said, infuriating him still further, and throwing him off, too, the way she did that—the way she could be back in the shtetl one minute, thinking she was a young girl running away from the Storm Troopers, and the next, remembering exactly every word he ever said.

"And anyway, that wasn't exactly recently," she said. "Wasn't that already two years ago?"

"You're killing me, Ma. I don't even believe you're doing it unintentionally. You just like—" He was going to say "yanking my chain," but didn't want to set her off on a new round of yanking-related free association. He started again. "You just like to—"

"What I like is hard rods."

"Jesus! Ma!"

"What? What did I say? It's a song. I heard it on the television."

Poor thing. She was ninety, shriveled, widowed, flat-chested, stoop-shouldered, and confused. She suffered from hemorrhoids, arthritis, bunions, dementia, and whatever horrors she'd lived through in Europe, not that she'd ever talked about them, or at least not to him. He'd grown up in a house of screamers: his mother screamed at him during the day; his father screamed, in his sleep, at night. It was a one-bedroom apartment, nice enough as far as one-bedroom apartments in Queens went. His parents had the bedroom. He slept in a corner of the living room, behind a screen decorated with Japanese ladies wearing kimonos against a flowered and golden backdrop. When he was very little the Japanese ladies, with their small mouths and hard black eyes, had scared him. When he got older they turned him on. He jerked off with his back to them, worried they'd be offended and equally worried that were he to face them, one of them might actually come down from off the screen and do things with him that he desperately wanted to do but not really. He was afraid of girls. It didn't matter how shy or friendly or fat or pretty or plain or desperate the girl was. He was afraid of them all. Then he grew up and his father died and he was still afraid of girls, but not so afraid of them that he didn't, on occasion, have sex with them. Sex he liked. It was women he wasn't sure what to do with.

He still wasn't sure what to do with them. On the other hand, that didn't stop him, mainly from being an idiot. He loved women. Always had. Unfortunately, the one he loved the most was married to someone else, didn't love him even a little bit, and on top of everything else had already dumped him—it was years ago, but still—and now here he was, back for more, and all because. . . but there was no reason. The thing had no future. It barely had a present.

Zoe's husband was old; he'd suffered two strokes and couldn't speak properly and she didn't love him anymore and hadn't for a long time. Sol didn't know why Zoe continued to stay married to him but all she said was "It's complicated." Then they went somewhere and had sex.

That night, when he asked her, again, why she bothered with the pretense of her marriage, she got up, began to dress, and said: "Don't."

"We need to talk."

"I disagree."

He appreciated her: she was sleek and mean and smart, without a drop of sentimentality other than the large diamond ring she wore next to her wedding band. Her blonde hair had dark brown under streaks. Her blue eyes were ice cubes. She wore perfume.

"I just don't understand it," he said. "You're sleeping with me for a reason, and I don't think it's my movie star looks."

"It's your charm," she said as she left the room. He didn't follow her. There was no point. The door closed. He was suddenly so tired that he didn't even bother to get up to take a piss.

"Will you marry me?" he said to the ceiling.

In the morning there was an email from his booking agent saying that the Boston affiliate of NPR wanted to talk to him about rising antisemitism in Poland—as if there were enough Jews left in Poland to be anti-Semitic over—and another from his agent, Daphne, who said that Ha-Aretz, English language edition, wanted to interview him for a round-up they were doing on what the editor there called "second generation Holocaustica," and would he be interested, and since when wasn't he interested because if he didn't keep doing this stuff he wouldn't be able to pay his mother's bills. At half past ten an email came in from Isa DeWitt, the chief administrator at Devorah House, with the subject heading: EMERGENCY. The email said to get in touch with her as soon as possible.

When he called, she said: "I don't want to alarm you."

"Alarm me," he said.

"I think your mother—" She stopped talking.

"Is my mother dead?"

"I think your mother may have—"

"A hearing problem? Dementia? Cancer?"

"A boyfriend."

"Please," he said.

"I think you need to come in," she said.

He sat across from her desk, trying not to look anywhere but her face, but kept finding his eyes sliding down her pretty neck to her even prettier breasts, pillowing and billowing under her red silk blouse.

"His name is Frank," she said. "But she calls him Hershel."

"Hershel," he said. "It means 'deer.'"

"Whatever it means, it has to stop. She's upsetting the other residents."

"What do you want me to do about it?"

She gave him a sharp look, the same look almost every one of his elementary school teachers had given him just about every day of his elementary-school education.

"Perhaps you could have a talk with her, explain things to her in a way she can take in."

"She doesn't listen to me."

"Mr. Zamesk," she said, "I must tell you, your mother is more than a handful. The staff here is highly trained. They're accustomed to dealing with all kinds of clients, including those who espouse racist views, or hurl racist invective, as your mother does."

"Ma's not racist," he began to say, but then, realizing that she was, stopped.

"They are trained to care for even the most debilitated of our seniors, those who are both physically and mentally impaired."

"Yes, of course."

"But we simply can't have our members engaging in any form of sex here," she said.

He, for one, didn't see why not. If the seniors were getting it on, they should get an award. At the very least, they'd be getting some much-needed aerobic exercise. His own mother, though—impossible. She couldn't even get out of bed without help. Not to mention her arthritis, her fingers bent like chicken claws, her joints swollen and purple and tender.

"I'll see what I can do," he said.

His mother's unit was on the ninth floor, at the end of the hall. He knocked and went in. She was wearing a spongy green dress that buttoned up the front, and watching TV. "Who's Hershel?" he said.

"Whoever he is, he's probably dead."

"Mrs. DeWitt says you're running around with someone named Hershel."

"Did you say Hershel?" she said.

"You know I said Hershel."

"Don't tell anyone!" she said, turning to look at him through her dim cloudy milky unfocussed confused gray eyes. "I met him at the pond."

"There's no pond, here, Ma."

"There is, and I met him there. Don't be a dunce! Oh, I see how it is! You're jealous of me, jealous jealous jealous! And if you tell Papa I'll tell him about what you do at night when you think no one is watching!"

"Ma! Ma! Look at me, Ma!"

"What?"

"Do you know who I am?"

"You're my homo son, the one who isn't married, because he likes to do it with boys, is why. Another *shanda fur die goy.*"

"Good God."

"And don't take the name of the Lord in vain! Didn't they teach you nothing at the fancy college where you went?"

"I went to Queens College, Ma."

"You went nowhere is where you went," she said.

Had she been this mean when he was growing up? What was he thinking? Of course she'd been this mean. That's how he'd gotten himself up and out of the house to begin with: he couldn't stand her. And yes, also, he loved her. But he mainly he couldn't stand her. A million years of therapy and finally he felt good about that, about how his little boy's tender heart had known from the outset that his mother, whom he loved with all the tender sweetness of his little boy's heart, was pure unadulterated venom. When he got his job at *Commentary* he was pretty sure she'd finally be impressed, that maybe she'd see fit to brag about him, but she didn't, she was too mean and twisted and ruined by being in the camps, and she couldn't do anything but sit in her own poison, spewing poison. Not that it was her fault.

"What do I do at night?" he said.

"What?"

"When I think no one is watching? What do I do at night?"

"You think I don't know? I only sleep next to you. You think I don't know what's happening when you start making those moaning sounds, those cat sounds, it's disgusting, and you're going straight to genom, and no one will marry you, and the matchmaker won't go near you, and if you think for one second that Papa won't tear you limb from limb you're sorely mistaken. You're ugly, too. Who will want a cow like you, an ugly deformed cow with a shriveled leg who plays with her own udders?"

"I'm not Leibka."

His mother's only sister hadn't survived. His mother never spoke of her except to say that she was "lame."

"Pervert," she said.

"I'm not Leibka," he repeated.

"Then who are you?"

"Sol. Your son."

"Then how do you know about the pond?"

"What pond, Ma?"

"We don't do anything there, anyway. We just meet. We talk. We..."

"Ma?"

"Come and get me! Catch me if you can!"

But now she was muttering in Yiddish and Sol could only catch a word or two—kish, opsh, shpet, zikher—and he just didn't know what to do, because as always, with his mother, he didn't know how much she was putting on, and how much was real. The trace-memory of Zoe's perfume lingered in his nostrils.

"Who's Frank?" he said.

"Frank? There is no Frank. Unless you mean Frank Zisk. Remember him? He was our neighbor, when we lived on 9th Avenue. You used to be scared of him. You were scared of everything. You were scared of your shadow. You were scared of your feet, that's how scared you were."

"Oh yeah, Frank," he said, remembering, for the first time in decades, the stoop-shouldered bald man who had lived on the other end of the hall, a man in an undershirt and baggy pants with bloodshot eyes and stained fingers.

"Okay then," he said. "Hershel. Who's Hershel?"

"Hesh? None of your business."

"Whoever he is," he said. "You need to know that if you continue doing—whatever it is you are doing—with Frank, or Hesh, or whoever he is or isn't, they're going to throw you out of here."

"Who, the shvartze? Let her try."

"I'm warning you, Ma."

"Let me ride a hot hard rod," she sang.

At dinner that night, he told Zoe about his mother, about her penchant for quoting, or misquoting, or pretending to quote rap songs she heard on TV. He said: "And on top of it all, apparently she's got something going with another resident."

"Meaning?"

"Some kind of monkey business," he said, and then, when she gave him one of her bright-blue looks, her two hard eyes looking at him as if her vision penetrated all the way into the fleshy workings of his brain, he said: "Sex."

"Sex sex?"

"I'm not sure. Maybe."

"I guess that's where you got your libido, then."

It was nice, and rare, having dinner like this, together like any other couple, out for a bite at a neighborhood restaurant and talking about the events of the day.

"Good for her," Zoe said.

"I agree. But she denies it. She obfuscates and denies it. She's a pro. Seriously. She missed her calling. She should have run the CIA."

"If you say so"

He paid the check. "Do I bore you?" he said.

She raised one eyebrow. "I'm not in it for conversation," she said.

She didn't give a rat's ass about him. He couldn't explain it, how he loved her.

"Did I ever tell you about the time my father chased me down the street with an axe?" she said, an hour later as she rolled out from under him, impatient as always to get away from his orgasm, his bed, his wet clinging love.

"Do you have to leave? Why do you have to leave? Can't you just make up some excuse? Is Branson so much as aware of your absence?"

But instead of answering, she continued down memory lane. "My dad was pissed at me, I think I may have talked back to him. And he flew into a rage. I can still see him, his face just flooded with rage, dark red rage like red wine. He told me he was going to kill me, and then I'm just running down the street, screaming my head off because my father was going to kill me with an axe." She perched on the side of the bed to pull her shoes on. "But he couldn't keep up with me. I was much faster."

"Why don't you stay?" he said. "I promise I'll never chase you with an axe."

"I have to be at work first thing tomorrow morning," she said. "And Branson gets sad when I'm gone too long."

Mrs. DeWitt kept calling and emailing with warnings about his mother, which he responded to with hiring yet another new one-on-one minder for her, another pleasant and pleasant-faced Jamaican or Nigerian or Haitian woman who managed to take all manner of shit without getting ruffled despite his mother's atrocious manners and outright abuse, but it was no use: she fired them all. She sent them packing! She sent them packing even after he'd explained to them, in turn, that his mother wasn't paying the bills and therefore had no power to fire anyone and if things got really bad to tell him know because he'd compensate for his mother's abuse with an extra something in the weekly paycheck etc. No dice. He kept telling her to cut it out and she kept telling him to mind his own business, but then again, that's what she said when he first told her the joyous and even wondrous news that his book, Son of Survivors, Child of Mass Murder: An American Story was being published.

"What do you say about that, Ma?"

"What I say is you should mind your own business," she said.

"Let me ask you a question," he said. "Should historians mind their own business too because maybe they weren't there during the fall of Rome?"

"You're not a historian," she said.

But that was then, when she was still, more or less, in her right mind; still, more or less, the same mean, cantankerous, spiteful, and undermining disparager of life writ large he'd always known her to be. Now that she was so old, who knew? He wanted her to be happy, and if her dalliance with Frank/Hershel made her happy, who did it hurt? So he tried not to think about it and tried not to think about it some more and then it was spring and then it was late spring and then it was summer and Mrs. DeWitt called him on his cell phone and said they needed to talk, it couldn't wait, could he come in today, or better yet, now.

"What can I do for you?" he said as he entered Mrs. Dewitt's office, noting again what a handsome, robust woman she was.

"Frank Benjamin died."

"What? Who?" he said.

"Your mother went to his room—apparently her aide had dozed off—and we don't know all the details, we're still piecing it together, but apparently she was—your mother was—well I'll just blurt it out: your mother was astride him—"

"Please no details," he said, shielding his eyes as if from a too-bright sun.

"But she was, and she apparently—well, the thing is, she kept going. I mean, that's what we think. She didn't even realize that he'd had a heart attack—she thought he was enjoying things. We've talked to her, and that's what she reported. That he was enjoying himself. But I must tell you, Mr. Zamesk, it's possible we're looking at criminal charges here."

"What? An old guy croaks in mid-nookey and that's a crime?"

"Frank Benjamin suffered from advanced Alzheimer's Disease," said Mrs. DeWitt. "He was unable to give consent."

"And my mother?" Sol finally said. "She must be devastated. I mean—does she know what happened?"

"We're not sure. As I said, when we questioned her, she merely said—"

"Got it," Sol said. He didn't want to hear any more about it. It was unseemly. He didn't want to know that his mother still possessed sexual feelings, let alone an active sex drive that, apparently, had blossomed into a full-throttled death machine.

"Isn't it possible," he said, "that the old gent would have had a heart attack and died anyway?"

"It's possible," Mrs. DeWitt said. "But that's not the point. The point is that he had a heart attack while she was—while they were—together like that."

"And all this happened when?"

"This morning," Mrs. DeWitt said, checking her watch. "Two hours ago. Around ten."

"I appreciate your tact," he said even though he neither thought she was particularly tactful nor what he himself meant by that. When she didn't reply, he got up and, tipping an imaginary hat in response to an imaginary interaction in which she'd said something either delightful or reassuring or sweet or encouraging, left.

Upstairs, his mother, dressed in a yellow sack that wasn't a dress but also wasn't a nightgown, sat in the Barcalounger that he'd paid an exorbitant amount of money to have moved to her two-room unit on the ninth floor, watching a cooking show on T.V. She'd never been much of a cook—perhaps she'd lost her appetite for food at the same time she'd lost her ability to love, or maybe not, maybe she'd just never cared—but over the past several weeks she'd become entranced with "The Great British Bake-Off." Her aide was nowhere to be seen. "And if you're looking for Lucinda," she said as he walked in. "She's toast."

"Why would that be, Ma?"

"She screwed up, but good," his mother said.

"What did she do, Ma?"

"I don't know exactly," his mother said. "But it was bad. The cops came. That's how I know it was bad."

"How many cops came, Ma?"

"And I swear to God, one of them wore a turban. Like a genie in a bottle. So now they have Arabs walking around with guns. This world."

"What did the cops say, Ma?"

"They wanted to know about my boyfriend."

"What about your boyfriend, Ma?"

"You promise not to tell anyone, right? Because I swear on everything that's holy, I swear on Papa's beard and Mamma's heart and on the Holy Torah and my own life, that if you squeal, I'll tell everyone about your—your disgusting business, the thing you do."

"Fine, Ma. I swear. I won't tell a soul. Tell me about your boyfriend."

He turned the TV off.

"Turn that back on!" she wailed. "They're making a plum tart."

He turned it back on.

"Tell me about your boyfriend," he said.

She leaned forward, so far forward over her own knees that she looked like she was about to buckle in two. She was like a hawk, on a branch, leaning forward, forwards—and all that stopped her from plunging into the air were the two claws that held her there.

"Hesh isn't like other boys," she said. "He's sweet, and kind, and gentle, and he thinks I'm the most beautiful girl in the world."

"So you are, Ma."

"We want to get married, but you know how stern Papa is, and also, just as soon as he can, just as soon as he's made a little money, Hesh is going to go to Warsaw, enroll in the university there. But he can't tell anyone! You know how they are about getting a secular education. He's going to go anyway, though. Nothing can stop him. And just as soon as he gets himself settled, I'm going to join him. We'll get married, of course. He's not like that—he's not like—he's a realist, he's forward-thinking, but he's not a socialist or God forbid a Communist. He wants to marry me."

"I see," Sol said.

"The thing is," she said in a low whisper. "I missed my monthly."

"Uh huh."

"So if I'm pregnant—I'm not saying I am pregnant, it's too early to tell, and sometimes I miss my monthly anyway or it's late—but if I am, then, obviously, we're not going to wait. We're going to go, together, to Warsaw. It's not that far from here, and I can get a job, he can too."

"Do you really think you might be pregnant?"

"Oh Leibkal!" she said, throwing her scrawny arms so tightly around Sol's neck that he had trouble breathing. "If only you knew how much I love him! And how much he loves me! It's wonderful, is what it is! Wonderful! Wonderful! Wonderful!"

And sure, some of what she said that day was in Yiddish, but enough of it was in English for Sol to have caught the drift, to have finally pierced the secret of his mother's secret soul, and how, for her, love had swept everything else away.

ABOUT THE AUTHOR

Jennifer Anne Moses is a multigenre author whose books include *Visiting Hours, Bagels and Grits, The Book of Joshua, Food and Whine, The Art of Dumpster Diving*, and *Tales from My Closet. The Man Who Loved His Wife* is her first collection of short stories. When she's not writing, she's painting or walking her beloved mutts. (*www. JenniferAnneMosesArts.com*) She and her husband are the parents of three children and live in Montclair, NJ.

Other Recent Titles from Mayapple Press:

Betsy Johnson, *when animals are animals*, 2021
        Paper, 62pp, $17.95 plus s&h
    ISBN: 978-1-952781-02-5
Judith Kunst, *The Way Through,* 2020
        Paper, 76pp, $17.95 plus s&h
    ISBN: 978-1-936419-98-2
Ellen Stone, *What Is in the Blood*, 2020
        Paper, 72pp, $17.95 plus s&h
    ISBN 978-1-936419-95-1
Terry Blackhawk, *One Less River*, 2019
        Paper, 78pp, $16.95 plus s&h
    ISBN 978-1-936419-89-0
Ellen Cole, *Notes from the Dry Country,* 2019
        Paper, 88pp, $16.95 plus s&h
    ISBN 978-1-936419-87-6
Monica Wendel, *English Kills and other poems*
        Paper, 70pp, $15.95 plus s&h
    ISBN 978-1-936419-84-5
Charles Rafferty, *Something an Atheist Might Bring Up
at a Cocktail Party*, 2018
        Paper, 40pp, $14.95 plus s&h
    ISBN 978-1-936419-83-8
David Lunde, *Absolute Zero*, 2018
        Paper, 82pp, $16.95 plus s&h
    ISBN 978-1-936419-80-7
Jan Minich, *Wild Roses*, 2017
        Paper, 100pp, $16.95 plus s&h
    ISBN 978-1-936419-77-7
John Palen, *Distant Music*, 2017
        Paper, 74pp, $15.95 plus s&h
    ISBN 978-1-936419-74-6
Eleanor Lerman, *The Stargazer's Embassy*, 2017
        Paper, 310pp, $18.95 plus s&h
    ISBN 978-936419-73-9
Dicko King, *Bird Years*, 2017
        Paper, 80pp, $14.95 plus s&h
    ISBN 978-936419-69-2
Eugenia Toledo, tr. Carolyne Wright, *Map Traces, Blood Traces /
Trazas de Mapas, Trazas de Sangre*, 2017
        Paper, 138pp, $16.95 plus s&h
    ISBN 978-936419-60-9

For a complete catalog of Mayapple Press publications, please visit our website at *www.mayapplepress.com*. Books can be ordered direct from our website with secure on-line payment using PayPal, or by mail (check or money order). Or order through your local bookseller.